"Will enthrall the reader and offer lots of satisfaction."
—*The Romance Reader*

"Returning to Dare Island is always a pleasure . . . Add to that the slow-burn sexual tension between Meg and Sam, and this series second really keeps things interesting."
—*RT Book Reviews* (4 stars)

CAROLINA HOME

"A story as fresh as the Carolina ocean breezes . . . It's always a joy to read Virginia Kantra."
—JoAnn Ross, *New York Times* bestselling author

"Kantra's *Carolina Home* is intimate and inviting, a feel-good story featuring captivating characters who face challenges as touching as they are believable . . . Contemporary romance at its most gratifying."
—*USA Today*

"It feels like coming home . . . Reading this book is like relaxing in a Hatteras hammock, gently swaying in the breeze."
—*Dear Author* (Recommended Read)

"Truly enjoyable."
—*All About Romance*

"A wonderful contemporary drama with great characters, a touching romance, and the beginnings of a fantastic series."
—*Romance Around the Corner*

"A sizzling good time. Kantra's story-building is excellent."
—*Publishers Weekly*

"A thoroughly wonderful read."
—*BookPage*

AND FOR THE NOVELS OF VIRGINIA KANTRA

"Brilliantly sensual and hauntingly poignant."
—Alyssa Day, *New York Times* bestselling author

Carolina Blues

VIRGINIA KANTRA

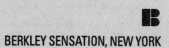

BERKLEY SENSATION, NEW YORK

THE BERKLEY PUBLISHING GROUP
Published by the Penguin Group
Penguin Group (USA) LLC
375 Hudson Street, New York, New York 10014

USA • Canada • UK • Ireland • Australia • New Zealand • India • South Africa • China

penguin.com

A Penguin Random House Company

CAROLINA BLUES

A Berkley Sensation Book / published by arrangement with the author

Berkley Sensation Books are published by The Berkley Publishing Group.
BERKLEY SENSATION® is a registered trademark of Penguin Group (USA) LLC.
The "B" design is a trademark of Penguin Group (USA) LLC.

For information, address: The Berkley Publishing Group,
a division of Penguin Group (USA) LLC,
375 Hudson Street, New York, New York 10014.

ISBN: 978-0-425-26969-5

PUBLISHING HISTORY
Berkley Sensation mass-market edition / October 2014

PRINTED IN THE UNITED STATES OF AMERICA

10 9 8 7 6 5 4 3 2 1

Cover art by Tony Mauro.
Cover design by Rita Frangie.

For Italian Guy.
You're my inspiration. Always.

ACKNOWLEDGMENTS

I want to offer the usual thanks to the usual suspects: to my patient editor, Cindy Hwang (I promise I'll never attempt another book about a writer with writer's block again), and the team at Berkley; to Robin Rue and Beth Miller at Writer's House; to artist Tony Mauro and cover designer Rita Frangie for another breathtaking cover; to Carolyn Martin and Michael Ritchey for invaluable input and advice.

Thank you to my wonderful readers.

And special thanks to Diane Spell, LCSW, for her insight, and to Patrolman M. Hall for coming through with stuff in a pinch.

One

LAUREN PATTERSON ENTRENCHED herself in the corner table of Jane's Sweet Tea House, barricaded behind her laptop, a latte, and a Glorious Morning muffin.

Facing a blank computer screen wasn't nearly as terrifying as confronting three masked men with guns, she told herself firmly. She hadn't frozen then. There was absolutely no excuse for her to be paralyzed now.

The July sun pushed past the HELP WANTED sign in the window to pool like syrup on her table. Beyond the shade of live oaks and loblolly pines, beyond the shrubs and shingled rooftops of the harbor, the waters of Pamlico Sound gleamed. Vacationers seeking an air-conditioned respite from the North Carolina heat packed the eclectic bakery. A young couple, broiled pink by the sun, held hands on a sofa. A father in line lifted his little daughter onto his shoulders. All of them happy. Together.

Lauren's muffin stuck in her throat.

Behind the counter, a pretty teenager in geek girl glasses struggled to meet the stream of orders for iced espresso drinks. Before Lauren's fifteen minutes of fame, she'd moonlighted as a barista to make ends meet. The psych department frowned on its graduate students taking outside jobs, but her stipend had barely covered her living expenses. Not to mention all the things her little brother Noah needed that Mom couldn't afford. Luxuries like game controllers. Athletic shoes. Meat.

Lauren swallowed hard. She couldn't do anything that would plunge her family into that state of financial uncertainty again. The advance from her publisher was already half spent, the publication date set. Late October, so the book would be shelved in time for Christmas but not lost in a sea of cookbooks and gift books. It was already selling briskly online.

She just had to finish it.

The cheerful silver bells on the door chimed, announcing the arrival of another customer.

She looked up, seeking a more positive direction for her thoughts. Or maybe, she admitted, she was simply searching for a distraction.

A man stood silhouetted against the brightness outside. Thick, close-cut hair. Lean, muscled body. Dark mirrored sunglasses.

Her heart beat faster. A cop.

Save me, she thought.

She took a deep breath and looked away. The sudden sight of the law was never good news. A uniform at the door, blue lights flashing in the rearview mirror . . . Anybody could get sweaty palms and a dry mouth. She was *not* having a panic attack.

She put her hand on her belly anyway, under the cover of the table, and drew a careful breath. *In through the nose . . .*

He entered the shop, moving between the artfully mismatched tables and chairs with a contained authority more menacing than a swagger. Among the pink, chubby, underdressed tourists, he stuck out like an assassin in a ballroom.

He promised safety. He promised danger. An irresistible combination.

She exhaled, pushing on her stomach. *Out through the mouth . . .*

He nodded to the young woman behind the old-fashioned register, the one with the fat blond braid and sleepy gray eyes of a princess in a fairy tale. The blonde nodded back, never losing her rhythm or her smile.

Lauren didn't understand why she wasn't melting into a puddle at his feet. Okay, so he wasn't Prince Charming. Not the kind of guy you wanted to meet at midnight, unless you intended to lose a lot more than your shoes.

But hot. Very hot. Smoldering, in fact.

Given the slightest encouragement, Lauren would have followed him home like one of the island cats that seemed to hang around the bakery's back porch, lean and hungry and hoping for handouts. *Pet me. Rescue me.*

She shook the thought away. She was not turning into a police groupie on top of everything else. She could take care of herself. *Without getting anybody shot in the process.*

Anyway, she tended to attract guys who needed her. Sensitive souls with lousy home lives or unsatisfying jobs, with full-sleeve tattoos and pierced tongues and nipples. Not law-and-order types.

"This isn't peppermint schnapps," complained a thin woman at the head of the line.

"No, it's Irish cream syrup and whipped cream," the blonde said.

"But I ordered Irish coffee. There should be peppermint schnapps."

Not in Irish coffee, Lauren thought. She noticed her heart rate increasing and took another deep breath.

The blonde blinked. "I'm afraid we're not licensed to serve alcohol," she said with doll-like calm. "But I can add a touch of mint syrup if you'd like."

"I don't want any damn syrup," the customer said loudly. "I want my drink. I want to speak with your manager."

The situation was escalating. The people in line behind the woman shifted away. Lauren had seen that kind of body language before. They didn't want to get involved. They didn't want the drama.

Lauren, on the other hand, had already proved she was a total sucker for other people's problems. Her faculty advisor had cautioned her about her tendency to get personally involved. *Empathy is a good thing*, Eleanor had said gently. *No one questions your ability to connect with clients. But our emphasis here is research, not therapy. You don't want to put your own future at risk by losing your professional focus.*

Which was great advice until, say, somebody drew a gun.

The band around Lauren's lungs tightened. Not a helpful thought. *Breathe in, two, three, four . . .*

"I'm Jane. The owner," the blonde was saying. "If you'd like me to make you another drink—"

"What I'd like is a real Irish coffee," the angry woman said. "It's false advertising, that's what it is."

The blonde flushed scarlet.

Lauren's face heated in sympathy. *The hell with it.* She abandoned her breathing and jumped up, grabbing her empty mug.

Hot Cop spoke. "This is a bakery, not a bar." His deep

voice raised all the little hairs along Lauren's arms. "You want a drink at ten in the morning, you'll have to take your business elsewhere."

Okay, so his by-the-book attitude wasn't going to win the bakery any patrons, Lauren acknowledged. But at least he was stepping in, defending the princess against attack.

The unhappy customer folded thin, tanned arms across her skinny bosom, and turned to give the interloper a piece of her mind. But faced with Hot Cop's cool air of authority, she faltered. "But I'm on vacation," she said almost plaintively.

He regarded her impassively from behind mirrored sunglasses. "Yes, ma'am. Have a nice stay."

"Carolina sea salt caramel latte to go," the owner, Jane, said, setting a drink with a clear-domed lid on the counter. "On the house."

The customer pursed her lips. "Skim?"

It was important in negotiations, Lauren had learned, to give the hostage taker an opportunity to save face.

Jane nodded. "And whipped cream."

The thin woman took the cup without thanks or payment. The door bells rattled in her wake.

Hot Cop looked at Jane. "You really want to start rewarding customers for bad behavior?"

Jane's flush deepened.

Lauren dumped her dirty mug into the bus tray. "I'm pretty sure she just wanted to get her out of here before she made a scene."

The sunglasses turned in her direction. "You don't stop bullies by appeasing them."

Memory tightened Lauren's chest, constricted her throat. Lying flat on the bank floor, her face pressed to the cool tiles, the smell of fear rank in her nostrils . . .

She pushed the memory away. Pushed down her nausea. *Helpful thoughts.* She smiled. *Focus on the positive.* "Sometimes you do whatever it takes to survive."

His dark brows flicked up. "Her survival isn't in question."

Right. Not every confrontation was a life-or-death moment. But . . . "It is if a customer decides to trash her bakery online," Lauren pointed out.

"Thank you," Jane said.

Hot Cop didn't budge. "So, in your opinion, she should compromise her principles to avoid a customer lying in a bad review."

"I think compromise is always a good idea. Especially if it gets you what you want."

"Here's your coffee," Jane said, setting it on the counter. "Black. No sugar."

"And two large to go, please."

Jane nodded and reached for the stack of cups.

Lauren glanced from the coffee on the counter to the cop's hard face. Humor tickled her mouth. "I guess you don't worry about stereotypes, huh?"

For a moment she thought that he wouldn't answer. That he didn't get it. And then his smile flashed, white, electrifying. "I didn't order donuts," he pointed out.

She tilted her head, enjoying the lightening of tension, like the drop in air pressure before the rain. "You don't like sweet things?"

He surveyed her coolly from behind his mirrored glasses. "I like them fine. I'm watching my weight."

Was he joking? Her gaze dropped to his lean waist. He had the flat stomach and disciplined body that came from serious gym time.

After the robbery, Lauren's faculty advisor had suggested she try exercise as a way to manage her anxiety. But every time she left her hotel room to go for a run, she started to gasp. Her shortness of breath, her rapid heartbeat, felt uncomfortably like a panic attack. She had visions of collapsing by the side of a road miles from home, followed by headlines: HOSTAGE GIRL SURRENDERS. BANK HEROINE PARALYZED BY PANIC DISORDER.

She didn't run anymore.

"Yeah, I can see how that would be a problem," she said dryly.

"Occupational hazard," he agreed, straight-faced.

She was almost sure he was kidding. She smiled back uncertainly.

"Jack is our chief of police," Jane put in from behind the counter.

Not just a cop. The top cop.

"I'm impressed," Lauren said.

"Don't be. We're a small department." He removed the glasses. His eyes were sharp and dark in a hard-featured face. Square jaw, strong cheekbones, bold, prominent nose. She sucked in her breath.

"Jack Rossi." He introduced himself.

Italian. It figured with that face.

"Lauren." *No last name.* To make up for her omission, she offered her hand.

His hand enveloped hers, sending a shock of warmth up her arm. Lauren swallowed, resisting the urge to tug back her hand. He did not recognize her. She'd made sure of that. Her new look bore little resemblance to the fresh-faced inset that had appeared at the bottom of the news footage or the polished, smiling image on her book jacket. Her hair was darker and longer, past her shoulders, and she flaunted her new piercings like self-inflicted battle scars.

His gaze skated over the tiny jeweled nose stud before

focusing politely on her eyes. "What brings you to Dare Island, Lauren?"

"Oh, you know," she said vaguely, waving her hand. "Work."

"What is it that you do?"

Even after all the media interviews, she hated that question. At thirty-one, she should be able to answer with certainty, *I'm a cop, I'm a baker, I'm a doctoral candidate in psychology.* Anything other than, *I'm famous for being in the wrong place at the wrong time.*

She couldn't be sorry that her presence in the bank that day had saved lives. But the whole hostage thing had changed her in ways her family couldn't see, her friends refused to accept. After her appearance on *Dr. Phil*, her book *Hostage Girl: My Story* had spent forty-eight consecutive weeks on the *New York Times* bestseller list. She was as isolated by her fame as she had been by her captors.

"I'm a writer."

Who couldn't write. Her stomach cramped. Her follow-up book, *Hostage Girl: My Life After Crisis*, was scheduled to release in less than four months. Before—her agent had explained with brutal honesty—no one was interested in her anymore.

That sexy little indent at the corner of his mouth deepened. Even his smiles were cool and controlled, she thought wistfully. She was jealous. Everything in her life felt so out of control these days.

"Guess you don't worry about stereotypes, either," he said.

What? She followed his gaze toward her table before understanding clicked. *The latte. The laptop.* Her lips eased into an answering smile. "The whole coffee shop scene is kind of cliché," she admitted.

Jane looked up. "We're a bakery. We're not a coffee shop."

Jack Rossi angled his body, shifting his attention to the woman behind the counter. His smile softened, making his strong features even more attractive. "I don't only come for the coffee, Jane."

Oh. *Oh.* Lauren glanced from his hard, dark face to Jane. The baker dropped her gaze, setting two large to-go cups in a cardboard tray on the counter. Right. If he didn't want donuts . . . and he didn't come for the coffee . . . Lauren snuck a quick look at his left hand. No wedding band. He must be after whatever else the pretty blond baker had to offer.

Her lungs deflated. So did her ego.

Which was stupid. Her lack of a love life had never bothered her before. She didn't date blue-collar cops with Italian-sounding last names. She didn't date, period. None of the grad students did. They hung out. They hooked up. They devoted themselves to their research, their course work, their clinical training. Occasionally she brought someone home to crash on her couch or in her bed until he found his feet again.

It was just that since the whole hostage thing, she'd lost even that casual companionship. Her romantic prospects had dwindled to marriage proposals from online weirdos and tired come-ons from seedy sales guys in hotel bars.

Which still wouldn't be a problem. She wasn't her mother, for God's sake, always needing the reassurance of another human being.

It was just that her defenses were low, her confidence shaken, her energy depleted. Was it any wonder she wanted to borrow someone else's for a while?

Don't overthink it, her publicist, Meg, had urged. *Everything will be fine. You'll be fine. Just move on.*

It was good advice. Lauren sighed. If only she could figure out how.

IT WAS A beautiful day. Too bad his job was to ruin it for somebody.

Jack sat in his SUV blazoned with the shield of the Dare Island Police Department, running the AC and the driver's license and registration of the seventeen-year-old who'd just blown through a stop sign on her way to the beach.

The ID checked out. The BMW belonged to her daddy. Jack could have let her off with a warning. He might have, too—he'd been young and dumb once—if so many other kids without cars didn't walk this road.

And if she hadn't tried so hard to flirt her way out of a ticket.

The law existed to protect everybody. The sooner Miss Teenage BMW learned the consequences of her actions, the better. He wasn't compromising his principles or public safety for some spoiled rich kid from out of town.

A face slid into his memory, that writer, Lauren No Last Name, her sharp, dark eyes with heavy black eyeliner, the winking nose stud, the silver wire that curled like a—snake? vine?—around her ear. *I think compromise is always a good idea. Especially if it gets you what you want.*

She reminded him of the college girls he used to watch walking down the street, always on their way somewhere, class or the library or some fucking foreign film festival. Smart girls, quirky girls who went to Bryn Mawr, who read poetry and smoked pot, who knew things a guy like him would never know.

After eleven months, Jack recognized most of the island's residents. Lauren No Last Name wasn't from around here any more than he was. Still, she looked familiar. Something about the shape of those eyes or the tilt of her jaw. His body tightened. She interested him, and not just as a member of law enforcement keeping tabs on his beat.

He shook his head, disgusted with the direction of his thoughts. Obviously, his dick hadn't learned the lessons of the past year.

He didn't do interesting women anymore.

Two

DARE ISLAND'S ENTIRE police force—three officers, if Jack counted himself, which he damn well did, since he worked more hours than anybody—were rarely all together in the same place at the same time. Only in the case of fires, natural disasters, and Thursday morning staff meetings.

On this particular Thursday morning, Jack walked into the police station to find Luke Fletcher, his new hire, on the phone. Hank, the part-time reserve officer, occupied the other desk.

Henry Lee Clark was gray-haired, rangy, and raw-boned, his face as deeply grooved as a tractor tire. His feet were propped on the desk, his collar unbuttoned against the heat. A thirty-year veteran of the county sheriff's department, he'd been the town's first choice to become the new police chief. Lucky for Jack, he'd turned the job down.

He was also Jane's father.

Lowering his newspaper, he regarded Jack over the top of his reading glasses. "You've been to Jane's."

Luke covered the mouthpiece of the phone and grinned. "Great detective work, Hank. How'd you guess?"

Jack set the cardboard tray on the corner of Hank's desk, the logo cups a dead giveaway. "I bought coffee."

"You should have brought donuts," Hank said.

Jack thought of that girl, Lauren Somebody, with her dark, aware eyes and three-cornered smile. *I guess you don't worry about stereotypes, huh?*

He shook the memory away. "Next time."

Hank grunted. "How is she?"

She was a pain in the ass. Somehow she'd gotten under his skin, into his head. Jack frowned. He was sure he'd seen that face before.

Hank was still watching, waiting for an answer.

Realization hit Jack like a slap. Hank was asking about *Jane.* His daughter. Hardworking, softhearted Jane, with her abundant blond hair and generous rack that set off a low-level hum of masculine appreciation every time Jack saw her.

He hadn't felt a hum around Lauren Whatever-her-name-was. More like a shock.

"She's fine," he said.

Jane was more than fine. She was perfect for Jack, for his new life. She'd grown up on the island. A young single mother, a natural-born homemaker, she was warm and nurturing and succulent as a muffin fresh out of the oven, the exact opposite of Jack's ex-wife in every way.

So why was he dragging his heels?

Hank set down his cup. "Coffee's cold."

Jack wasn't going to excuse himself by explaining the traffic stop. "It's still better than that sludge Luke makes."

Luke hung up the phone and leaned back in his swivel chair. He was a Marine vet, like Jack. An islander, like Hank. A real hometown hero, a genuinely good guy who'd come through hell with all his shiny principles intact. *Not* like Jack. He wore his brand-new police uniform with military precision, his pants sharply creased, his shoes polished. "You can take over the coffee-making duties anytime, Chief."

Jack smiled without answering.

"You need a woman," Hank said.

Jack met his gaze impassively, hoping Hank couldn't spot the heat crawling in his cheeks. That was part of his long-range plan. Find somebody supportive and sane to pick out a couch and curtains with, to raise kids and plan vacations with. Maybe Jane. But she lived with her father and her six-and-a-half-year-old son. Two good reasons for taking things slow.

Jack wasn't dumb enough to blame every woman for the wreck of his marriage. Hell, he didn't even entirely blame his ex-wife. But he'd been a cop long enough to know you don't shit where you eat. If they got serious and things didn't work out, Jane would have to cope with the reactions at home. And Jack would have to deal with the fallout at work.

Luke grinned. "I've got one, thanks. You're both invited to the wedding, by the way. Monday after next."

"Looking forward to it," Jack said.

"It's the middle of tourist season," Hank said.

Luke shrugged. "At least we'll miss the weekend turnover. The restaurant was free. And the priest is willing."

Renee had insisted on a big white wedding, six bridesmaids and Jack's nephew in a ring bearer's suit. Half the cops in Philly had packed the church, like an officer's funeral. The only thing missing was the bagpipes.

Jack cleared his throat. "I'll call the sheriff's department."

"It's a small wedding. Mostly family," Luke said. "Not much need for traffic control."

"We still need somebody to cover our calls."

"Which is why you ought to hire a girl to answer the phones," Hank said. "Make coffee."

Luke raised his eyebrows.

Right. Making coffee wasn't only a woman's job. But Jack understood where Hank was coming from. There wasn't much difference between rural North Carolina and the blue-collar suburbs of Philadelphia when it came to gender equality. Law enforcement was still largely a good ol' boys club, despite the fact that Jack had known competent women who could and did kick ass.

Women like his ex-wife.

Renee used to complain about sexism on the force, back in the days when she still talked to him about anything besides whose turn it was to empty the dishwasher or take out the trash. Jack had sympathized.

Renee never let her sex or anything else stand in her way. But the truth was Jack had never really gotten over worrying about her. Sometimes an officer had to depend on sheer size to control a situation. Making a traffic stop on a dark road. Walking into a bar full of drunken rowdies. Jack still occasionally tangled with some asshole who figured he could take him.

"I requested a dispatcher in the new budget. We'll see what the town council says." Jack looked at Luke. "Speaking of calls . . ."

"Dora Abrams," Luke said, referring to the call that had just come in. "She heard a noise under her house."

"What kind of noise?" Jack asked.

"Like a banging. Water pipes maybe."

"Or a possum," Hank said.

"Or she just wants somebody out there to change her air filter again," Jack said.

"I'll go take a look," Luke said.

In Jack's old job, he would have suggested eighty-three-year-old Dora call a plumber. Or animal control. But small-town policing didn't work like that.

The islanders were an independent lot. When they had a problem, they were more inclined to take matters into their own hands than to call the police. As the new police chief, Jack had to earn their trust.

Even if it meant crawling under Dora's house again.

"I've got it," Jack said.

"Let me know if you need backup," Luke said. "Or a trap."

"You have a possum trap," Jack said.

"Sure," Hank said, his drawl thickening. "Possum's good eating. Mostly we just scoop 'em off the road with a shovel, but—"

Jack's expression must have betrayed some reaction, because Hank wheezed with laughter.

"It's a humane animal trap," Luke said, grinning. "Kate bought it to catch Taylor's cat."

Taylor was Luke's daughter, the unexpected legacy of a high school girlfriend. Nice kid. She'd had a rough time before coming to live with the Fletchers a year ago.

"How's she doing?" Jack asked. "Taylor."

"She's good. Well, she's pissed at me right now because I won't let her play Grand Theft Auto, but I told her that didn't have anything to do with my being a cop."

"At least you're home now," Jack said.

"Until you start working overtime," Hank said. "And holidays."

Luke shrugged. "Beats being deployed. Plus, she's pretty happy about Kate coming to live with us."

"Wait until she gets older," Hank said. "That's when the real trouble starts."

"I've already told her she's not allowed to drink, date, or drive until she's twenty-one."

Hank grunted. "Better make it thirty-five."

Jane was twenty-nine. Jack didn't know much about their relationship except that Hank had raised his daughter alone and took her back in when her husband took off.

Luke grinned. "I'll keep that in mind."

He'd missed this, Jack realized. The camaraderie of a station house, the dumb-ass jokes, the bullshit. He missed Frank.

His ex-partner.

His right hand curled reflexively into a fist. His knuckles tingled with remembered pain.

Shit.

Slowly, he loosened his fingers. Shook his head.

And went off to deal with somebody else's problems.

AT THE END of another unproductive day, Lauren let herself in the front door of the Pirates' Rest, a gorgeous two-and-a-half-story Craftsman built above the bay around the turn of the century. The Fletcher family had renovated the old house into a gracious bed-and-breakfast. The leaded glass transom threw bars of colored light on the faded William Morris carpet.

Each of the eight guest rooms was decorated in the Arts and Crafts style and named after a pirate of the North Carolina coast. Lauren was staying in the William Kidd Room on the second floor, with a view of the water and easy access to the coffee-and-tea service set up in a converted wardrobe on the sunlit landing. Maybe she'd curl up in the window seat with her laptop after dinner and try to get something done.

E-mail. Free Cell. Candy Crush.

The kitchen door swung open. Lauren stopped with one foot on the stairs as Meg Fletcher emerged carrying a plate of cookies.

Lauren's publicist was casually dressed in jeans and a T-shirt that cost more than Lauren's entire graduate student wardrobe. Her dark hair was cropped in a short, chic cut that revealed her strong jaw and big diamond earrings. She sported another massive rock on her left hand that hadn't been there when Lauren had hired her nine months ago.

Patricia Brown, Lauren's agent, had not approved of her choice. *So she went to Harvard. Big deal*, Patricia had said. *She doesn't have any experience.*

She was a vice president of marketing, Lauren had pointed out.

Patricia sniffed. *At an insurance company. For God's sake, darling, when I said you needed help, I meant a psychiatrist or life coach or someone who understands the business. Meg Fletcher doesn't know the first thing about publishing.*

But Meg had learned.

And Lauren had felt comfortable with her from the start. Meg was as cool, brisk, and bracing as a breeze from the sea. When Lauren hit the wall last month, unable to leave her hotel room, Meg had flown to her rescue. Within hours, she'd reorganized Lauren's schedule, cutting back on her speaking engagements and offering her parents' inn as a refuge.

"Lauren." Meg flashed a smile, setting the cookies on the table in the hall. "How'd it go today?"

It. The writing? Or the panic attacks?

Lauren made an effort to breathe. To smile. "Oh, you know. It's going. Sort of. Nowhere."

"Well, you just got here. You need to give yourself some time." Meg's tone was encouraging, but her eyes were worried. "It'll take a while for you to find your rhythm."

As if a change of pace or place would fix what was wrong with her.

"I'm sorry," Lauren said humbly. "I'm screwing things up for you, too. Did you hear back from that writers' group in Maryland?"

"Don't you worry about that," Meg said. "I'm handling your schedule. You concentrate on your writing. No pressure."

Lauren pressed her lips together to stop a hysterical bubble of laughter from escaping. *No pressure.* Except she was letting everybody down. Not just Meg and her editor and agent. Everybody. Including herself.

For the last twelve years, ever since her dad died, Lauren had been the responsible one, the one Mom and Noah could count on. Dad's life insurance hadn't even paid off the mortgage on the house. And with Noah applying to colleges . . . And the other obligations she'd taken on . . .

Lauren felt her chest tighten, smothered by the press of obligations. She was dying inside.

"Oh, I almost forgot," Meg said. "You got a letter."

Lauren froze. *A letter.* Not a bill. She paid those online. Reader mail went to a PO box, almost everything else to her mother's house. *Thirty-one years old, and my permanent address is the house I grew up in.* The only person she knew who wouldn't contact her by e-mail was . . .

Meg emerged from the office alcove, waving a thin white

envelope with the Illinois Department of Corrections prisoner number printed neatly in one corner. "Here you go."

Ben.

Lauren swallowed and took the envelope.

Meg continued to watch her with those too-perceptive, too-sympathetic eyes. "Everything all right?"

Lauren forced herself to smile. "Fine."

If anything was wrong, Ben would have called. He had her number. She was on his approved list of contacts. She took a slow, deep breath.

"Want a cookie?" Meg asked.

She shook her head mutely.

"Oxygen?"

Lauren's breath sputtered out on a laugh. "I'm fine."

"How about a glass of wine?"

Alcohol, the drug of choice for self-medicated clients everywhere. The traditional antidote for writer's block.

She had a sudden vision of Jack Rossi's strong, dark face, his flat Philly accent. *Guess you don't worry about stereotypes, either.*

Her smile this time came more easily. "Sure," she said. "Why not?"

The letter would keep. Ben wasn't going anywhere. He wouldn't be out of prison for at least another six years. She winced.

"Right this way," Meg said.

Lauren followed her down the cozy paneled hallway toward the kitchen. The inn guests took breakfast in the dining room. She hadn't visited the family quarters before.

"Wow." She stopped, taking in the sleek granite counters and warm oak cabinets, the stainless steel appliances and wide-planked wooden floor. Herbs bloomed in pots on the windowsill. Peaches shared a bowl with the mail on the long farm table. "This is really nice. Homey."

Meg pulled down two wineglasses. "Well, it's not your average hotel."

"You're telling me," Lauren said with feeling. "When I was on my book tour, I was grateful for peanuts in the minibar."

Especially on those days when she couldn't summon the courage to leave her room.

She pressed her hand under her rib cage. *Breathe in, two, three, four . . .*

Her mother wanted her to live at home again. As if being together under one roof would magically return them all to the time when her father was alive, when their family was safe and secure and whole. If Mom had her way, Lauren would never go back to school, never run another errand, never go anyplace where armed men could take her hostage ever again. Barbara Patterson needed to believe that it was over. She wanted to pretend that everything was all right. But her anxious looks every time Lauren left the house pressed on her heart like a bruise.

Lauren got it. Mom had already lost Dad. She didn't want to lose Lauren, too.

But Lauren couldn't live at home. She couldn't write. She couldn't breathe. She felt her world gradually shrinking to the walls of her bedroom, still decorated with the wallpaper border she'd picked out at thirteen, frozen forever on the cusp of adolescence. Swaddled by familiar surroundings, it was too easy for her to give in to her mother's fears, to sink into the stultifying comfort of childhood. To crawl under the covers and never come out again.

She'd thought that things would get better once she was back at school. That *she* would be better. But she'd found, to her shame, that she couldn't handle living alone, either. She had trouble focusing on her dissertation, difficulty sleeping in her tiny apartment. Every creak and car horn sent her bolt upright, gasping for breath.

Her faculty advisor suggested counseling and then a leave of absence. Her fellow graduate students were sympathetic and then impatient.

The last time a total stranger had approached Lauren on the street, her friend Brandon had rolled his eyes. *No offense*, he'd said, which was what someone always said when they wanted to say something offensive. *But we've all heard it before. Not everybody wants to relive your fifteen minutes of fame over and over.*

Her life had been divided in two, Before and After the robbery, and it felt sometimes as if everyone she loved was on the other side of an unbridgeable chasm with the girl she used to be.

Lauren watched Meg dig in a drawer. At home, she took care of her mother and Noah. At school, she took care of herself. She still wasn't used to being waited on. "I don't want to put you out."

Meg dug in a drawer for a corkscrew. "You're not."

"It's not your job to look after guests." Or me, Lauren thought. She paid Meg to be her publicist, not her babysitter.

"Not usually. I'm helping out today while Mom runs wedding errands with Kate and Taylor."

Lauren had met Meg's eleven-year-old niece Taylor. But . . . "Kate?"

Meg glanced over from opening the wine. "My brother's fiancée. They're getting married in two weeks."

Meg had two brothers, Lauren remembered.

Before the robbery, she'd always imagined she was a good listener. A useful skill for a clinician. Even more useful for a crisis negotiator. Anyway, it had kept her and seven other people alive. But she realized she knew next to nothing about Meg's personal life. Maybe she was a little intimidated by Meg's easy assurance.

And maybe she was becoming as self-absorbed as Brandon accused her of being.

"Is that your brother the fisherman?" Lauren asked.

"No, that's Matt. Luke's the cop."

"Oh."

Meg lowered the wine bottle. "Should I have mentioned it before? Do you have issues?"

"Issues," Lauren repeated blankly.

"With cops. Because of . . . You know. The bank thing. The shooting."

Lauren flushed. "Oh. No." She tried to make a joke. "I'm anxious, not paranoid."

Meg's brow creased in concern.

Lauren sighed. "The police have a job to do," she said and tried to shut down the memory of Ben's face as they'd swarmed over him on the floor, jerking his arms, cuffing his hands behind him. The smells of flop sweat, urine, and blood.

She cleared her throat. "It's natural for them to see things in black and white. Us versus Them. Me or Him."

"And that's not how you see it," Meg said.

Lauren smiled crookedly. "I must. I mean, I'm here, aren't I? I'm alive." She took a gulp of wine, swallowing the taste of betrayal. "Anyway, I'm grateful to the cops for doing their job that day. That doesn't mean I'd sleep with one."

Meg's eyes widened.

"No offense to your brother. I didn't mean him," Lauren added hastily. Crap, that came out wrong. "Not that I'd sleep with your brother, either."

"I'm sure that's a relief to his fiancée," said a flat, deep voice behind her. Jack Rossi's voice.

Lauren's stomach sank. Her cheeks burned.

She turned and there he was, Jack Rossi in uniform and in the flesh, dark and lean and oozing pheromones on the other side of the screen door, having obviously heard every word.

Double crap.

JACK GRINNED, ENJOYING her blush. My point, sweetheart, he thought.

And then wondered why he was keeping score.

He wasn't interested in playing games anymore. He was thirty-eight years old. Ready to settle or at least to settle down. He wanted calm, companionship, stability. Kids. Not some Goth wannabe with painful piercings and her whole life ahead of her.

She was . . . interesting-looking, though. Not deliberately sexy like the girls from his neighborhood, with their fake nails and fake hair and breasts served up like apples on a plate. Her plain black tank top showed off her arms and the delicate bones at her throat. Her eyes were smudged, her lips bare, like a woman after a night of sex.

She caught him looking and smiled back crookedly, her eyes dark with rueful awareness. His dick shifted from neutral to first. Yeah, definite spark of awareness there.

He inhaled carefully.

That doesn't mean I'd sleep with one.

"Jack. Come in." Meg gave him her public relations smile, friendly and sharp. "What can I do for you?"

"Meg." He shut the screen door behind him. Nodded to both women. "Luke told me you had an animal trap."

"If we do, it's in his cottage." Meg tilted her head. "Do you have a problem?"

"Not me." The island grapevine operated just fine without any input from him. If Dora Abrams wanted to tell the neighbors she had possums or intruders or even ghosts under her house, Jack figured that was her business. But since he was asking Meg for a favor, he owed her some kind of explanation. "I didn't want to bother Taylor. In case she was home alone."

Meg's smile warmed. "She's shopping today with my mother and Kate. But I'm sure I can find it for you."

"Thanks. If you want to tell me where to look—"

"No, I'll get it. Have you met Lauren?"

"Lauren . . ." He let the word drag out.

"My client, Lauren Patterson. She's staying at the inn."

So now he had her last name. He smiled. "Nice to see you again, Ms. Patterson."

"You, too, Chief Rossi." Her tone was wry. Aware.

There was that jolt again, like a shock from a live wire. It had been a long time since he'd felt that kind of gut-level response to any woman other than Renee. Except for his time in the service, they'd been together since high school. One woman in twenty years. Like he was imprinted on her, the way he'd read baby ducks attached themselves to the first thing they saw coming out of the egg.

"Great," Meg said briskly. If she caught the vibe in the room, she didn't let on. "Well, I'll let you two chat while I dig up the trap. Can I get you anything? Cookie? Wine?"

"I'm good, thanks," Jack said.

He didn't drink on duty. Not anymore.

He stood there, not saying anything, while Meg bustled out. He'd always found the silent routine worked pretty well in getting other people to talk. Suspects. Women.

Lauren Patterson. He'd heard that name before. Where had he heard that name?

It wasn't like he was interested in her personally, he told himself. He was the chief of police. It was his job to know what was going on.

She regarded him over her glass of wine. She had pretty hands. Short, dark painted nails. Twists of silver curled around three fingers and the thumb of her left hand. To match the ear cuff?

When the silence stretched on too long, he asked, "So how long are you staying?"

"I don't know yet. I just got here a couple days ago."

"Nobody waiting for you at home?"

Lauren shook her head.

"Kids? Family?" he persisted. *Husband? Boyfriend?*

"A mother and a younger brother. Noah's a high school senior this fall." She leaned back against the counter, which did nice things for her breasts under the thin ribbed tank top. "You?"

"No kids."

He'd supported Renee when she said she wanted to wait. *I am not your mother. Or your fucking sister-in-law, pumping out a kid every two years. I have things I want to do with my life.*

Yeah.

Turned out one of the things she wanted to do was his partner, Frank.

Lauren was still watching him, still waiting, doing her own version of the silent routine. Where had she learned that?

"Two parents," he offered. "Two brothers, one sister."

"And you're the oldest."

"Good guess."

She shrugged. "Not really. You have that whole overde-veloped sense of responsibility thing going on. Plus you don't cut yourself any slack."

She sounded like one of those talking heads yapping on *The View*. And yeah, he had definitely seen too many hours of daytime TV during his months on leave.

"You don't know me well enough to judge," he said.

"I know you're chief of police. That's a responsible job. And you turned down a glass of wine because you were on duty."

Point to her, he decided. "What about you?"

"What about me?" she asked, turning the question back on him.

That was a cop's trick. Or a shrink's. Jack had seen one of those, too, during his leave. "You have a younger brother. Does that make you the responsible one in your family?"

"Yes," she said. No explanation, no excuses.

He could respect that. The silence stretched. He shifted his weight. She studied her glass.

Okay, this wasn't an interrogation. Once upon a time, he used to be good at talking to women. *Say something, dickhead.*

She beat him to the punch, looking up from her wine. "So, Jack Rossi, where are you from?"

"Philly."

She gave him that three-cornered smile. "Like Rocky."

He suppressed a sigh. It was the accent. Or the fact that for the past twelve months he'd been taking out his aggres-sions on a heavy bag and it showed. His chest and arms were heavy with muscle. He was down a belt size, too. He wanted to tell her there was more to him than that, that he used to read books and listen to blue-eyed soul. But maybe that part of him was gone, along with his marriage and his collection of Hall and Oates CDs. Maybe she got off on muscle-bound guys in wife-beater T-shirts. So he told her what she expected to hear.

"I worked a township just south of the city. Three generations of Rossis all living in ten square blocks, most of them cops, all of them baptized, married, and buried at Our Lady of Your Grandmother's Gravy."

It was kind of like a police interview. You disclosed a little truth to get a bigger truth in return. The only difference was there wasn't anything he wanted from her.

Was there?

"Gravy?" she asked.

"Old school red sauce with meatballs," he explained. "Cooked low and slow and served every Sunday."

"Very nice."

"Yeah."

It had been. After he hit bottom, his family had stuck by him. But it got so he couldn't stand the talk around the station house, the looks around the dining room table, his father's silence, his mother's sighs. The way conversations broke off when he walked into the kitchen.

"So what made you decide to exchange family and red sauce for North Carolina barbecue, Chief Rossi?"

He rolled his shoulders, uncomfortable with the turn of the conversation. He preferred being the one asking the questions. "It was time for a change."

"I can understand that." Her voice was soft. "Everybody has somewhere they're going. Or something they're running away from."

Their eyes met.

Right on the button. Maybe she did understand.

And maybe he needed another session with his shrink. Or the punching bag. This was not the kind of girl he should get involved with.

What is it you want, Jack? That was the shrink's favorite question. *Is this the behavior that will get you what you want?*

Fuck, no.

But he couldn't deny that he was interested. Turned on. By Lauren Patterson. Jack frowned. *Where* had he heard that name before?

Meg pushed through the back door, the trap bumping against her legs. "Sorry. That took longer than I expected."

He smoothed his expression. "No problem." He took the heavy wire cage from her. "Thanks for taking the time."

Lauren smiled wryly. "I was just telling the chief the story of my life."

Meg glanced from one to the other. "Swapping hostage stories?"

Lauren froze. "No. God, no."

"What?" Jack said.

Meg grimaced. "Oops. Sorry," she said to Lauren. "I thought he knew."

Jack narrowed his eyes. "Knew what?"

Meg shrugged apologetically at her client before answering. "Lauren was involved in a bank robbery last year. She was taken hostage. She wrote a book about it."

Hostage. Last year.

Shit. *Lauren Patterson.* He remembered the story now. Right about the time his personal life went down the crapper. It had been on the news and later the talk shows—the pretty psych student who'd talked the would-be robbers into releasing her fellow hostages, one spot of bright news in a dreary reporting cycle. Even as he sat alone in his rat-hole apartment, ripe with whiskey and resentment, the story had compelled his attention.

He couldn't recall all the details through the fog of Jack Daniels. But he remembered her, a pixie-faced blonde smiling out of an inset photo on his TV screen.

Before his suspension, Jack had been a sniper on the county emergency response team, the guy you could count on in a crisis when negotiations went sour. In his experience, a hostage's best chance of survival lay in staying calm and staking out a middle position—not too passive, not too assertive—while the professionals did their jobs. But Lauren Patterson had defied expectations and the odds. She'd actually taken an active role, befriending the bad guys and persuading them to surrender.

Even mired on his couch, Jack had found her courage foolhardy. Admirable. Dangerous.

Her hair was darker now and she'd let it grow in the intervening months, scooping the slippery strands into a messy bundle on top of her head. Her face was older and thinner than in her photograph. But he remembered her. The smile. The strong, arched brows. The dark, intelligent eyes.

"You're 'Hostage Girl.' "

A flicker crossed her expression. Not quite a wince. "Guilty."

Interesting word choice. "What are you doing here?"

Meg answered. "She's writing her next book."

"About what?"

"That's sort of my problem."

"It's a follow-up," Meg said firmly. "*Hostage Girl: My Life After Crisis.*"

Jack kept his eyes on Lauren. "And that's a problem, how?"

"Maybe because I don't have a life." Her voice was low

and amused, a late-night radio voice. But he didn't think she was joking. "I don't know where I go from here."

"So which is it?" he asked. "Are you moving forward? Or running away?"

Her head snapped back. And then she aimed a smile like a punch. "You'll have to buy the book to find out. Excuse me."

She nodded to them both and slipped through the door into the hall.

Definitely running. Jack frowned, watching her go.

"Here's your trap."

He turned.

Meg held out the cage, a gleam in her eyes. "Happy hunting."

Three

THE BANK ROBBERY had left Lauren too aware of her surroundings. She tensed at loud noises. Froze like a stupid rabbit when someone walked into a room. Sometimes she got anxious just walking down the street. Oddly, the constant bustle of the bakery acted as a kind of white noise, screening out distractions, allowing her to concentrate.

But today the shop was almost empty. The sky outside was a cloudless, brilliant blue. Everybody was at the beach, squeezing in one last, glorious sunlit day before the rental week ended.

"Sweet." The man's voice cut easily through her absorption. From his tone of voice, low, suggestive, he wasn't talking about cupcakes.

Lauren flicked a glance toward the cash register. Some guy in a ball cap was chatting up Jane. As distractions went, he was no Jack Rossi. Good-looking, though, in a rough and scruffy way. Dirty blond hair, lean, stubbled face, long, lanky body in ripped jeans and a torn T-shirt. He looked like a grad student who'd spent too much time at the lab, or a homeless guy who'd been sleeping in the park.

He leaned across the counter, pressing in close, stroking Jane's arm. "You done real good for yourself, Janey."

Jane closed the cash drawer with a little snap and said something too quietly for Lauren to hear.

It was none of her business anyway.

She dropped her gaze to her laptop, staring blindly at the blank screen, willing the words to come.

Hostage Girl: My Story had spewed out of her in a matter of months. *Honest and raw*, *Publishers Weekly* had praised. *An intimate portrait of courage and compassion*, wrote the reviewer in the *Washington Post*.

Nobody would say that about her writing now.

Jack Rossi's hard face popped into her head, his dark, deep-set eyes, his sardonic mouth. *What is it that you do?*

I'm a writer.

She closed her eyes. *I'm a fraud.*

Overgeneralizing. Focusing on the negative, chided her therapist training. *Choose a positive, helpful thought.*

Fine. She would think about Ben, who had written to her yesterday to let her know that his brother, Joel, had enlisted in the Army and was now at Fort Jackson, South Carolina, doing his Basic Combat Training.

She could write to Ben. That would really be helpful.

She clicked to open a new document. She knew her letters gave Ben a kind of status in prison. Any mail did. She tried to write at least once a week. It hadn't been easy, at first, finding things to say. Her days were all the same. His, of course, were worse.

They didn't have a lot in common, except the robbery, which they never mentioned. And her dad was dead, and his dad was gone, and they both had younger brothers. So she wrote to him about her brother, Noah, about to start his senior year, and he wrote to her about Joel. Sometimes the contrast between their brothers—their situations, their opportunities—overwhelmed Lauren, despite the money she sent to his mother every month.

Ben's mother never wrote to Lauren. Never acknowledged her checks or her existence, never forgave Lauren for getting rich off the story of their ordeal while Ben rotted in jail.

Breathe.

"Travis, please," Jane said. "I can't talk to you now."

"Then I'll come by later. To the house."

"No."

Lauren looked up, nerves skittering over her skin.

"I have a right to see him," Scruffy Blond Guy said.

"You left him."

"That don't change my rights."

Lauren's heart beat faster. She didn't like his tone of voice. She *really* didn't like his grip on Jane's arm or the sudden tension in Jane's body. She'd seen that same body language too many times in clinical settings, in controlling men and battered women. She knew how suddenly a situation could turn and go south.

Jane pressed her lips together. "We've been through all this before. There's nothing else to say."

"I'm not leaving you, darlin'."

"Bit late for that. Darling," Jane said with unexpected spirit, tugging her arm free.

Lauren forced herself to relax. Not every confrontation was a crisis. She was not involved, it was none of her business, Jane had the situation under control . . .

"Come on, Janey, don't be like that." His tone turned

wheedling. "I'm not asking for much. You want to have this discussion in front of Aidan and your daddy? Or we settle things now."

"Fine." Jane yanked her apron over her head. "Thalia, I have to go to the bank. Can you keep an eye on the shop for a minute?"

The teenager put down her book. "Sure, Jane."

"I won't be long."

The girl glanced curiously from Jane to the waiting man. "Yeah, no problem. It's pretty quiet anyway."

In the doorway, Scruffy Blond Guy tried to take Jane's arm again. She averted her face.

The teenager—Thalia—watched them stalk out, a little pleat between her eyebrows.

Not your clients, Lauren told herself. *Not your responsibility.* She was not the girl in charge anymore, the one who stepped in to quiet the screaming kid at the grocery store, who organized every department birthday party. Who talked three gunmen into laying down their weapons and got one of them killed.

Keep your mouth shut and your nose out of it.

And heard herself ask, "Who was that guy?"

The teen met her gaze, unconsciously seeking reassurance from the only adult around. Lauren had volunteered as a youth leader in a homeless shelter. She knew that look.

Thalia opened her mouth. Shut it. Shrugged.

Because, yeah, dishing about your boss's love life with total strangers was not cool at any age.

Lauren waited. Nature abhorred a vacuum. Silence was one of a therapist's most effective tools for getting clients to talk.

After a minute, Thalia said, "I don't know. He came in once before, I think."

Lauren nodded encouragingly. When that didn't provoke a response, she tried again. "He and Jane seemed . . ." She searched for a word. Not *friendly*. "Close."

"Yeah." Thalia hesitated and then added, "I don't think he's from around here, though."

Lauren smiled. "Well, you would know." On an island with a year-round population that hovered around two thousand, everybody must know everybody else. "Maybe he's here on vacation."

The dirty clothes, the scruffy beard . . . He looked like he might be camping. Sleeping out. Living rough.

"I guess." Thalia's eyes behind her Smart Girl glasses were wide and troubled. "It's not like she has a lot of options."

"There are always options," Lauren said, slipping automatically into therapist mode.

Thalia's slightly round face set. "Maybe if you live someplace else. It's bad enough when you're my age. But Jane is *twenty-nine*." From the tone of her voice, this was ancient.

Lauren winced. She was thirty-one. "Twenty-nine isn't old."

"It is on Dare Island," Thalia said. "Most guys her age are already married."

"What about Jack Rossi?" Thirty-eight and still, according to Meg, single. Virile. Lauren's pulse picked up just thinking about him.

"The chief? He's not married. But he's not that into her."

Lauren's pulse fluttered again. "He comes in all the time."

Thalia snorted. "So does old Mr. Rogers." Lauren recognized the name of one of the older bakery regulars. "That doesn't make him Jane's boyfriend."

"So Jane and Chief Rossi aren't . . ." *Dating? Sleeping together?* "A couple?" Lauren hazarded.

"Nope." Thalia tilted her head. "Why? Are you, like, thinking of going out with him?"

Was she? The thought was intriguing. Terrifying. That would certainly get her out of her rut.

And into emotional quicksand.

"I don't know. Probably not," Lauren said.

"Why not? The chief's kind of hot. For an old guy."

He hasn't asked me. But that was a—*haha*—cop-out. "We're too different," Lauren said.

Thalia grinned again, perfectly comfortable now that they were off the subject of her boss's love life and onto Lauren's. "Well, you know what they say. Opposites attract."

"On a biological level, certainly. Women are hardwired to respond to chemical cues. Basically, we use smell to find mates who are genetically different from us, increasing the chances of survival for our potential offspring."

Maybe that explained her response to Jack Rossi. *It's not me, it's my DNA.* Not that she was going around offering to smell his armpits or have his babies or anything.

"Cool," Thalia said. "So is that, like, what you're writing about?"

No, because that would be interesting.

"Not exactly," Lauren said.

The chimes jangled as two young mothers, six kids in tow, came into the shop.

Thalia gave them a quick look before turning to Lauren. "Can I get you anything?"

"Um." Back to work. For both of them. However fascinating this discussion of Jack Rossi was, Lauren couldn't take up Thalia's time when she had other customers. On the other hand, she couldn't sit for hours using the WiFi, taking up a table, nursing a single cup of coffee. You had to buy. "Maybe iced tea? And . . ." She surveyed the bright, glistening pastry case. "A chocolate croissant, please."

Thalia smiled. "You got it."

Lauren took her croissant, retreating to her table so that Thalia could serve the bakery's other customers. But as the lunch crowd began to straggle in, it was clear that the teenager had more than she could handle. She shuttled between the register, the panini grill, and the espresso machine, making change, sandwiches, drinks, struggling to keep her head in the rising tide of orders. Lauren felt a twinge of sympathy. Jane's errand must be taking longer than either of them had expected.

A buzzer went off somewhere in the back of the bakery. Thalia threw a panicked glance toward the kitchen.

Lauren moved without thinking. "I've got this," she said to Thalia, sliding behind the counter. She pulled the portafilter from the espresso machine. "Go do what you need to do."

Thalia wavered. "But—"

Lauren grinned and dispatched the spent grounds into the knockbox with a well-placed *thwack*. "I used to be a barista. But I can't bake worth a damn. You'll take to take care of whatever's buzzing back there."

"It's the bread."

"Okay." Lauren tamped fresh coffee into the portafilter. "Don't let it burn."

"Right." Thalia smiled. "Thanks."

Thank you, Lauren wanted to say. It felt good to be busy. Helpful. Heck, it felt good simply to be moving again.

Jack Rossi's dark, sardonic eyes gleamed. *Moving forward? Or running away?*

She shoved the thought aside and turned to help the next customer.

JANE CLARK LEFT the tiny branch bank, shaking in the aftermath of conflict.

She'd promised herself that she wouldn't give in again. That Travis was out of their lives forever. But like most promises in her life, this one had crumbled like a piecrust under pressure.

It's only money, she told herself as she walked away. A couple hundred dollars was a small price to pay for her stupidity ten years ago.

She would have paid a lot more to save face with her father. To protect her son.

She inhaled slowly, breathing in the familiar island smells, sand shoals and shell banks, mudflats and rolling sea. Above the electric lines and utility poles, the sky was as bright and blue as an inverted mixing bowl.

She set off toward the bakery, resisting the urge to walk by the school where six-and-a-half-year-old Aidan was in camp. He needed normalcy. Routine. Not a mother who embarrassed him in front of his friends by hanging around the playground, hoping to reassure herself with the sight of him.

The buildings were a jumble of shingle, brick, and cinder block, separated by sandy strips of short, thick grass. Jane was born on this island, one of a tough, perennial breed as hardy as the daisies blooming beside the road. Her roots were here, in the island brogue that occasionally haunted her speech, in the centuries-old gravestones marked CLARK. After her mother left them, Jane's life had totally changed. But the island was constant.

She belonged here. And so did Aidan.

Maybe sometimes Jane dreamed of a second chance, a fresh start, a cooking apprenticeship in New York or Paris. But she'd never *act* on it. A sense of belonging, of continuity, was critical to a child growing up with only one parent.

Besides, as her father once pointed out, who would watch Aidan if she left?

It took a village to raise a child. On the island, there was always a neighbor around to provide snacks, supervision, and car pool rides. Jane was grateful for the help of other single moms like Cynthie Lodge. And she absolutely depended on her dad. She had to leave for the bakery at four every morning. She catered weddings on weekends. Somebody had to be home to see Aidan off to school, to be backup in an emergency.

No matter how bad things got between Jane and her father, Hank was always there for her son.

She swallowed against the ache in her throat. Maybe Dad's semiretirement gave him more time. Or maybe he was simply more comfortable with his grandson than he had ever been with his daughter.

After her mother took off, Hank's days went on the same as before. He went to work, came home, ate in front of the TV, fell asleep after dinner in his old recliner. At twelve, Jane was already taking care of herself and the house, washing the dishes and their laundry, doing her best to fill her mother's place.

She was lonely, haunted by the awareness that she was somehow unworthy of her mother's love and her father's attention.

Most island kids worked, at least during the season, waiting tables, babysitting, helping out in their parents' shops or on their fathers' fishing boats. But Jane had felt isolated, set apart by her father's job as deputy sheriff, hedged by rules, afraid of letting him down. Mortified when he stopped her friends or moved them along when they hung out under the pier or on the sidewalk.

She would never marry a cop.

Jack Rossi, lean and dark and tough-looking, was not for her. If only he'd been a little more approachable or a little less dedicated, if only he'd reminded her a little less of her father, she might have . . . But no. She was done living with *if-onlys*. Because they never worked out. Jack's quiet attention was flattering, but she wanted more in her life than another man's neglect.

By the time Jane was eighteen and Travis sauntered into her life, she had been starved for affection and ripe for rebellion. Hank had tried to warn her. *Shiftless son of a bitch.* But her father's disapproval only increased the thrill of her first romance. Travis was four years older, already— at least in her mind—a man, a carpenter following construction work up and down the coast. *He* had paid attention to her, Jane remembered. To her breasts. Her body.

She could still remember a time when she had wanted that. Welcomed it. When she hadn't been so tired and preoccupied and terrified of her own bad judgment that sex still seemed like a good idea. Or at least a possibility.

Those times were gone.

Jane's Sweet Tea House came into view, the blue tin roof and wide, welcoming porch just visible between the trees. The corners of Jane's mouth softened.

For six years, she had slaved, saved, and borrowed to turn the bakery into the home she'd longed for as a child. To build a future for her son filled with warmth and smiles and the smell of good things wafting from the kitchen. She'd painted the walls herself, chocolate brown and wheat yellow, and scavenged, stripped, and repainted every table and chair. The resulting décor was as eclectic as the buildings around the harbor, a comforting blend of old and new, weathered charm and practicality, from the antique cash register to the sleek refrigerated cases.

Maybe it wasn't perfect. But it was hers. Hers and Aidan's.

She ran a practiced eye over an unbussed table under the trees, the fingerprints smearing the front window. Since Jane's part-time help had decamped last week to follow her boyfriend to Wilmington, the bakery had been short staffed.

And at the moment, it was crowded with business. Her errand had taken longer than she had planned. Poor Thalia must be swamped.

Grabbing the dirty plates from the picnic table, Jane hurried inside.

And stopped.

There was a customer operating the espresso machine. Behind the counter, which was totally off-limits. Lauren Something, with the piercings and puckish smile.

She'd been in every day this week, Jane recalled, occupying the same corner table with her laptop and her phone. Always alone. Unlike some patrons who thought a single cup of coffee entitled them to sit all day, this one actually ordered food—a scone or muffin in the morning, a croissant and fruit at lunch, sometimes a cupcake in the afternoon.

Jane appreciated every one of her customers. She liked feeding people. She was proud of her pastries. And she had overhead to pay.

None of which excused a customer's presence behind the Cimbali machine.

Jane normally cringed from conflict. But the Sweet Tea House was hers. "What are you doing?"

And where on earth was Thalia?

"Oh, hi." Lauren looked up, smiling, before setting a tall glass on the takeaway counter. "Iced mocha cappuccino."

"And an Americano," added the woman waiting for her order.

"Coming right up," Lauren said cheerfully. She glanced at Jane. "If that's okay with you."

"Um." Jane blinked, fascinated and frankly envious of the other woman's ease. "All right. Where's Thalia?"

"Kitchen," Lauren said. "The timer went off."

"Right." Jane slid behind the register to take the next order, watching out of the corner of her eye as Lauren tamped and pulled two shots.

She seemed to know what she was doing. Was she looking for a job? Was that why she sat day after day in the shop, manning her computer and phone? But no, she'd said she was a writer.

Unless that was the sort of thing people said when they couldn't get other work. Real work.

Jane rang up and plated two croissants—ham and Swiss, spinach and feta, a side of fruit, a chocolate chip cookie—as Lauren poured the espresso over hot water, put a lid on the cup, and set it on the counter.

"You look like you've done this before," Jane said.

"I used to work as a barista." Lauren stroked the gleaming Cimbali, the way Jane would pat a loaf of bread. "Your grinder needs adjusting, but you've got yourself a great machine here."

Jane flushed, torn between pleasure at the compliment and defensiveness at the implied criticism. She ran a bakery, not a coffee shop. She'd researched her equipment, buying the best she could afford. But there was no one on the island to teach her how to use it.

"The grinder was adjusted when I bought it," she said.

"Mm," Lauren said noncommittally. "You know, changes in humidity and temperature affect how coarse the grind should be."

"Seriously?"

Lauren nodded. "You should probably adjust it every day."

Jane puffed out her breath. "Right. Okay. Thanks."

She studied the woman in front of her. She couldn't afford to make mistakes. But . . .

"How long are you here for?" she asked abruptly.

Lauren shrugged. "I'm not sure."

"Where are you staying?"

"The Pirates' Rest."

"I know it." The Fletchers' bed-and-breakfast. Not the most expensive place on the island. Not the cheapest, either, especially in midseason. Obviously, Lauren Whatever-her-name-was didn't need to sling coffee to get by.

Which was too bad. The HELP WANTED sign still hung in the window. If only Jane could afford to pay more than a measly hourly wage . . .

No more *if-onlys*.

"Well, it was nice of you to help out. Do you want . . ." *A cup of coffee. A cookie. A muffin.* "A job?"

"Oh, I—"

Jane saw the uncertainty gather like clouds across her face and hurried into speech before she could refuse. "Not full-time or anything. Maybe ten hours a week? Just around the lunch rush. You're here then anyway."

"But I'm working. Writing."

Right. Jane sighed. Well, it had been worth a shot.

Lauren's dark gaze fixed on hers. "Only ten hours?"

Jane nodded, afraid of sounding too eager. Too desperate.

Lauren bit down on her lower lip. "I have been in kind of a rut," she admitted.

"We could give it a couple days. See how it goes. You'd really be helping me out," Jane added.

That didn't sound too needy. Did it?

And maybe it was the right thing to say, because Lauren's smile broke like the sun through clouds. "Sure. Why not?"

JACK DROVE THROUGH the center of town toward the bakery. Fifteen months ago, he'd been a plainclothes detective with an unmarked car. Driving the big, department-marked SUV made him feel like a beat cop again, like a giant leap back.

But he had a chief's responsibilities now. Bottom line, the shield on the door, the lights on top, were a visual deterrent to crime. For every tourist speeding through town, for every island kid with too much time on his hands, the official-looking vehicle and uniform served as a reminder. *Slow down. Think twice.*

Jack parked the SUV near the road, where it could be seen by passing motorists. Gravel and oyster shells crunched underfoot as he stepped out into the lot.

He climbed the steps to the porch, anticipation tightening all the muscles in his abdomen, like he was about to take a punch to the gut. Like he didn't need coffee, his heart already pounding.

The over-the-door bells chimed. He stood a moment silently inside the doorway, eyes adjusting to the light.

Jane was coming out of the kitchen with a tray, a smudge of flour on one flushed cheek, pink and white and delectable as one of her own cupcakes. He looked past her toward the corner table, Lauren's table. Empty.

She wasn't there.

The unnamed hope in his chest collapsed, leaving him deflated.

Jesus Christ. He wasn't a fourteen-year-old boy anymore, hanging around some girl's locker after class, waiting for her to show.

Even at fourteen, he'd never had to wait. Females had been coming on to him since first grade when Tina Zanelli offered to show him her underpants if he'd be her boyfriend. He couldn't remember how that had worked out. He might have taken her up on her dare. She could have delivered on her promise. More likely, he'd said something rude and the opportunity had been lost.

Proving he hadn't learned a damn thing in thirty years. What the hell had he been thinking, busting Lauren's chops the other day, making that crack about her running away?

Relationships were supposed to get easier when you got older. More supportive or sophisticated or something.

Maybe Renee was right. *You only see what you want*, she used to say. *You don't think about what I need. You don't know how to make a woman happy.*

His jaw set. He'd known how to make her come, though. For a while, that had been enough.

"You look like you could use a cookie." Lauren's voice broke into his thoughts.

He turned his head and she was there, her dark hair slipping its messy bundle, the stud on the side of her nose winking at him like a tiny exclamation point: *Here I am!*

Something inside him contracted like a fist and then relaxed. "You sound like my mother."

Her brows rose in question.

"Ma believes most of the world's problems can be solved with food."

Comprehension lit her eyes like laughter. "Well, it's a place to start."

He met her gaze. Held it. Today she wore a cuff shaped like a snake with jeweled eyes, coiling under her hair, whispering in her ear. Tempting her. Tempting him. Where else was she pierced?

A rush of heat washed through him. He wanted a lot more from her than a cookie.

He took a deep breath. *Slow down. Think twice.* She wasn't some shiny image on his television anymore, the one bright spot in his boozy, miserable world.

He forced himself to step back, to remember their surroundings. And saw her hands full of dirty glasses, the apron around her neck.

"What are you doing?" he asked. Rookie question.

She shrugged. "Working."

"Bussing tables." Not a question this time.

"Among other things," she said lightly. "I also make coffee. Don't judge."

She had it all wrong. He admired her, her courage, her willingness to put herself out there. *Hostage Girl.*

"Coffee's good," he said. "I wish we had somebody around the office who could brew a decent pot of coffee."

"Then you wouldn't have an excuse to drop by here anymore."

He went still. She'd heard him say he didn't come by for the coffee. Did she think he came by to see Jane? He didn't want her to think that, for reasons he wasn't prepared to examine. "I don't need an excuse. It's my town."

She smiled suddenly. "I thought maybe you were going to ask why I'm not working on my book."

He shook his head. "It's not my job to rag on you about how you spend your time."

"Gee, thanks."

Her droll tone made his lips twitch. "I'll leave that to Meg."

Her smile lost some of its shine. "She doesn't know yet."

He frowned. "You haven't told her?"

She regarded him thoughtfully, her pupils wide, like she was trying to see inside the darkness in his head. "I'm not hiding anything. I just haven't had a chance to talk to her."

"I only offered Lauren the job half an hour ago," Jane said. "She hasn't even filled out the paperwork yet."

Not hiding, Jack thought with relief. Not lying.

Not that it was any of his business.

"You might want to mention it," he said. "Unless you want Meg to hear about it from somebody else."

"Who's going to tell her? Nobody even knows who I am. That's why I came down here."

"You'd be surprised. On an island, everybody knows everything."

"And what they don't know, they make up," Jane said, her tone bitter.

He took another look at her. Her smoke gray eyes were shadowed, her soft face strained.

Well, hell. Maybe there was something to the talk after all.

"Heard your ex-husband's back," he said.

She blinked and then sighed. "How did you know? Who told you?"

He wasn't ratting out Hank. "Word gets around. He giving you any trouble?"

Her lashes swept down, veiling her eyes. "Nothing I can't handle."

Lauren threw her a quick, uncertain glance.

Interesting.

Jack gave them both a minute in case they had anything

to add, but Jane remained stubbornly silent. And Lauren, who until this moment had shown no hesitation in butting into things, kept her mouth shut.

Jack wasn't here to stir up trouble. "If anything changes, if he bothers you, you let me know," he said.

A blush suffused Jane's face like heat inside a cup. "Why? So you and my dad can discuss my lousy judgment in men? I don't need that kind of help."

"This isn't about your father, Jane."

Jane crossed her arms at her waist over her apron. "Can you honestly tell me Hank didn't ask you to check up on me?"

No, he couldn't tell her that. And he couldn't explain, even to himself, why, if Hank was worried about his daughter, he hadn't come by to see her himself.

"He cares about you," Jack said instead.

"I know." Her head dipped, in acknowledgment or defeat. "You tell him I'm fine. I'm making ham and collards for dinner. Aidan has T-ball practice tonight, but you tell him I'll leave him a plate. He'll know what that means."

Girl code. Dinner in the oven meant Jane cared about Hank, too. Jack frowned. And that they wouldn't be discussing anything when her father got home that night.

She escaped into the kitchen, her rubber-soled shoes squeaking on the old wooden floor.

Lauren handed him something wrapped in a napkin.

Jack narrowed his eyes in surprise. "What's this?"

"A cookie."

He could see it was a cookie. "I meant, why are you giving it to me?"

"I told you. You looked like you needed one. And . . ." Her eyes met his. "That was nice, what you said to Jane. Nice of you to look out for her."

He wasn't nice.

He was closed and uncommunicative and angry most of the time. If she imagined he was nice, she was only going to be disappointed.

"I'm just doing my job," he said, more harshly than he intended.

But she didn't back down. Damned if he didn't like that about her. "Take it anyway. You should never leave a bakery empty-handed."

He shook his head. "Thanks. But I already got what I came for."

She searched his gaze. "Information?"

You, he almost said. *I wanted to see you.*

But the admission made him deeply uneasy. Hell, the thought made him deeply uneasy.

So he took the cookie and left, the big, bad police chief running from the quirky writer with the pierced nose and too-perceptive eyes.

Four

THE FOLLOWING MONDAY, Jack borrowed a bucket and supplies from the fire station and hunkered down in the parking lot to wash the department SUV. The sun beat down, heating the hood, leaving water spots on the paint.

"Hell of a way to spend your day off," Hank observed.

Jack hosed the vehicle's roof. "You're one to talk."

"A man your age should have better things to do."

An image surfaced of Lauren Patterson, holding out that cookie like Eve with the fucking apple. And that tiny stud in her nose, winking, irresistible . . . She tempted him on more than one level.

He'd like to do her. Hell, he just liked her, her expressive face, her crazy earring, her dark, intelligent eyes.

Tension shivered through him, rippling through his muscles, like he was a sleeper waking to arousal. She made him remember how it felt to be alive.

He ran the dripping sponge over the windshield, dissolving the bloom of salt. He finally had his life under control again. He had himself under control. All the time. *Take a breath, go for a run, hit the heavy bag instead of the bottle.* He wasn't looking to lose it all again over a woman.

No more emotional highs and lows. No games. No lies.

Hank was still watching him, waiting for a response.

"Take care of your gear and it'll take care of you," Jack said evenly.

"Couldn't find another sucker for the job, huh?"

He dropped his sponge into the bucket of sudsy water. "You volunteering?"

"Hell, no. I'm fifty-eight, boy. I'm too old, too mean, and too tired to volunteer for anything."

A smile tugged Jack's mouth. "That why you turned down the chief's job?"

"Pretty much." Hank's face creased in a grin. "Plus I didn't want to spend my remaining years kissing the town council's ass."

"So you became a reserve officer instead."

"Said I was old. Didn't say I was smart." Hank watched Jack pick up the hose, playing water over the hood. "You know, you could have gone to the Soap and Suds."

The Soap and Suds Car Wash and Beer Barn was half an hour away on the other side of the bridge. Off island. Out of Jack's jurisdiction. Too far away if the officer on duty—it was Luke today—suddenly needed backup. Not to mention the public relations fail of taking a police vehicle to a drive-through liquor store.

Jack picked up the sponge again. "You didn't come out here to critique my car-washing technique."

Hank grunted in acknowledgment. "Heard that low-life scumbag asshole Tillett's still in town," he said after a pause.

And there it was. The real reason Hank was out here in this heat instead of inside reading the paper. Travis Tillett, Jane's ex.

"I ran him through the database," Jack said. "Vehicle registration checks out. No outstanding warrants."

"He doesn't belong here."

Neither did Jack, according to half the island's old-timers. He smiled thinly. "If that was enough to lock him up, I'd have to arrest the entire tourist population."

"Not a bad idea," Hank said.

Jack didn't respond.

"He giving Jane any trouble?"

Jack thought of Jane's veiled look, Lauren's quick, uncertain glance.

If he bothers you, you let me know.

Why? So you and my dad can discuss my lousy judgment in men? I don't need that kind of help.

"You could ask her yourself," he suggested. *Leave me out of it.*

"It might have escaped your notice," Hank said, his drawl thickening, "you being a big-city detective and all, but my daughter and I aren't exactly what you'd call close."

"I noticed. I just don't understand why. Seeing as how you're so easy to get along with," Jack added dryly.

A snort of laughter escaped Hank before his face relapsed into its usual gloomy lines. "I should have put in more time at home when she was growing up."

Jack shifted, uncomfortable with the direction the conversation had taken. He didn't think Hank was the type to stand around jawing about his *feelings*. But you never could tell. "You can't change what's past."

He was pretty sure the shrink had said that. Something like that anyway.

"She always seemed to be doing okay. Never any trouble, that girl. Not until *he* came sniffing around."

Jack reached for the hose again to avoid answering. Maybe Jane had been a model daughter before Tillett. Or maybe Hank was kidding himself. In Jack's experience, you didn't see what you didn't want to see.

Look at the way Jack had fucked up his marriage. He'd known Renee wasn't happy. The signs were all there. Work . . . Well, they'd both always worked too many hours. And the sex had been good, at least until the very end. But there had been plenty of clues, if he'd been willing to see them—the calls she didn't take, the simmering silences, the snide comments in front of their friends. He'd chosen to ignore them, and that was on him.

He'd never suspected his wife was fucking his partner, though. *Don't shit where you eat.* And that was on them.

His hand flexed on the sponge. He could still feel the phantom throb of his knuckles where they'd connected with Frank's jaw. Still remember the impact in his chest, betrayal blooming like blood from a gunshot wound.

He stared down at the sponge, dripping over the hood. He was going over and over the same spot, scrubbing at an invisible stain.

The inside phone rang, jerking at his attention.

Hank straightened from his post against the rail. "I got it."

When Jack started this job, the one cop in a one-cop town, unanswered calls to the department were forwarded either to his cell phone or to his backup—Hank, if Hank was around, or the dispatcher in the county sheriff's office. But there were three of them now. Jack had been talking to Nick O'Neal, head of the volunteer firefighters, about developing a coordinated emergency response, police, fire, medical. But that would demand a hell of a lot more sophisticated system than they had now.

Hank came out, his face creased in heavy lines. "That was Grady Real Estate. Somebody busted the air conditioner over at the bakery. Repairman's saying it's vandalism."

Jack went still, his skin tightening. *Lauren*. "Everything else okay?"

"Fine. But Grady wants a police report so he can file an insurance claim."

"Right." Jack drew a careful breath. *Don't overreact*. Vandalism was a common problem on the island, where big vacation homes sat empty half the year. "You want to take it?"

Since you're so concerned about her ex. Jane was Hank's daughter. It was her bakery. Nothing to do with Jack at all.

Was Lauren there?

"She won't want me," Hank said gruffly. "Luke's on duty."

"He's on a call." The Crowleys' dog, barking again, disturbing the renters next door. Nothing that required much time. But maybe Luke's absence would give Hank the excuse he needed to go.

Hank's face set. "So he can handle it on his way back."

Of course he could.

And in the meantime, Jane was fine. Lauren was fine. It was only vandalism. Nothing dangerous. Not like, say, getting caught in a bank robbery and being held hostage for three days.

The thought made his gut clench.

How was Lauren handling this? She was a crime victim. She might act like she was over it now, but you didn't walk away from what she'd been through without it affecting you. Jack had been a sniper. He knew.

He dried his hands, reached for his keys. "I'll check it out."

THE BAKERY WAS hot as hell. Condensation dripped on the outside of the steel-and-glass refrigerated cases.

Behind the counter, Lauren was dripping, too. Sweat slid down her spine; soaked the band of her bra. She wiped her face with the back of her forearm.

The bakery had nearly emptied, the climbing temperatures inside driving patrons outside to the tables under the trees. Apparently the heat was more bearable outdoors away from the ovens. But the shift meant that she and Thalia were kept running, serving orders, bussing tables, as Jane dealt with the repairman out back.

Lauren scraped the last scoop of ice from the cooler, her mind leaping ahead. They couldn't make drinks without ice. She glanced toward the kitchen door. If Jane didn't come back soon, Lauren might have to close, if only to run out and buy more ice.

God, it was hot, a blanketing heat that smothered her in exhaustion.

The silver bells over the entrance jangled. Her stomach tightened like a fist. More than a year after the robbery, she still tensed sometimes at sudden entrances. She looked up, forcing a smile to her lips.

Jack stood in the door of the bakery wearing jeans and a damp white T-shirt, projecting an air of cool authority.

And she just . . . melted. Like the icing on the cupcakes.

Wow. Just . . . Wow. He looked different out of uniform, younger, tougher, more aggressive. Everything that was soft and weak and fluid inside her just flowed toward him, attracted by his power and sense of purpose. As if he could stamp her, mold her, shape her somehow into something stronger and more durable. He had all the confidence she lacked right now. How was she supposed to resist him? Did she even want to?

The jeans rode low on his narrow hips. The T-shirt molded to his heavily muscled chest. Beneath the thin white cotton, she could see the shadow of his body hair. She flushed all over as if she'd been scalded.

He came toward her with that fluid walk she admired so much, all contained power and masculine grace. *Oh, God.* She was abruptly aware that her face was hot and undoubtedly shiny. She probably stank, too.

Most individuals selected partners of comparable attractiveness. At her best, Lauren was, well, interesting-looking. And right now, she was *not* at her best.

Be cool. "Hi, Jack."

Those black Italian eyes met hers. "Lauren."

Save me, she thought, and then chided herself. He wasn't here for her. "Jane's in the back with the repairman. You can go out through the kitchen."

He nodded once, his gaze sharp on her face, like he was waiting for something.

"She, um, she didn't want to call you. But her landlord said she needed to get a police report so he could file an insurance claim."

"Okay. Thanks." But he didn't move on. "You doing okay?"

His concern made her throat clog. She worked enough moisture into her mouth to swallow. "I'm fine."

A smile touched his lips. "Because you look like you could use a cookie."

Something inside her eased and bloomed into a smile.

His eyes warmed. "That's my girl," he murmured.

Her breath caught. Okay, he didn't actually say that. She must have misheard him. *Thattagirl*, maybe?

He smiled again, a brief curve to that hard mouth, and walked away, leaving her hot and longing and bewildered.

"Crap," Thalia said. "Are we out of ice?"

"I'LL STAY." LAUREN squeezed Jane's hand. Despite the sweltering heat inside the bakery, Jane's fingers felt cold. "At least until Thalia gets back with the ice."

Jane's fingers tightened once, convulsively, before she pulled away. "I'll be fine. You've done enough already. I probably have to close for the rest of the day anyway."

Lauren pushed back her hair with her wrist. "What about tomorrow?"

Jane sighed. "I don't know. The temperature will drop enough overnight that I can get some baking done, but there's no way I can decorate cakes in this heat. And it's going to be miserable in the shop."

It was miserable now.

"I'll be here," Lauren said staunchly.

"It will be a light day." Jane pressed her trembling lips together. "If we open at all."

"I can still help out," Lauren said. Although she didn't want to take Jane's money if there weren't going to be any customers. "Or just, you know, hang out. If you want company." *If you need support.*

Jane met her gaze, gray eyes soft and grateful. "Thanks."

They weren't friends. But they could be. It had been a long time since Lauren had connected with anyone outside the bubble created by the bank standoff. With someone who needed something from her besides a sound bite or a book.

"No problem," Lauren said warmly. And it wasn't. She *wanted* to help. Whether that help would be welcome or not.

"Jane." She hesitated, trying to figure out her approach. They weren't therapist and client. And questioning your boss about her potentially vengeful ex was definitely not in the employee handbook. "Do you have any idea who could have done this?"

Jane's gaze dropped to the counter. She moved a glass a quarter of an inch to one side. "No."

She was lying. But confronting her directly would only make her more defensive.

"I'm not judging. I want to help," Lauren said honestly. Sometimes sharing the truth, even a small, personal truth, created trust between strangers. It had worked before with Ben. *Ben, who was in prison now, so maybe that hadn't worked out so well for him.*

Not a positive thought. Think positive.

Jane's lips parted, as if she might actually speak. And then her gaze caught on Jack, entering silently from the kitchen, and her lashes swept down again.

"Thanks," she said. "But I'm fine."

The breakthrough moment—if that's what it was—slipped away. Lauren bit her lip in frustration.

Jack prowled closer, his black eyes alert. "Everything okay here?"

Jane raised her chin. "Yes. I was just telling Lauren she should go home."

His gaze switched to Lauren. "You need a lift?"

She tilted her head. "That depends. Do I have to sit in the back of the patrol car?"

Black laughter leaped in his eyes like flames, sending flickers of warmth through her. "It's my day off. You promise to be a good girl, you can sit up front. I might even let you play with the siren."

Her heart thumped. She wanted to play. The flickers kindled and spread, heating her from the inside out.

But it didn't feel right, lusting over the chief of police when Jane had just been vandalized. "I don't want to take you away from your crime scene."

"I'm done here. I need to get back to the office and type up my report." He looked at Jane. "Grady has the case number. He'll be able to file the claim today."

"Thank you."

"I'm giving you the phone number for Island Security Systems. They do alarm systems for a lot of local businesses. Sam Grady says they'll give you a price break if you want to get something installed."

Jane took the piece of paper. "Thanks."

Jack tucked away his notebook. "Somebody from the sheriff's department will be by tomorrow to process the scene. They'll be out of your way before the repairman gets here."

The paper crumpled in Jane's grasp. "Is that really necessary? I mean, if the insurance company is paying for the damage—"

"It's just routine," Jack said evenly. "You got a problem with it, you need to take that up with your landlord."

Jane's mouth snapped shut.

"What was all that about?" Lauren demanded as she slid into the front seat of the department SUV.

Jack closed the passenger door—at least he hadn't put his hand on top of her head as she climbed in—and walked around to the driver's side. "Buckle up."

She fumbled for the seat belt. "What's the sheriff going to do, search for fingerprints?"

"That's the idea."

She raised her head to look at him in disbelief. "Seriously?"

"Guy did a couple thousand dollars' worth of damage. Around here that constitutes a major crime." Something that might have been a smile touched the corners of his mouth. "You're not in the big city anymore."

"Neither are you." She studied his Great Stone Face, trying to read him. "Do you miss it?"

Jack started the engine without answering. The air-conditioning whooshed on. Lauren jumped as the dashboard blasted her with heat.

"What time did you come in this morning?" he asked.

She adjusted her vent, uncomfortable. "I don't know. Nine?"

"You notice anything unusual?"

Her mouth twisted. "You mean, besides that it was getting really hot?"

"Any unfamiliar cars, any suspicious characters . . ."

She stopped fussing with the vent long enough to shoot him a disbelieving look. "Wait a minute. Did you just offer me a ride so that you could *question* me?"

"I offered you a ride because you look ready to fall over." He reached between the seats and handed her a bottle of water. "Here."

She blinked, off balance. "What's this?"

"You've been working in the heat for hours. Drink."

"Thank you." She unscrewed the top, touched and taken aback by his care. It was so . . . sweet. So at odds with his hard-boiled appearance. *Rescue me.* She swallowed, searching for some defense against her own vulnerability. "You know, most plastic bottles end up in landfills or the ocean," she announced suddenly. "Tap water is just as good for you and better for the environment."

He looked at her sideways. "Have you tasted the tap water on the island?"

The air from the vents was cooling, evaporating the sweat on her forehead and between her breasts. Her spine wanted to melt into the deep leather seat. She forced herself to sit up. "The water at the inn tastes fine."

"Probably filtered."

"Oh." This was one of the most inane conversations ever. But he was playing along, giving her time to recover. She was grateful for his patience. And the water. She swigged from the bottle. Licked her lips. "What about the bakery?"

Jack raised his gaze from . . . Was he looking at her *mouth*? "Same thing. Pretty much anyplace that caters to visitors is going to have filtered water."

Well, that made sense. She drank some more, holding the water in her parched mouth, absorbing it into her tissues.

The inn was within walking distance of the bakery, a little over a mile, but the number of tourist cars and bicycles on the narrow road made the trip take much longer. She didn't mind. The AC lapped her in comfort. She felt herself reviving like a plant out of the heat.

Jack sent her another dark, assessing glance. "You doing okay? No bad effects?"

She shook her head. "Thanks," she said again. "I guess I was a little dehydrated."

"I meant from the vandalism."

She stared at him, shocked by his understanding.

She'd learned from experience that nobody—not the reporters or radio interviewers or her fellow students or her mother—really wanted to listen to Hostage Girl being insecure. They wanted her to be brave. They wanted her to inspire them. And then they wanted her to get over it, because anything else demanded too much of them.

"I'm fine," she said, relieved because it was almost true. "I wasn't even there when it happened."

She wasn't the one whose space, whose trust, had been violated. It wasn't her trauma.

"So you didn't see anything. Anybody."

She rolled the wet bottle between her hands. What could she say? How much should she tell him? Not her trauma. Not her secret, either. She wasn't bound by client confidentiality in this case. But maybe she was bound by friendship? Jane had quite clearly avoided naming her ex as a potential suspect.

"There are people in and out of the bakery all the time. I couldn't tell you who's a regular or who's just visiting or who . . . or if anyone is likely to cause a problem. You need to ask Jane."

"Her ex ever drop by? Travis Tillett."

Lauren bit her lip. Not so much of a secret after all. "Not today."

Jack just looked at her, the way she would look at a client who was being evasive. She would look and wait and then say, *I can't help you if you don't let me know exactly what's going on.*

What would help Jane?

Lauren didn't know Jack well enough to trust him. But she could at least cooperate in his investigation. "He came in on Friday to see Jane. She didn't want to talk then, but she didn't want him coming by the house, either. She left with him. She was gone about an hour. An errand at the bank, she said."

There, Lauren thought, relieved. She'd even managed that last bit—*an errand at the bank*—without a hitch, as if the words didn't cause a blip in her heartbeat.

She hadn't been inside a bank building since the robbery.

Jack didn't say anything.

"What are you going to do?" she asked.

"What you said. Talk to Jane."

That sounded promising. But . . . "You know, she may not want to talk with you."

He made a noncommittal noise. Lauren used the same sound when she worked at the family clinic, an acknowledgment token, a signal to the client to continue. It was oddly reassuring to hear it from him. Like discovering they spoke a shared language.

She took a breath and forged ahead. "A lot of women are reluctant to report harassment to the police. Especially in domestic cases."

He slid her a look. Amused? Annoyed? "You think I don't know this? I've been a cop a long time."

"I'm sure that makes you a model of sensitivity," she said politely.

His lips twitched.

Encouraged, she continued. "Maybe Jane thinks she can handle the situation. Maybe she's afraid of what could happen once the authorities are called in. Once you tell someone, it's out of your control."

An image of black-clad figures burst into her brain. Pounding feet. Pandemonium. Voices shouting, *Police! Stay down, stay down.*

She curled her hands around the bottle, holding it tight, the condensation like cold sweat against her palms. *Once the authorities are called in . . .*

"If her ex is vandalizing her place, she's not controlling shit," Jack said.

Lauren pulled herself together. They were talking about Jane, she reminded herself. It wasn't personal. She shoved down the memory of blood sinking into the bank's blue carpet, the betrayal in Ben's eyes.

She took another sip of water. "You know that," she said. "Jane doesn't."

"She should. Her dad's a cop."

Lauren's brows drew together in confusion.

"Hank Clark, retired sheriff's deputy," Jack explained. "He's part-time now with the police department. Jane and her kid live with him."

Something clicked in Lauren's memory. *That don't change my rights . . . You want to have this discussion in front of Aidan and your daddy?*

"Jane has a child."

Jack nodded. "Little boy. Aidan."

"Do you know if her ex has visitation rights?"

"I'll find out."

"How does Jane's father feel about all this?"

Jack shrugged.

Of course, Lauren thought. Never ask a cop how he feels. Because they were *guys*. They didn't sit around discussing their *foolings*.

But then Jack surprised her. "He's worried about her. I get the impression he thought this guy was bad news from the beginning."

"So asking for help means admitting to her father that he was right all along."

"That's no reason to protect this asshole."

"Maybe she's protecting her son. Or herself."

Another glance from those almost-black eyes. Definite amusement this time. "You sound like a shrink."

"I am a shrink. Although 'counselor' works. Or 'therapist,' " she said lightly.

Jack frowned. "I thought you were a psychology student."

It had been in the news coverage. She was surprised he remembered. "Graduate student. I'm getting my doctorate." *If I ever go back.* "I see patients in a supervised clinical setting."

Jack shook his head, like he couldn't believe it. "A *shrink*," he repeated.

Her heart sank a little. "Is that a problem?" she asked.

He didn't answer right away. *So, yes.* She suppressed a sigh. And here she'd been thinking they spoke the same language. "A lot of people could benefit from counseling," she said.

He raised one dark, sexy eyebrow. "Present company included?"

"I was talking about *Jane.* Mediation could help her if there's a custody issue."

"Yeah, maybe. Or I can find this guy and talk to him."

He sounded so confident, Lauren thought wistfully. So sure of himself and the situation. Maybe he wouldn't mind if she borrowed a little of that confidence for a while.

God, she was pathetic. She barely knew him.

And maybe that was part of his appeal. She was free to imagine anything she wanted, to invest him with all kinds of magical qualities. He could be the man of her dreams.

Harmless enough, as long as she kept him a fantasy.

"Don't you need some kind of proof first that he's involved?"

"I'm not going to drag him in and beat him up," Jack said stiffly. "But there's nothing to stop me from approaching the guy on the street and starting a conversation."

He looked so hard and dangerous. He made her feel so safe. *Jack Rossi to the rescue.*

She fought a shiver of longing.

He must have caught the movement, because his eyes narrowed. "What?"

As if she were accusing him of police brutality when in fact she admired his ability to do his job within the constraints of the law. "I'm just wondering where you draw the line between your personal and professional life."

His jaw set. "I don't."

He still sounded stiff. Defensive. Her insides squeezed in sympathy.

She nodded, emboldened by her understanding. "I guess that's something we have in common. It's hard sometimes to maintain an appropriate emotional distance. I mean, you have to care to do your job."

He was looking at her oddly. "I meant I don't have a personal life."

"Oh." She was embarrassed. "I find that hard to believe." He was so attractive.

"Then you haven't ever dated a cop."

She didn't date. She hung out. She hooked up. But never with a cop before.

"Cops can't have personal lives?"

"When? Days I'm on, I work split shifts, do the rounds in the morning, another at the end of the day. So I don't get home 'til seven, eight o'clock. I work weekends. I'm on call nights."

"You must get some time off."

"Sure. A couple hours in the afternoon to do paperwork, run errands." A corner of his mouth kicked up. "And I made it a rule that if I get called out in the middle of the night, somebody better be bleeding or somebody's going to jail."

She smiled. "Setting boundaries."

"Yeah."

"I'm not very good at that."

Another sidelong glance. "You got problems with your fans?"

"My . . . Oh, my readers? No, not really. My readers are wonderful. Aside from the occasional creepy guy at book signings. I was talking about my clients." *And Ben.* But she never talked about Ben.

The peaked roof of the Pirates' Rest emerged through the trees. They were almost at the inn. Disappointment curled inside her. Her moment-out-of-time with Fantasy Man was almost over.

"My wife was a cop," Jack said out of the blue.

My wife.

The two words punched into her midsection, robbing her of breath. A doorknob moment, they called it in therapy, when a client dropped a major bombshell admission on his or her way out the door.

Was. Past tense.

"She's not . . ." Lauren trailed off tactfully.

"Dead?" He pulled the SUV into a parking slot under a blooming crepe myrtle. "No. We're divorced."

"Oh. Good."

He gave her an unreadable look.

Oops. "I mean, not *good*, just . . ." She pulled her thoughts together, trying to hear what he would not say. "Do you blame your job for the difficulty in your marriage?" *Your wife? Yourself?*

"I'm not blaming anybody." The flowering branches shielded them from the back of the house, filtering an incongruous pink light through the windshield. "I'm just telling you how it is."

"Why?" Her heart slammed. Her stomach fluttered. *Why are you telling me this?* Was he trying to warn her? Or to warn her off?

Maybe she was jumping to conclusions. Other than offering her a ride—*purely in his role as public servant?*—Jack hadn't done a thing to signal that he was interested in her personally. Which was really too bad, because he had that whole good cop/bad cop thing going on, all in one tightly wrapped masculine package—the brute muscles and cool control, the brooding intensity of his dark, deep-set eyes, the wry, amused curve of his mouth. When she climbed into the SUV, his scent had wrapped around her, soap and sweat and pheromones, until she wanted to bury her nose in the damp soft cotton of his shirt and sniff him all over.

He shrugged. "I thought you should know."

She sat a moment, absorbing that. "How long?"

"Since the divorce? Six months."

"But you've been down here a year."

He cut the engine. "Yeah. So?"

She took a breath. The rush of oxygen made her light-headed. Her chest expanded with possibilities. "And there hasn't been anybody since."

"No. What the hell difference does it make?"

Adrenaline spiked her blood. Not fear. This anticipation was warm and easy. "If I invite you in for a drink, would that violate your professional or personal boundaries?"

He went still, his hand on the keys. The inside of the vehicle heated up. The air felt charged.

Lauren's face flushed as the silence stretched. She wondered if he could hear the wild beating of her heart. "I'm not trying to pressure you. I just think you're probably ready for a rebound relationship."

He met her gaze, his dark eyes intent. Predatory. "Let's find out."

Five

JACK STRODE UP the flagstone walk, following the movement of Lauren's smooth, round butt beneath her short, snug skirt. No lines.

She wasn't his usual type. Before he met her, he didn't consider himself the kind of guy who was in the market for a casual hookup.

But his dick didn't care.

The sunlight struck glints in her dark hair like charcoal sparks. She glowed with life and perspiration, warming him in places that had been dead cold a long, long time. She appealed to something dark and animal inside him, a darkness he usually hid, an animal he was doing his damnedest to control.

At least until they got into the house.

Anticipation surged through him, heavy and thick. His skin tightened.

She didn't use the back door—the family entrance. She

led him around to the shaded porch on the side of the house instead, where the inn guests sometimes took breakfast or sat at the end of the day. Inside the French doors was a butler's pantry with a coffee service and refrigerator for guest use. Through the access on the other end, he could see the Fletchers' kitchen.

Lauren stretched to open a glass-fronted cabinet above the counter, her little top riding up to expose a narrow band of pale skin and ink, curling lines following the sexy lower curve of her back. A rush of heat slammed into him, blinding him with lust like a teenage boy. He wanted to press his mouth to the base of her spine, to trace her tattoo with his lips.

She turned, holding two glasses. "Drink?"

Hell. He'd figured the drink was just an excuse. A ruse. Like inviting somebody up for coffee after a date. But what did he know? He hadn't been on a date in years.

She was dehydrated, he reminded himself. And maybe it was better if he didn't fall on her like a pit bull. He didn't know if this was a one-off thing for her or if there was going to be a repeat performance. If he wasn't going to get a second shot, he wanted to make this last.

"Sure."

She smiled—*right answer*—and turned away again, reaching into the mini fridge. When she bent over, her skirt and top separated again, revealing the vulnerable bumps of her vertebrae and that lick of ink against her skin. He crossed his arms over his chest and settled back, determined to take this at her pace.

She straightened, a bottle of wine in her hands. "White okay? Or would you like a beer?"

"Wine's fine."

He wasn't planning on drinking anyway. He didn't drink in the afternoon. Not anymore.

She turned back to the counter to open the bottle.

With another woman, he'd figure she'd pulled out the alcohol to relieve her nerves, to ease the awkwardness of sex with a near stranger. But Lauren didn't look nervous. Maybe the wine put a gloss of civility over the whole thing. Maybe she was making a point to him or to herself that he wasn't just here for the sex.

He felt a twinge of . . . something. Conscience? Which was stupid. He'd been honest. They both had.

I'm just telling you how it is.

You're probably ready for a rebound relationship.

They were both going into this with their eyes open. But her hands on the corkscrew weren't quite steady. So maybe she was a little nervous after all.

Tenderness uncurled inside him.

He came up behind her as she poured the wine and rested his hands at her waist, his thumbs riding that half inch of warm, exposed skin. She jolted, gripping the bottle, and then released it to relax against him, her muscles loosening, yielding. He loved that, that she yielded. To reward her, to indulge himself, he bent his head to her throat. Her hair brushed the side of his face. Her scent was warm and musky like sex. Opening his lips, he pressed his mouth to the soft hollow of her neck. Her shudder rocked them both.

His fingers tightened on her waist. He had enough control to do that, to keep his hands from sliding to her breasts. His erection lodged against her bottom. She made a soft, assenting sound. Turning in his hold, she twined her arms around his neck and pulled his head down for her kiss.

And hello, yeah, she could kiss.

Her mouth was hot and slick and sweet. Her kiss cut into him like a knife into butter, melting him with her response. Well, except for the part of him that definitely wasn't melting, that jutted, hard and eager, against her stomach.

"Jack." The interruption dashed over him like a bucket of cold water. "Luke didn't tell me you were coming by today."

Tess Fletcher. Luke's mother.

Reluctantly, Jack raised his head. Lauren stared back up at him, her eyes wide and dark, her lips pink and wet.

His mind blanked. Stumbled.

Lauren was a guest of Tess's inn. Okay, so the Pirates' Rest wasn't the no-tell motel next to the trailer park on the other side of the bridge. But the inn had a goddamn honeymoon suite. Guests probably had sex there all the time. Just because Tess Fletcher found him kissing the shit out of a guest in the pantry was no reason he couldn't . . . They shouldn't . . .

Fuck.

Or not.

He turned, sliding his hand to the small of Lauren's back, shifting her in front of him like a shield to hide his obvious erection.

"Tess." Even to his own ears, his voice sounded husky.

Luke's mother, Teresa Saltoni Fletcher, was a slim, attractive woman in her fifties with a smile-lined face and dark Italian eyes. Her gaze met Jack's. Her eyebrows rose, very slightly. A mother's look. Ah, hell. This woman knew him, had invited him to Christmas dinner at her house. He felt fifteen again, sneaking Amy Wolacek down to the basement rec room to have sex on the gnarly brown couch.

Lauren grinned, unabashed. "It was kind of an impulse thing."

"I see." Tess regarded them thoughtfully.

Jack bet she did. The woman was married forty years with two sons. He was pretty sure she didn't miss a trick.

She smiled. "I didn't realize you two knew each other."

Jack's brain still wasn't working properly, his dick still focused on getting upstairs and into Lauren. He was determined to keep things compartmentalized, to separate sex and the job, *Lauren here, Dare Island there, no problem.* But Tess's arrival had blurred his neat divisions.

Before he could formulate a response, he heard quick, firm strides cross the kitchen floor and Luke Fletcher walked in.

"Hey. Hi, Mom." His sharp blue gaze cut to Jack. "I saw the patrol vehicle outside. Mom acting drunk and disorderly again?"

Tess rolled her eyes, clearly accustomed to her son's teasing.

But Jack heard the concern beneath the gibe. If he'd been thinking with his big head instead of his little one, he would have realized that a police vehicle parked outside the Pirates' Rest in the middle of the afternoon would be a red flag to Luke.

But he hadn't thought at all. And now Tess and Luke were both looking at him, speculation in their eyes.

"Everything's fine." Everything but his dick, pressing insistently against his fly. He cleared his throat. "I gave Lauren a ride home."

"Lauren Patterson." She offered her hand to Luke, a smile in her voice, like she was delighted to meet him. Like she wasn't embarrassed at all to be caught tangling tongues with the town's chief of police.

Maybe she did this all the time, brought men back to her room. Jack realized he was clenching his jaw and relaxed it deliberately. He'd been only too happy to follow her upstairs. He was in no position to judge.

"I'm a client of Meg's," she was saying to Luke.

Luke shook her hand. "Nice to meet you. I'm Meg's brother."

Her smile broadened. "I guessed. You're getting married soon, right?"

Luke's pleasure showed in his grin. "Next week."

"Congratulations," she said warmly.

"Thanks." Luke threw a wicked look at Jack. "Are you Jack's date for the wedding?"

Jack narrowed his eyes. He might have to put up with Tess mucking around in his personal life. He didn't have to take that shit from his subordinate.

Lauren came unexpectedly to his rescue. *Hostage Girl, taking action in a crisis.* "We're not thinking that far ahead yet."

Tess lifted her brows again. "It's only a week until the wedding."

"I just meant . . ." She shifted, throwing Jack a laughing, help-me-out-here look over her shoulder.

He let her go reluctantly, keeping his expression impassive. *What* did *she mean?* Maybe he would have invited her. If he'd thought about it. Which he hadn't. She wasn't part of his life here. It wasn't like they were *dating.*

Which was kind of Tess's point.

Shit. He was thirty-eight years old. Tess was not *his* mother. His sex life was his own business.

"I'm sure it's too late to add someone to your guest list," Lauren said when he didn't say anything.

"Always room for a plus one," Tess said blandly.

"What is this, a party?" Meg Fletcher stood in the doorway, surveying the half-filled glasses of wine on the counter. "Why wasn't I invited?"

Tess waved a hand. "Help yourself."

"Seems like everybody else is," Luke said.

Jack made himself stand still. Never let them see you sweat. Or squirm.

Lauren's gaze met his, her eyes alight with laughter. And the tension that had been part of him for the past year and a half, the coil that was so tightly wound *all the time*, suddenly relaxed. She made things so . . . easy. Because, yeah, okay, the situation was pretty funny. Frustrating as hell, but bearable, as long as Lauren smiled at him with laughter in her eyes.

A corner of his mouth curled in response.

"I was looking for you," Meg said to Lauren, picking up the wine bottle. "Your agent called."

The laughter in Lauren's face died.

Jack fought an absurd impulse to go to her. To comfort her. But he didn't know if the gesture would be welcome. He had no real place in her life, any more than she had in his. He didn't know what she wanted from him, besides sex.

"Guess I better get to work, then, huh?" she said in a bright, brittle voice.

Jack frowned. *Was that what she wanted?* "We all should," he said.

"You okay to drive, Chief?" Luke asked with a glance at the wine.

Jack gritted his teeth. He hadn't touched the wine. Or anything else. Hardly.

This was why he didn't have a personal life. It was too damn messy.

"I'm good. We need to talk anyway." He needed to bring Luke up to speed on the bakery situation.

He glanced at Lauren. She was watching him with those dark, observant eyes, her chin slightly higher than usual.

She would be all right, he thought with relief.

His gaze dropped to her mouth, still pink and swollen-looking, and the ground shifted under his feet just enough to let him know that he was not, in fact, *good*. He was not in control.

And maybe she wasn't as all right as she pretended, either, because she wasn't smiling anymore and there was a pucker between her brows.

Hell. He was not kissing her good-bye with an audience. Wasn't making a date in front of one, either.

"I'll . . ." What? *I'll call you* was out. "I'll see you," he said.

Her lips firmed. She gave him that look, like she could see right through his excuses to the back of his skull. The look that promised they weren't done here. "See you."

He said his good-byes and left with Luke. It wasn't like he was running away, he told himself. He had things to do. Real things. Paperwork. E-mails. Finding Tillett.

Things he could control.

"So, YOU AND Jack Rossi . . ." Meg's voice trailed off as she settled into the cushions of the lounger. Sunlight streamed through the jasmine twining over the porch trellis, firing the pollen in the air to floating motes of gold. "Is that a good idea?"

Lauren gulped her wine. She couldn't believe he'd left her like that. Well, yes, she could. *I don't have a personal life*, he'd said.

Yeah, because he was running from one as fast as he could. His rejection flicked heat to her face.

Okay, not rejection. What was he supposed to do, say *Excuse me*, throw her over his shoulder, and haul her upstairs so that the entire Fletcher family could listen to her headboard banging against the wall?

The thought made her warm all over for entirely different reasons.

It was just bad luck that Tess had interrupted them before they went upstairs. Just bad timing.

Kind of like everything else in her life.

Lauren knew better than anyone that sometimes things didn't work out as planned. Fathers died. Educations were put on hold. A simple run to the bank turned into a three-day ordeal in front of television cameras. Life was too uncertain for her to get hung up on some guy. Any guy.

But somehow all the relationships that had come before—the missed connections and botched communications and guys who failed to follow through—had not prepared her for Jack. He was different.

Or maybe she was the one who had changed.

She shifted uneasily on the couch. "Couldn't we talk about something else? You said Patricia called." She really had it bad if talking about her agent was preferable to dwelling on Jack Rossi.

"I was leading into that. Gently."

The idea of Meg approaching any subject gently tickled Lauren's humor. "Like a dentist starting a root canal."

Meg grinned. "So tact isn't one of my strong points."

"It's okay," Lauren said. "I can guess what she wanted anyway." *The book. It was always the book.*

"She just wants to know if you're on schedule," Meg said.

"Why didn't she call me herself?"

"She doesn't want to pressure you."

Too late. The suffocating feeling was back, pressing on

Lauren's chest, squeezing her lungs. She forced herself to inhale. "So she got you to do her dirty work."

"Only after I plied you with wine."

Lauren stared down into her glass. "I am writing." *Trying to write.* "Every day." Even to her own ears, the words sounded weak. Like an excuse.

Meg raised her eyebrows. *She* didn't make excuses. After she'd been fired from her Fortune 500 job, Meg had formed her own very successful boutique PR agency. Her drive and determination made Lauren feel even worse about her own floundering panic. "And how are you feeling?"

Think positive. "Good."

Meg didn't say anything. She didn't have to. She'd been in that hotel room.

Lauren sighed. "Better," she amended.

"So . . ." *What's the matter?* The words hung silently in the air like a thought balloon in a comic strip.

What's the matter with you?

"I think . . . I need to do more," Lauren said.

Meg frowned. "Lauren, when I came down to Saint Louis, you were exhausted." And that exhaustion had brought on a full-scale panic attack. "The whole point of you coming here was to give you a break. To give you a minute out of the spotlight so you could concentrate on your writing."

"I know. And I'm grateful." She was, too. Meg had *saved* her. "But . . ."

"You just need a chance to relax. Until things get back to normal."

Lauren's hands tightened on her glass. She set it down carefully. There was no "normal" anymore. Not one she recognized. Her old life was gone.

At least when she was on tour, she'd had a role to play.

She could be, for hours at a time, the person that her audience expected. Hostage Girl, clear-thinking and brave.

But away from the SWAT teams and television cameras, who was she?

Only with Jack she had felt briefly, intensely, herself. Present. *Alive.*

"I need to do more with my *life*," she explained.

"Like work at the bakery?" Meg asked dryly.

Lauren winced. "You heard about that."

"Sweetie, you're on an island now. The two main occupations are fishing and gossip. And since my nephew's girlfriend also happens to work at the bakery . . ."

"Your nephew's dating Thalia?" Lauren asked, diverted.

Meg's eyes narrowed at the change of subject. Lauren smiled ruefully. No one could ever accuse *Meg* of being unfocused.

"Not that my nephew's love life isn't my top priority," Meg said. "But let's stick with you for the moment. Why are you working for Jane?"

"It's only for a couple hours a day," Lauren said defensively. "And Jane's short staffed."

"But what do you get out of it? Besides free pastries."

"It's something I can do. Something I'm good at," Lauren said with growing assurance. "I need to help."

"That's why you quit school after your father died," Meg said.

Lauren's heart jolted.

"It's not a secret," Meg said. "It's in your book. Which I read. You're my client. You left college because your mother wasn't holding it together and your brother, Noah, needed you."

"He needed counseling," Lauren said.

"Which you made sure he got," Meg said. "And then

when you did go back to school, you chose psychology as your major."

Lauren hadn't realized she had revealed so much of herself, her old self, on the page. Or maybe Meg, with her Harvard education and tight-knit family, was very good at reading between the lines. "Noah went through a really tough time after Dad died. The counselor made a huge difference in his life. It made me realize that that's what I wanted to do."

"That's great. But, Lauren." Meg met her gaze. "You can't save everybody."

"I know that." She sure hadn't saved Ben, despite her promises to him that everything would be all right. She hadn't saved his family, even if she did still send them money every month. Somehow she had to learn to live with the guilt and move on. "It makes me feel better to try," she said. "To give back, even if it's just a cup of coffee."

"Where does Jack Rossi fit into all this?"

Lauren hesitated. This wasn't the kind of thing you discussed with your publicist. Only with your therapist. Or maybe a friend.

She was so very tired of being isolated in hotel rooms. Of presenting a front to strangers. Of hiding her hurt from the people who knew her best.

But she wasn't sure enough of her relationship with Meg to know what to say. She wasn't sure of *herself.*

Are you moving forward? Jack had challenged her. *Or running away?*

Lauren took a deep breath. She'd come this far. She wasn't going to back down now. "He makes me feel better, too."

"Really." Meg sounded disbelieving.

"You don't think he's hot?"

Meg shot her a droll look. "I'm engaged, not dead. Of course I find him hot. I'm just surprised you do."

Lauren smiled wryly. "To use your expression, I'm messed up. I'm not dead."

Meg turned pink. "I wasn't going to say messed up. Fragile maybe. And Jack is kind of a bad ass. A cop. An ex-sniper. Are you really sure he's the best person for you to be with right now?"

A *sniper.* The word conjured visions of black-jacketed, goggled figures swarming through smoke like demons from the mouth of hell. Of Ben's uncle, George, one blind eye staring up at the ceiling, lying in his blood on the nubby bank carpet.

"Jack was a sniper? In Philadelphia?"

"In the Marines. In Afghanistan. Luke told me."

Lauren's heart beat faster. "Don't they screen them? To be, like, super emotionally stable or something?"

Meg shrugged. "Maybe when they go in. God knows what happens when they come out. My point is, I just don't see Jack as the nurturing type."

Nurturing? No. Blunt and honest and uncompromising. A man of principle, Lauren thought, remembering how he'd tried to warn her off. *I'm just telling you how it is.*

But he'd given her water. Driven her home. Cared for her. She remembered those dark, assessing eyes on her face. *No bad effects?*

"He's been nice to me," she said.

"Good for him. I still wouldn't have pegged him as your type."

He could be her type. Well, once he got over his unfortunate tendency to walk away after kissing her brains out. But Lauren could work with that.

"He's a fixer-upper," she said.

"A what?"

"That's my type," she explained. "I sort of collect them. Musicians, tattoo artists, fellow grad students. Guys who need a place to crash after their parents or their girlfriends kick them out. Nice guys, but not long-term relationship material. So they stay with me until I can fix them."

Meg narrowed her eyes. "You fix them."

"Mm." She helped them find their feet or their mojo, gave them haircuts or research help, got them into rehab or out of debt. "And then, when they don't need me anymore, they move on."

"And you're okay with that?"

"I was." Lauren blinked. *Past tense.* Why wasn't she now? Was it Jack who was different?

Or was the change in new Lauren? Not only the result of trauma, not simply a matter of survival, but a choice.

Meg was frowning, staring into her glass, swirling the contents gently. "You know," she said slowly. "Jack isn't some twenty-something couch dweller you can launch after he learns to tie his own shoes. He's older than me. Older than Matt, even. He's not going to change for you."

"I know. I'm his rebound girl," Lauren said.

"Excuse me?"

"He hasn't been with anyone since his divorce. He isn't ready for a committed relationship."

Meg raised her brows. "And that's enough for you?"

Lauren looked at Meg, with her New York haircut and three-carat rock, blissfully engaged to the hunky contractor she'd crushed on in high school. So sure of herself, so confident about her life and Sam's place in it.

It must be nice.

"It has to be," Lauren said. "My life is a hot mess right now. I have no idea where I'll be or what I'll be doing in two months. I'm not looking for true love. I'm just hoping to get laid."

Meg was silent.

"You don't approve."

"Not for the reasons you think. Lauren . . . Before I was with Sam, I wasted six years of my life on a guy who was more interested in what I could do for his career than in who I was or what I wanted. So I have to ask, what do you get out of this?"

Jack, Lauren thought with a stab of pure longing.

She got Jack. All that tough strength, all that tempered control, all that sublimated passion, to wrap herself in like a down comforter, his hard hands and broad shoulders and smoldering dark eyes.

Rescue me.

"Maybe just the chance to feel connected again." She looked up. Smiled. "It's been so long since I've had sex, I'm practically a virgin."

Meg laughed and leaned forward to refill her wineglass. "Okay. I think it's great that you're rejoining the living. Everybody deserves a summer fling. As long as you know going in that that's what it is."

"That's all it is," Lauren said.

She was pretty sure she was okay with that.

Six

"HEARD YOU DITCHED my daughter for some gal with a nose ring," Hank said two days later.

Jack's jaw clamped. He'd kissed Jane one time at Matt Fletcher's wedding four months ago. Maybe he'd thought about doing more, but the chemistry had never been there. On either side, he admitted.

Defending himself to Hank, though, would only make him sound like a jerk. *Never mix sex and the job.*

"Lauren Patterson." Luke looked up from typing a list of items stolen from Lois Howell's clothesline. "And if you ask me, Jack's the one with the ring in his nose."

Hank snorted. "If a woman's leading him around, it's not by the nose."

A police department was like a locker room, the same smell of sweat and pine cleaner, the same playground hierarchy. Ribbing was good, a sign of acceptance, evidence that they were playing as a team. But he was the coach. Time to get everybody's head back in the game.

"How's Jane?" he asked.

Hank scowled. "She doesn't talk to me. I figured you'd know. You're the one at the bakery all the time."

"The bakery was closed until this morning," he reminded Hank. "I went out yesterday to take a look at the new security system."

He'd met up with the crime scene tech from the sheriff's department. He'd seen Jane and the repairman fixing the air conditioner unit. He'd looked for Lauren.

But she wasn't there.

Of course. She had work to do. And so did he.

His disappointment at her absence was strong enough to make him uneasy. He wanted her. He didn't deny it. A good detective didn't ignore the facts to suit his own theories. Or in this case, his life.

But he didn't want to need her. So after leaving the bakery, he hadn't gone to the inn to see her. He held back, just to prove to himself that he could, like a smoker going a whole day without a cigarette.

Her dark gaze met his, her perception lightened with humor. *If I invite you in for a drink, would that violate your professional or personal boundaries?*

He almost shuddered. You couldn't put yourself out there like that. You couldn't let people in. Because if you did, they would mess you up.

But somehow she did it. Invited him in, left herself all raw and naked and open and vulnerable.

She was incredibly brave.

And dangerous.

"What about that piece of shit Tillett?" Hank asked.

Jack dragged his mind off Lauren. "Is that what you called him when he was your son-in-law?"

"Worse than that. Not that Jane ever listened," Hank said. "You find him?"

Reluctantly, Jack shook his head. Beneath Hank's gruff manner, he was obviously concerned. "Not yet."

"He could've left the island," Luke said.

Maybe. The locals looked out for their own. No one remembered seeing Tillett in the last two days. But at the height of the tourist season, one scruffy, long-haired guy could easily blend in with the fishermen, surfers, and campers on vacation. Without a warrant, there was no way to track the guy's movements, especially if he drove across the bridge instead of taking the ferry.

"I'll take his photo around again when we're done here. Grab the other side of this desk," Jack said to Luke. "I want to move it by the entrance."

Luke pushed back his chair to comply.

"Why do we need another desk?" Hank said. "We're crowded enough already."

Jack wedged the desk beside a bank of file cabinets. "Town council finally approved the new budget. We've got ourselves a dispatcher, someone to take over the permits and filing and handle calls."

Luke whistled. "What did you do, twist their arms?"

"More like knocked their heads together." Hank eyed Jack with rare approval. "When does she start?"

"I have a candidate coming at ten today. That's why I asked you to come in on a Wednesday. I wanted you both to meet her."

"What's her name?" Luke asked.

"Marta Lopez."

"Sounds Mexican," Hank said.

Jack shot him a hard look. Working in law enforcement, your world became divided into Cops and Everybody Else. *Us versus Them.* The distinction became easier and uglier when prejudice crept in, when "They" had darker skin or different last names or spoke another language. It used to make him sick sometimes back in Philly, the way some cops talked about the people they were sworn to protect. The words they used. The attitude.

He wouldn't tolerate it. Not in his office, not in the field. And if Hank thought otherwise, he was out of here.

"She's Hispanic, yes," he said evenly. "We could use somebody who speaks Spanish in this department."

"My nephew Josh is friends with a Miguel Lopez," Luke said easily. "His mom works at the realty office."

Jack nodded, keeping his eyes on Hank. "That's the one. According to Sam Grady, she's been with them twenty-five years. Worked her way up from the cleaning crew to the office. He says she's smart, organized, and used to handling calls and pressure."

"So why's she leaving them?" Hank asked.

"She says now that her boys are older, she's looking for more of a challenge." Jack wondered how she'd deal with Hank and his redneck attitude.

"Sounds like you already made up your mind," Hank said.

"She's qualified," Jack said carefully. "Not experienced, but most dispatchers train on the job."

Hank grunted. "Let's hope she can make coffee."

"I can make coffee." A woman's voice, assured. Amused. "As long as you don't expect me to serve it to you."

Hank turned to the doorway, shoulders bunching like a bulldog's at the sight of a cat.

Marta Lopez stood in the door to the office. Early fifties and confident in her skin, with generous curves and thick, dark hair and a handsome face. What Jack's dad would call a nice handful. And then Ma would dig him in the ribs with her elbow.

Jack bit back a smile. "Marta, this is Hank Clark. Our reserve officer."

She pursed bright coral lips. "I know who he is. I've seen him driving around in his car. You used to be with the sheriff's department."

Hank nodded, apparently strangled by his collar.

"And Patrol Officer Luke Fletcher." Jack continued the introductions.

Marta cocked her head. "Josh's uncle? You're Tess Fletcher's son."

Luke, over six feet of Marine Corps muscle, grinned at her like the Boy Scout he'd undoubtedly been. "Yes, ma'am."

"You're just back from Afghanistan, then. Welcome home." She smiled with genuine warmth, offered her hand. Bright nails, no rings. "Thank you for your service."

The phone rang.

Before Luke could pick it up, Marta looked at Jack, raising dark, elegant brows. "You want me to get that?"

In a few sentences, she'd established her island pedigree and her ability to hold her own. Good for her, Jack thought. And good for him. If she handled calls as easily as she'd handled introductions, she was in.

He gestured toward the desk. "Please."

She took off one big gold earring and laid it on the desk before tucking the receiver to her ear. "Dare Island Police Department, how can I . . . Oh, hi, Dora. It's Marta Lopez. What's up?" A series of sympathetic hums, and then, "When did you notice? Hold on. I'll check." She punched the hold button. "Dora Abrams on Teach Street. Something's caught in the trap under her house. Since this morning, she thinks, but it could have been last night. When can someone go out there?"

"I'll go," Luke said.

"I've got it. You stay and get acquainted," Jack said.

In emergency situations, communication was key. Hank might have reservations about their new dispatcher, but they all had to work together. If there was going to be a problem, Jack needed to know now. And if Marta couldn't change Hank's attitude, Jack would.

"If you don't mind me leaving you with these two for a while," he said to Marta.

"Whatever you say, Chief." She hit the button again. "Dora, it's your lucky day. The chief is on his way."

"Great," Jack said when she ended the call. "We'll talk when I get back. In the meantime, Luke here can give you the tour, take you next door to meet our friendly firefighters."

"Luke's a rookie." Hank's voice scraped like barnacles over rock. He cleared his throat, his dark eyes fixing on Marta. "I'll show you around."

They all regarded him with varying degrees of surprise.

Marta's eyes crinkled at the corners. "I did say I wanted more of a challenge," she murmured.

Red crept into Hank's craggy face. His jaw hardened.

Jack narrowed his eyes, picking up some vibe in the room. Trouble? Flirtation?

He shook his head, dislodging the thought. *Don't over-react.* Hank was simply pulling rank on Luke. Or he was making amends for that remark about the coffee.

They would be fine. Everything was under control.

"Don't worry, Dad." Luke's blue eyes gleamed with laughter. "I'll referee 'til you get home."

Hank snorted. "More like I'll be babysitting."

And after that, what choice did he have but to trust them and go?

Moving forward? Or running away?

His fist curled on the handle of the door, the metal pressing into his palm. Damned if he knew anymore.

HE DIDN'T CALL.

Probably just as well, Lauren told herself as she trailed up the stairs of the Pirates' Rest, her stomach churning with disappointment. The evening sun slanted through the windows, throwing rose-colored bars across the wooden treads and faded floral carpet.

Snipers were hardly known for their warm, nurturing personalities. If she wanted to salve her ego or recharge her energies, she could certainly find a less demanding hookup than the recently divorced, chip-on-his-shoulder, stick-up-his-butt chief of police.

What could Jack Rossi give her that she truly needed?

Jack, behind her, his hands at her waist, his lips at her throat, his body a solid wall at her back . . .

Well, except for that. She fumbled for her room key. Anyway, she didn't expect him to call. Guys never did. But she'd thought—okay, maybe she had really *hoped*—that Jack would be different. All that confidence and control, the hot, disciplined body, the cool, assessing eyes. A man who knew what he wanted, she'd thought.

Two days ago, with him pressing hard and urgent against her, she had thought he wanted her.

My mistake.

She opened the door to her room. The stale air wrapped around her, smelling faintly of guest soap and bathroom cleaning products. The scent of a hundred hotels, reminding her how far she was from home. For a moment she couldn't breathe.

She crossed to the window and dragged up the sash. The evening air flowed in, humid and alive with the scent of salt and a chorus of tree frogs.

Jack hadn't said he would call. In fact, she'd gotten the impression that he was carefully avoiding saying much of anything at all.

She was the one who was trying to make that flare of attraction—that instant of connection, that moment when she'd felt vibrantly, achingly alive—into something more, projecting her own yearnings onto him. *See you. See* you. She wanted that so desperately, to be seen. Not through a television screen or the halo of celebrity, but seen for herself.

But he hadn't even dropped by the bakery this afternoon, when he knew she would be there.

Fine. She didn't need Jack kissing her. She didn't want him judging her. She didn't need a guy to make her feel inadequate. She felt bad enough all by herself.

She pressed her forehead to the screen, the metal mesh biting into her skin.

She'd been stuck on this book for months, unable to let her words or feelings out, afraid of revealing what a hot mess she was inside. Editing her emotions, fudging the truth, until all her words were empty. *Hostage Girl: My Life After Crisis* was a joke. Hostage Girl was a fraud.

She wasn't anyone special. How could she expect to help or inspire anybody when she couldn't help herself?

She took a shaky breath. Held it.

Okay, that had just used up her entire quota of negative self-judgment for the day. She needed to grow a thicker skin. Or a spine. Positive thoughts, she reminded herself.

Outside her window, over the tops of the trees, the sea shimmered like a promise out of reach. The sun lay down a trail of fire across the water. Lauren blinked hard and climbed to her feet, looking around for her laptop.

It wasn't there.

Crap. She looked again, on the bed, under the bed, by the dresser. She'd had it with her this morning at the bakery. And then . . . Had she put it under the counter while she worked? Or left it charging on the corner table? She couldn't remember. And now she'd forgotten it.

Unless . . . The thought bloomed inside her, the tight bands easing around her chest. *Unless someone stole it.*

The relief was shameful.

No more laptop. No more pressure to find the words to put her soul on paper. Nothing she could do about it.

Anyway, her laptop was there, at the bakery. It had to be there, in one place or another. And even if she lost her computer, her work was backed up on the cloud. *Like some giant black thundercloud looming on the horizon. Threatening. Inescapable.*

She shook the image away. She wasn't trying to escape. She wasn't running from her responsibilities or her deadline or anything else.

However much she might want to.

She glanced again out the window to where the sky was turning pink and gold. *Red sky at night, sailor's delight.* Plenty of time to walk to the bakery and back before dark. Of course, Jane's would be closed by now. But Lauren had a key. *Just in case,* Jane had said, pressing it into her hand a week ago, and even though Lauren couldn't see why she would need one—she was never there alone—it felt so good to be trusted that she'd taken the key anyway. *Just in case.*

At least retrieving her laptop would be doing something. Not sitting alone in her room or hanging around the guest parlor, intruding on the vacationing couples, hoping Meg or somebody—*not Jack, screw Jack*—would notice and take pity on her.

She closed the window and locked her door before slipping downstairs and outside into the gilded summer light.

Opening the garden gate, she felt a touch along her spine like the finger of her mother's fears. She hesitated, looking up and down the empty road. Maybe she should call Jane or Meg. Or at least let Tess know where she was going. But that was anxiety talking. This was Dare Island. Nothing was going to happen to her here. Unless she got run over by a random cyclist.

Anyway, the walk was good exercise, past Fletchers' Quay and along the harbor before turning inland through more residential streets. Lights blinked on in windows as she passed. A dog barked and was hushed. A line of pelicans glided over the rooftops, black against the radiant sky, and her heart lifted.

She turned into Jane's drive.

It was . . . darker under the trees. Chairs loomed out of the shadows. Lauren hurried up the wooden steps, clutching her shiny new key. A security light—new since the vandalism?—threw the spindles of the porch into sharp relief.

Through the front windows, she could make out the silvery glow of the refrigerated cases, a faint spill of light from the kitchen. No laptop in sight.

Swallowing, Lauren unlocked the dead bolt and nudged open the door.

Beep beep beep. A soft, warning sound.

Startled, she looked around. Red lights on the coffee machines. Red EXIT signs above the doors. Nothing unusual, nothing alarming. She ducked behind the counter. *There.* Her breath whooshed out. Her laptop was there, safely tucked away on a ledge under the register.

She grabbed it.

Beep beep beep from the kitchen. Had Jane left an oven on? A timer?

Still holding her laptop, Lauren crossed to the shadowy kitchen. Dim lights gleamed on stainless steel. Beside the back door, a panel glowed. *Beep beep beep.*

She sucked in her breath. *The security system.*

Her heart hammered. She should have called Jane. She should have . . . Should she just leave? Or was there some way to turn it off? She hurried closer to take a look. Text blinked on the tiny screen. ARMED. ARMED. ARMED. Like a missile or something.

Oh, crap. She stared helplessly at the keypad.

The kitchen exploded with sirens.

She gasped and flung her hands over her ears. Her laptop cracked against the panel and slithered to the floor. *Shit, shit, shit.*

The sirens blared, stabbing her ears, vibrating through her body like electric shocks. Her chest tightened.

Don't panic. She forced her eyes open. *Breathe. In, two, three . . .*

Another blast shattered her concentration. She was nearly blind. *The dark, the sirens . . . Get down! On the floor!*

A phone shrilled from the wall, tearing against the horns. She stumbled toward it, her breath choppy, desperate for relief. For silence. She fumbled for the receiver, her hands shaking. "Hell . . . Hello?"

"This is Island Security." She could barely make out the words through the deafening brays. "Can you give me the passcode, please?"

Her mind blanked. Her head pounded. *Passcode?* "You need . . ." She tried to think. "Jane."

"Is she there?"

More sirens. Black spots danced before her eyes. *Make it stop. Please.* "No."

"The passcode, please," the voice said implacably.

She gripped the phone, her palms sweating. "I don't have it. I . . ." *Work here*, she wanted to say. But she had no air.

"If you can't give us the passcode, we will notify the police."

Rough voices shouting, glass breaking. Gunfire.

Stay down! Police!

She curled in on herself, struggling to breathe.

"Ma'am, the police are on the way."

She slid to the floor, holding the receiver to her chest, the sirens blaring in her head.

Seven

THE SECURITY ALARM blared like a damned air raid siren, covering the sound of Jack's entrance. He swept a look around the kitchen. Lauren curled on the tiled floor, her back against the wall, gasping for breath.

The sight of her hit his chest like a bullet.

He pushed down his instinct to go to her. As a sniper, you learned to control your reactions, to get into the zone where you were calm. Controlled. You couldn't make assumptions. Especially ones that could get you killed.

Senses alert, heart pumping, he scanned the room for potential targets, the corners, the shadowy aisles. *Nothing.* Lauren was alone.

He relaxed his grip on his weapon and stepped deliberately into the dim light.

Her head jerked up as she saw him. No blood, but she was definitely not all right. Her body shook. Her eyes were dark and cavernous in her flushed face.

He strode down the narrow work aisle and plucked the phone from her chest. "Ned, it's Jack Rossi." He cupped the receiver, pitching his voice below the screaming sirens. "Yeah, everything checks out. You want to—"

The alarm cut off. *Relief.* In the sudden silence, he could hear Lauren wheeze.

"Yeah, it's her." Her eyes met his. He held her gaze as he spoke into the phone. "Front door was open. Have you reached Jane yet? Well, keep trying . . . Thanks. Yeah, I'll lock up."

Lauren wrapped her arms across her chest, as if she could physically hold herself together.

He'd seen Marines freeze like that in battle, their systems on overload, flooded with adrenaline and cortisol. And after battle, too. The body had no way to distinguish between real and remembered danger. The reactions were the same. *Fight or flight.*

He didn't tell her to calm down or suck it up. If she could have calmed herself, she would. And telling her there was nothing to worry about would just make her feel crazier.

He hunkered down beside her, his weight on the balls of his feet. Not crowding, not threatening, not even touching her the way he wanted to. Just there. Her dark, dilated gaze fixed anxiously on his face. He began to breathe slowly in and out. In through the nose, out through the mouth, deeply, deliberately, again, regulating her breath with his, until the rhythm caught and held, until she realized what he was doing and began to breathe in time with him, in and out, in an intimate cadence like sex.

Until they matched, sharing the same rhythm, the same breath. The tension screwing his insides slipped a half notch.

"You must have really wanted a muffin," he said.

Her breathing broke on a laugh. Something turned over in his chest. Like his heart.

She got to him. Not her vulnerability, not just that. He'd never been attracted to weak women. But the strength and humor she found to face and fight her fears.

She stretched out her hand and patted the computer on the floor beside her.

"You left your laptop," he guessed.

She nodded. "I . . ." Her lungs wheezed.

"Give it a minute," he suggested.

"I'm fine." A pause, measured in breaths and heart-beats. Her color deepened. "I feel stupid."

In his years as a cop, he'd responded to a lot of false alarms. It wasn't her fault that Jane hadn't prepared her for the new security system. "At least you got your laptop."

"Probably busted. I dropped it. When . . ." She ran out of air and flapped her hand toward the back door.

Understanding twisted him up. *When the sirens went off.*

Her breathing was easier now. Jack straightened, reaching out his hand to help her to her feet.

Her fingers were like ice. She gripped him—*I've got you, it's okay*—and lurched to her feet.

"Oops." She staggered.

He steadied her with an arm around her waist and then gave in to temptation and pulled her close. Instead of resisting, instead of fighting to get away, she pressed her face against his chest and held on as if she wanted him there, as if she needed his strength and reassurance. As if he were worth holding on to.

She was still recovering from a panic attack, he told himself. Her pulse was too rapid, her breathing choppy. He was support, nothing more.

But it felt so good to be wanted like that, to be held like that. She was warm and soft against him, her skin hot and sweet. She made a little sound, burrowing against him, pulling him around her like a blanket, and he went hard.

Taking advantage. *Hell.* He loosened his hold, easing himself away before she noticed his dick trying to get in on the action, pressing for her attention. *This isn't about you, you bastard.* "You want to test it?"

She raised her head, her eyes dazed and dark. "What?"

Test me, his body begged.

He cleared his throat. "The laptop. You want to check if it's still working?"

She blinked like a woman waking up after sex. "Oh. Okay."

She stooped unsteadily to pick it up, flashing the tattoo before she straightened. A crack zagged across a corner of the case. The DVD drive stuck out slightly.

She took a deep breath.

"I'm sorry," Jack said. Not that he'd done anything to apologize for. But he'd been married ten years. You couldn't go wrong with *I'm sorry.*

She shook her head impatiently. "It's fine. Everything's backed up to the cloud. Not that it was worth much anyway."

It. The laptop? Or her work?

She tapped the power button. The laptop ticked like the timer on an explosive device before the screen flickered to life. "It works," Lauren said hopefully.

Something—a fan?—clunked and whirred. Not a good sound.

"Turn it off," Jack said. "Save the battery."

She nodded and closed the lid. Her head bent. Her fingers tightened on the plastic.

That small, betraying gesture ripped him up inside, made him want to go forth and slay dragons. Or hit something. Anything besides dealing with actual tears, actual feelings.

"Sorry." She straightened her shoulders. "I'm really glad you're here. I'm not usually like this."

She was talking. Not crying. That was good. "You're doing great."

She gave him a disbelieving look and he bit back a grin. She was coming back.

"How often does this happen?" he asked.

"Me breaking into places where I work?"

But he wouldn't be put off by her wry tone. She *was* coming back. But wherever she'd been, in her thoughts, in her head, was a dark place. "The PTSD."

She opened her mouth. Shut it. "That's not . . . It's not the same. I'm not a Marine."

"But you have flashbacks," he guessed.

Her breath hitched. "Not as often as I used to."

He didn't say anything.

"It was just a panic attack," she said. "I'm not . . . I'm fine."

He wondered if she'd been saying that for so long she actually believed it. Or if she was only concerned with what other people believed. "You got something you can take for them?"

The doctors in Afghanistan were always pushing pills. To sleep, to stay awake, to relieve pain or push the demons away.

She shook her head. "They never last long," she reassured him. "I'll be better in a minute."

She was the shrink. She should know. But her hands on the laptop trembled.

He leaned against the counter, crossing his arms against his chest so he wouldn't grab her and upset her careful equilibrium. "Take your time. I'm not going anywhere."

LAUREN CLOSED HER eyes against temptation. She was aching and shaking inside, and he looked so good, he sounded so calm, so confident and controlled. She wanted to lean on him, to sink into him. To burrow into his chest and absorb him through her pores, make him part of her. Hers. *I'm not going anywhere.*

She shut the laptop with a little snap. He didn't mean the words that way. She forced a playful note in her voice. "No hot date tonight?"

He shook his head once, side to side. "You shouldn't be alone. Have dinner with me."

Oh. Heat swept through her again, burning her up from the inside.

Her mind whirled. He was asking her out? Now, when she was sweaty and nauseous. Why was he asking her *now*? Her armpits stank. All she needed to cap off her evening—and his—was to puke all over him at some restaurant. "I'm hardly dressed to go out."

His eyebrows lifted, very slightly, and she flushed. Because the truth was nobody dressed up on Dare Island. Not even to go out. She simply wasn't confident that she could handle food right now.

Or noise.

Or people.

She just wanted to be alone. Except that wasn't true, either. She stared at him helplessly, her insides churning. *Rescue me.*

Those dark, dark eyes watched her. "We could go to my place. I'll make dinner."

Shock and pleasure zinged through her. Okay, she knew what *that* meant. She didn't have to be alone. She could go home with him and have sex. *Yes*, said her body. Her brain spun like the little blue circle on her computer screen, struggling to keep up. She looked at him from under her lashes, hungry for his strength, stealing glances like he would catch her and make her give them back. "You cook?"

A corner of his mouth curled. "Well enough."

"Okay." *Come on, Lauren, you can do better than that. Deep breath. Smile.* "Are you going to make red sauce?"

"Not this time."

Implying there might be a next time. The thought made her giddy.

Or maybe that was the residual effect of her panic attack.

She wanted this, she thought as they went outside. Wanted Jack, filling her up, taking her hard, making her whole and complete.

It wasn't like he wasn't getting something out of the deal, too, she told herself as she locked up, as he placed a quick call to the security company. At least . . .

She slid him another glance as he got into the vehicle beside her. That had definitely been his erection, pressed up against her. Twice. Once when they'd kissed at the inn, and just now, after he helped her off the floor. So he must want her, too, she thought hopefully. Even if he hadn't called.

She settled into the passenger side, reaching for the seat belt. Something scrabbled in the back of the SUV like a rat in a Dumpster.

"Ohmygod." She jerked and grabbed at the dashboard. "What was that?"

Jack's lips twitched. "Dora Abram's intruder."

"What?"

He gestured with his head. "Behind you."

Cautiously, she turned. The top of the Fletchers' big animal trap stuck up from the cargo space. The backseat in between prevented her from seeing inside.

"If that's a snake, I'm out of here," she said.

Definitely a smile this time. "It's a cat. The island has a big feral population."

She relaxed back into her seat. A cat was a million times better than a snake. "We have the same problem on campus when the students go home for the summer. They don't think about what it means to a pet to be forced outside and left behind."

"I don't think this one was a pet. The locals say the island cats have been around since the early shipwreck days. Like the island ponies. They're wild animals, not house pets."

She turned again, but she still couldn't see inside the cage. "What will happen to it?"

"Tomorrow a volunteer will take it off island to the humane society. They have some kind of spay-and-release program for adults. This one's young enough, though, it'll probably be adopted."

Her instinct—to *do* something, to help—stirred. "What about tonight?"

His shoulders rolled in a shrug. "I'll take care of it."

Warmth glowed in her midsection, broke on her face in a smile. "You are such a nice guy."

He grimaced. "Not really. There's no animal control officer on the island. I'm just dealing with a problem."

Right. Guys did not appreciate being called *nice*. Nice guys did not get the girl. Nice guys finished last.

And maybe he really saw his actions that way. Maybe he was so used to doing the right thing that it wasn't a big deal to him. But she didn't know a lot of guys who would put themselves out like that, who would choose the right thing, the compassionate thing, over whatever was convenient.

He was kind of amazing, actually.

"Uh-huh. Just doing your job," she teased.

His eyes narrowed. "Where are you going with this?"

She wasn't sure. She'd been so glad to see him when he walked into the bakery. She was so grateful she didn't have to be alone. But this wasn't all about her. Or it shouldn't be. She didn't want to burden him with obligations. With expectations.

She took a breath. Released it. "I'm just wondering if you brought me home out of a sense of duty or because you felt sorry for me."

"Jesus."

"I don't mind," she assured him hastily. She'd had no objection to being his rebound relationship. Why not his pity fuck?

Meg's voice played in her head. *As long as you know going in that that's what it is.*

A muscle flexed in his jaw. "I asked you to dinner," he said very deliberately, "because you shouldn't be alone."

"It's okay. I get it."

He shot her a hot, dark look. "No, you don't. You shouldn't be alone. And I want your company."

That was nice of him to say.

"I want your company, too. Thank you for inviting me." She smiled crookedly. "Us."

"Lauren." His voice rubbed over her, making all the little hairs on the back of her neck stand up in warning or pleasure.

"What?"

"You're not some stray I'm bringing home for the night."

She made herself smile. "As long as you're not dropping me off at the shelter tomorrow to get spayed."

Unexpectedly, his hand left the wheel and covered both of hers, pleated together in her lap. Such a simple, human touch, warm and reassuring. His kindness made tears burn at the back of her eyes.

"Stop worrying," he said.

"Okay," she said promptly.

And worried for the rest of the drive.

THE GNARLED OAKS and stubbly lawns had given way to dense vegetation, thickets of dark shrubs that followed the shape of the sandhills on either side of the road. A bat cut across the sky, a fluttering triangle against the fading light. Ahead, a heavy metal chain blocked their way. A sign dug into the soft sand read, CONSTRUCTION ONLY. DO NOT ENTER.

Jack got out of the vehicle.

She should have offered to do that for him, Lauren realized as he unlocked the chain, drove forward, and then fastened it behind them again.

"I guess you don't worry about trespassing," she said as he slid back behind the wheel.

His teeth showed briefly in a smile. "I live here. Sam Grady—that's Meg's fiancé, old Grady's son—is developing this whole area. Having a cop around discourages theft from the construction site."

They emerged from a tunnel of twisted trees to open sky and grassy hillocks rolling down to a long wooden wharf, obviously new, its planks even and unweathered. The patchwork waters of Pamlico Sound, green and blue and brown, shone like beaten copper, the gleaming surface broken only by a jetty of tumbled rock and the thin, dark line of the mainland in the distance. *A world away.* A few fishing boats, bristling with antennas and fishing rods, floated like pelicans on the water.

There was only one building. A big one, shingled like most of the island homes, but shaped like a warehouse. Lauren raised her brows. "You live . . . here?"

"No, that's the new fish house for the watermen's association Matt Fletcher's heading up." Jack parked the police cruiser in the broad, pebbled strip bordering the wharf. He nodded through the windshield. "I live there."

She leaned forward, squinting against the golden glare of the sun. Painted on the blunt back end of the nearest fishing boat was the name *Rossi's Wreck.*

Her heart lifted like a seagull, in pure delight. "You live on a *boat*?"

He walked around the front of the cruiser. "For now."

She could not wait for him to open her door. She stumbled out onto the gravel, pushing her hair back with her hand. "That is so cool." The breeze off the water stirred the lines, striking the bridge of the boat with a faint *ting ting*. She turned to him, beaming. "Did you buy it when you moved down here?"

He shook his head. "My pop and my uncles liked to fish down the Jersey shore. They went in on the boat together about twelve years ago. We used to go out together weekends."

She had never had an extended family to do things with.

Or any family at all. Her mother was too lost in grief and her television programs, and Noah was too young, and Lauren was too busy trying to keep things together, making sure the bills got paid and dinner got made, and Noah did his homework. *Maybe if Dad hadn't died . . .*

She pushed the thought away, out of habit and self-defense. "It sounds very manly. You all must have been very—"

"Drunk?"

She laughed. "Close," she said. "Your family must be very close."

He looked away, his lips tightening. "Yeah."

She'd said something wrong. But she didn't know what. "What happened?" she asked softly.

"Hurricane Sandy. The boat survived the storm okay, but my uncles were getting tired of the insurance and upkeep." Jack shrugged. "So I bought it from them in a shrewd business move. When I moved down here, the boat was ready housing."

She hadn't been asking about *Rossi's Wreck*. But maybe the boat represented a tie to the family he'd left behind. "What do you do if there's another hurricane?"

Those dark eyes crinkled. "Pray."

She laughed again. He took his job so seriously that his humor was a pleasant surprise, like biting into a hard candy and finding the soft liquid center. The thought distracted her. She'd like to bite into him. Her breathing quickened.

". . . help with evacuations," he was saying. "Bunk down at the school if I have to."

He was still talking about hurricanes. And she was helpless, caught in a sudden storm of longing and desire.

She watched him open the back of the SUV and lift out the animal cage, muscles sliding under his shirt, his back smooth and powerful, his movements efficient and controlled. A kitten huddled in a corner of the trap, a thin, striped shadow with enormous eyes.

"Oh, it's a baby," she said, her voice melting. "It's so cute."

Jack glanced down, a grin tugging his mouth. "Looks like a rat. It probably bites."

You and me both, kitty. She felt a blush rising and looked away.

Water slapped the pilings. The smells of fish and fuel and algae rose from the dark gap separating the boat from the dock. The cat mewed once, piteously, as Jack stepped down into the boat and then turned to offer Lauren a hand. His palm was broad and firm, his wrist thickly muscled. She felt her balance dissolve in another wave of lust and gripped his hand tightly.

"Easy, tiger," Jack murmured. "I've got you."

Was he talking to her? Lauren wondered, amused. Or the cat?

He helped her aboard and set the cage in the shelter of the bridge. "You want something to drink?"

"Thank you." She balanced in the middle of the small, square space, unsure of her footing. She knew what to do when she brought a guy to her place. Make him a meal and then either find him some pillows and the remote or take him to bed. But with Jack, she was all at sea. Literally. "What can I do to help?"

"Not much room in the galley. Have a seat. I'll be right back."

He ducked into the cabin, leaving the door open. She could hear him moving as she perched on the edge of a padded bench, taking her bearings. The skinny gray kitten watched anxiously from the shadow of the cabin wall.

"Do you have something I can give the cat?" she called through the open door.

"I'll take care of it." Jack's voice was patient. Amused. "You like fish?"

"Sure. I used to live on tuna fish." *Cats ate tuna, right?* "Well, that and ramen noodles."

"No tuna. Bluefish or Spanish mackerel."

"I've never had either one. I'm from Chicago, remember?"

"Chicago's on a lake."

"Sure. Ask me about whitefish. Or smelt. Oh, hey, wait. Did you catch the fish yourself?"

"Not today. It's in the freezer."

"You did catch it. That's so cool."

"Until you fry it," he said. "Then it's hot."

Wow. Chief Law-and-Order Rossi had actually made another joke. And he was cooking her dinner. She wasn't sure which impressed her more.

She'd never bought into traditional dating models, the exchange of dinner-and-a-movie for sex. But something about Jack preparing her food satisfied her on a deep, biological level. Like he'd bagged a woolly mammoth and dragged it back to the cave. Her DNA wanted to have his babies.

Condoms, she thought suddenly, and looked around for her purse.

Jack emerged on deck holding a wine bottle. He'd taken off his uniform shirt, revealing a thin-ribbed sleeveless undershirt. A wife-beater, her brother Noah would call it, and even though Lauren scolded him over the term, it conjured images, dangerous, beautiful, male. Marlon Brando in *A Streetcar Named Desire*, Sylvester Stallone in *Rocky*, Channing Tatum in, well, anything. The intimacy of Jack's undress—his broad, smooth, muscled shoulders, the dark tufts of hair under his arms—struck her like a blow. She opened her mouth to breathe.

He handed her a thick-stemmed wineglass. "Pinot grigio okay?"

She pulled herself together. "You've obviously never been to a graduate student party. It's not box wine in a red plastic cup, but I can adjust." She watched him pour. "None for you?"

"I'll have a beer with dinner."

Her brows twitched together. "On duty?"

He set the wine bottle beside her. "I like to keep a clear head in the kitchen."

Maybe that was it, she thought as he returned to the galley. She wasn't his therapist, required to read deeper significance into every word or gesture. She didn't have to take care of him or fix him. He wasn't drinking to relieve stress, he wasn't drinking alone, he obviously was in excellent health, and his work clearly wasn't suffering. So he didn't have a drinking problem.

She smiled to herself. Control issues, maybe, but not a drinking problem.

The air was soft and humid, scented with salt and diesel. A warm breeze slid over her bare legs. Cautiously, she sipped the crisp white wine, settling back against the bench seat, more relaxed than she had felt in months. Years.

A year ago, a man like Jack, an Italian Catholic cop with his black-and-white view of the world and rigid self-discipline, would have been completely outside her experience. Outside her comfort zone. But now . . .

Lulled by the lap of the water and Jack's presence a few feet away, her hypervigilance eased. As if her body recognized she was safe. If danger threatened, Jack could deal with it. She didn't have to be the hero when he was around. Or a victim. She could just sit here and breathe. Be. Be herself.

Whoever she was anymore.

He came on deck, carrying two plates. "I figured we'd eat out here. Unless you want air-conditioning."

"Out here is perfect," she answered honestly.

She accepted a plate. After an attack, she usually didn't have much appetite. Would Jack be offended if she shared part of her dinner with the cat?

Before she could ask, Jack set his food on the small table and picked a piece of fish from his plate. He approached the trap. The kitten flinched from his heavy footsteps and then stuck its skinny neck out, nose twitching, obviously drawn to the scent of food. Its pink mouth yawned in a silent mew.

Jack crouched, poking the fish through the cage. "Here you go, pal."

The rough murmur of his voice stroked Lauren's nerves inside and out. Creeping to the wire, the tabby began to bolt the food, shoulders hunched, eyes cocked for danger.

"That's the way." Jack stuck a finger through the wire, ruffling the fur on the kitten's head.

Everything in Lauren melted and yearned, swamped in a wave of awareness. She was suddenly, excruciatingly conscious of Jack. The size of his hands, the long muscles of his thighs, the deeply tanned skin at the back of his neck.

He straightened and met her gaze. His eyes went dark.

Her blood drummed in her ears. *Say something*, she ordered herself. *Anything*.

Touch me. Pet me.

"How's the fish?" he asked.

"Um." Were they just going to ignore it, that moment of

humming awareness? She swallowed and glanced at her plate. Flaky white fish. Green salad. A roll. "It looks delicious. Are you this good at everything?"

Dark laughter gleamed in his eyes. But all he said was, "Not much to cooking fish. A little butter, a little salt and pepper."

She kept trying to figure him out, and he kept eluding her neat definitions. *A Manly Man who was comfortable in the kitchen?* "I don't know a lot of guys who cook. Did you learn from your father?"

"Yeah. Pop always cooked Saturday night dinner. Pork chops. Pasta. Said it relaxed him." Jack sat with his plate on his lap. "I was probably twelve or fourteen before I figured out he did it to give Ma a break."

"That's so nice."

"Yeah." This time, she noticed, he did not object to her choice of the word. "Only on Saturdays, though. The rest of the week, Ma ruled in the kitchen."

Lauren dug into the fish. "My parents were the same. Very traditional gender roles."

"That must have made it tough on your mom."

"No, she loved fussing over Dad. That's all she ever wanted."

"Hard when he died, I mean."

Yes. Her throat closed. She stared down blindly at her plate without answering.

"Who stepped into his role?" Jack asked. "You?"

Lauren swallowed. "Somebody had to take care of things."

"You were a kid, though, right?"

"Nineteen."

"So who took care of you?"

Nobody. She shook her head. "I don't need anybody to take care of me."

"Okay."

"I'm fine," she insisted out of habit. Out of instinct. Because that's what she always said. That's all she allowed herself to be.

He looked at her, his black eyes unreadable. "So why are you here?"

Her face, her whole body, flamed. She raised her chin and glared. "Because I want . . ."

You. I want you.

"Sex," she said.

Eight

AROUSAL GRIPPED JACK'S balls like a fist. His blood beat low and thick.

Lauren raised her chin, simmering with nerves and determination. He warmed at the sight of her, the setting sun smoldering in her hair, her face flushed and damp. *She was so hot.* So bright with life. Embarrassed, maybe, and still wobbly after that panic attack, but she still had that essential spark he'd lost.

I want sex.

Hunger, savage and dark, surged inside him. His stomach muscles tensed. *I can give you sex.* On that bench, on the floor, bent over that table. He wanted to yank that little skirt up to her waist and find her creamy and ready for him. He wanted to sink inside her, to make her come and come and come until her eyes lost her questions, until all she could see was him.

He ground his teeth so hard his jaw ached. *Not him.* He

didn't want her to see the real him, the angry, crazy man or the cool, controlled bastard. Until she saw what he wanted her to see, then. Somebody capable of giving her what she needed.

I want sex, she'd said.

But that wasn't what she needed.

Who took care of you? he'd asked, and seen the answer dark in her eyes. *Nobody.*

He didn't have her courage. He couldn't put himself out there the way she did, spilling his guts and his goddamn feelings all the time. But he could be the guy who took care of her for now, who made her problems go away for a while. He could provide her with a refuge. Not simply his boat, not just dinner, but the sweaty, dark oblivion of sex.

As long as he stayed in control.

"You need to call the inn," he said. "Let them know you won't be home tonight."

Her mouth jarred open as his meaning registered. He'd surprised her. *Good.* He surprised himself, how much he wanted her to stay.

She rallied swiftly, like the survivor she was. "I'm thirty-one years old," she pointed out wryly. "Past the age for curfews. Or bed checks."

"Right." He took her almost-empty plate.

At least she'd eaten something, he saw with satisfaction. He'd done that much for her. Thoughts of other things he'd like to do for her, with her, to her, fired his brain, crackled through his body.

He set the plate down carefully, precisely, on the table.

Her eyes crinkled at the corners. What did she see when she looked at him that way? "Want help with the dishes?"

She was teasing him. Did she guess how close he was to the edge of his control?

"The dishes can wait." His voice was rough. "I can't."

She laughed a little breathlessly. "You do know that's ridiculously flattering, right?"

"Honest," he corrected. He could do honest. To a point. Detectives did it in interrogation all the time. Admit just enough of the truth to coax the response you needed.

He took her hands and drew her smoothly to her feet. Their bodies brushed, hips, belly, thighs. She was warm and solid against him. The tiny stud in her nose winked like an ember. She tilted her head back, her pupils dilating to take him in until he felt himself falling into her gaze. He kissed her in self-defense, closing her eyes, opening her lips. She tasted cool and crisp like the wine with a touch of hot, a hint of sweet, a bite of salt. She kicked all his senses alive. He kissed her again, deeper, wetter. Her hands came up, shaping his shoulders, her fingers imprinting his skin, and his whole body surged and lunged like a dog on a leash. His dick was like iron.

He raised his head. *Control.* "Let me show you the cabin." *Before I take you out here.*

She blinked once, lashes sweeping those wide, dark eyes. "Okay."

He could make it to the cabin. He could take her on a bed. He could be what she needed him to be.

He guided her with a hand at the small of her back, reluctant to lose hold of her completely. His thumb found the gap at the top of her waistband, and his hand tingled liked he'd stuck his finger into an electrical outlet. Her skin was moist and warm.

"Wow." She turned slowly in the cramped space, her gaze traveling over the no-frills cabin as if she could catalog his character along with all his stuff. "So this is you, huh?"

"My place. Yeah." He hoped like hell he didn't sound as defensive as he felt.

He kept it clean. He'd made a few upgrades—a flat-screen TV mounted on the wall, a new microwave in the tiny U-shaped galley. But the *Wreck* was a fishing boat, not a yacht. Even the rosy light of the setting sun could not disguise the bench seats' fading navy upholstery, the scorch mark on the countertop from his uncle Tony's cigar. Sea-worthy and comfortable, but not the place you brought a woman. He had steam cleaned the spilled beer from the carpet, but memories still saturated the air, his pop's big laugh, his cousins playing poker around the table, his brother Paul puking in the head.

"I like it," Lauren pronounced. "It's very cozy."

"Thanks."

She went down a step into the galley, her bare feet quiet on the smooth floor. He followed after her, trying not to loom, to make her feel trapped or stalked. Although, hell, he was a cop. Using his size to intimidate was part of the job. And maybe he was a dick, but her awareness of him, of his size, of his closeness, was kind of a turn-on. Anyway, the boat didn't leave him much space to maneuver.

She peered through the narrow stateroom door. His bed, with storage underneath, took up all the available floor space. He had just enough headroom to get dressed in the mornings if he stood in the middle close to the door.

She smiled at him over her shoulder. "It's all mattress."

He came up behind her, settling his hands at her waist, his thumbs riding the curve of her ass. She gave a little sigh and relaxed against him by degrees, the steel slowly leaving her spine, all the tension in her muscles surrendering to him. It was unbelievably erotic, feeling her yield against him.

He rubbed his jaw against her hair. "You want to test it

out?" He kissed her neck, his lips barely parted, all breath and moisture. *See? Controlled. No pressure.* "Try it on."

"Try it on?" Her voice shook with laughter and nerves.

He grinned into her throat. "For size."

JACK'S DEEP VOICE sank into Lauren, vibrating in her ear, sending ripples through her like echoes in a pond.

Test it out.

Try it on.

Try me on. For size.

She shivered deliciously, feeling him hard behind her, the slight abrasion of his jaw ruffling her senses, prickling all her nerves to attention. Waking all her numbed emotions, all her bruised and stunted feelings, to life. She tingled with an almost painful awareness, as if her whole body was coming awake with returning circulation.

She turned in his arms. They stood toe-to-toe, close enough that she could feel his arousal. She smiled up at him. "It's awfully big."

His gaze darkened at her teasing. "You can handle it."

His roughened voice stroked over her. She could do this. He made her feel as if she could do anything. "Okay," she whispered and reached for him.

His stomach muscles jumped under her touch. His big hands covered and caught hers, lifting them away. "Hey, easy, there."

"You said I could handle it."

His laugh was husky. "I'm not sure how much I can handle, sweetheart. It's been a while."

His admission filled her with an odd combination of tenderness and power. "I'll be gentle."

His eyes kindled with laughter and heat. "How about

we try something different? Let somebody take care of you for a while."

Her mouth opened on a quick breath, her lungs expanding in excitement and a terrible, yearning hope.

For most of her life, she'd been the responsible one. Giving up that role, even in bed . . . She exhaled. How would that work exactly? Letting it all go sounded tempting, sure, but there were too many things that had to be managed. Egos. Orgasms. Birth control.

"I'm not really the lie-back-and-relax type," she confessed.

"Why don't we try it and see?" Jack murmured and lowered his head.

In Lauren's experience, the way a guy kissed said a lot about him. Her college pals were mostly friendly, enthusiastic, and slobbery as puppies. Her grad student hookups were perfunctory and distracted, already thinking ahead to the main event. The slackers mostly stabbed with their tongues, like they had to get inside you somehow and never mind if you were ready.

Jack kissed like . . . well, like a detective searching for answers, alert for reactions, following up the clues of her response. As if what she felt, how she felt, were pieces of a puzzle he could take apart and solve.

It made her feel funny to be kissed that way, warm, coaxing, tasting kisses that explored every sensitive surface, that exploited every nuance of response. Her stomach quivered. Or maybe that was her heart. She swayed against him, wanting, needing . . . more. More pressure. More kisses. His hands tightened at her waist, holding her close. Not nearly close enough. His thumbs skimmed lazily up and down, soothing and inciting at the same time. Up to tease the lower curve of her breast, down to dip beneath the waistband of her skirt. She held her breath in anticipation. *Up and down.*

Up and . . . His thumb brushed metal, and his body twitched as if he'd been electrified.

"It's okay," she whispered reassuringly. "It doesn't hurt."

His fingertips dug in before he eased her away. Darn. Not the reaction she was hoping for.

His eyes narrowed intently as he stared down at her piercing: a small gold bar dangling a trio of gemstones like a shower of sparks.

She couldn't read his face. Her heart sank a little. *Too slutty? Too Goth? Too much?* She moistened her lips. "It's agate. To calm anxiety. And—"

"It's hot." He dropped to his haunches in front of her and pressed a kiss to the bare curve of her stomach, just beside the glitter of stones. The hot, wet suction of his mouth weakened her knees.

"And, um, blue topaz. For protection." She swallowed as he worked her skirt up her thighs. Her heart pounded in excitement. "And tourmaline for . . . uh, tourmaline . . ."

His hot breath gusted across her sex, covered only by a thin triangle of cotton. She squeezed her legs together, overcome with lust and embarrassment. *Oh God.* She couldn't remember what tourmaline was for.

"Jack . . ."

He leaned forward, holding her close and still in his strong hands, and kissed her *there* with the same attention he'd given her mouth, licking, flicking, chasing her response. In minutes, she was gasping, shaking. She couldn't stand it. She couldn't stand. Her head rolled back and hit the wall.

He raised his head, his black eyes narrowed and gleaming, his mouth wet. "You okay?"

Oh God, oh God, oh God. "Fine," she said weakly. She waggled her fingers. "Carry on, don't mind me."

He laughed, a vibration through her flesh, and went

back to what he'd been doing. *So good.* She grabbed his shoulders, his muscles too hard and smooth for her fingers to find purchase. She clutched his hair. Too short. He slid his finger inside her and she cried out, her body jolting in pure, mindless pleasure.

Selfish pleasure.

She couldn't just stand here and let Jack do all the work. She gripped his head, rubbing little circles, massaging his scalp, and he made a dark sound low in his throat and surged to his feet. Wrapping her in hard arms, he nudged her back on the bed and followed her down.

"Jack." She twisted under him, her skirt scrunching around her hips. Too many *clothes.* She wriggled in frustration.

He levered off the bed in one smooth movement, stripping his shirt over his head, shucking his pants and underwear.

And he was just so . . . Whoa. Wow.

Jack in uniform, armed and dangerous, was enticing enough. Naked, he was all hot, honed strength. His chest was broad and deep, lightly dusted with dark hair, his torso solid with muscle.

He wasn't like any man she'd been with before. No hint of adolescence, no sign of self-indulgence, nothing pale or soft or uncertain about him. She wondered what her friends back at school would think of him, this plain-spoken cop. What he would make of them. Would he find them, well, lacking in some way?

Would she?

Jack, in contrast, was all grown up. Fully adult, fully functioning, all male. She smiled. Hard to miss that, with the impressive evidence right there in her face.

She started to reach for him and then stopped. "I have birth control. In my purse."

"I'll take care of you."

Yeah, she'd heard that before. "I'm not on the pill."

"I said I'll take care of it."

He slid out the drawer under the bed and pulled out a box of condoms. *A new box.* Not that she was reading anything special into that, but . . . Cellophane crinkled as he broke the seal.

"When did you buy those?" she asked.

His mouth quirked in that wry half smile. "After I didn't follow you to your room the other day."

Her breath went as something in her chest expanded, pushing out the air. Maybe he hadn't called her. But he'd wanted—he'd *planned*—for this.

He met her gaze, his eyes dark. "You are so damn beautiful."

Heat rushed through her. She blushed and opened her arms. He joined her on the bed, pulling her close, shaping her breasts through her blouse, pushing his knee between her thighs. The friction made her crazy. She wanted the texture of his chest on her breasts, his hot sleekness everywhere.

Clumsy with desire, she struggled to raise herself, yanking at her top. Jack's warm hands moved deftly to help her, sliding her top over her head, working her skirt down her legs. While he was down there, he kissed her ankle and then the inside of her knee and then . . .

Her hips jerked against his mouth as he worked her, as he kissed and sucked and stroked, reading every hitch of her breath, every twitch of her body like a blind man reading Braille. She panted. *So close.*

"Jack!"

He dealt efficiently with the condom and then moved over her, his heavy legs tangling with hers. Her hands fell from his shoulders and grabbed his ass hard.

He laughed low and rubbed against her, his hot sex gliding where his mouth had been. He slid the first little bit inside her, the feeling so good, so intense, she contracted and moaned.

His eyes gleamed. "Is this what you want?"

She arched helplessly against him, trying to take him in, desperate to have all of him inside her.

"Here you go, baby. Take it." He pressed deeper, his dark voice filling her head, his hard sex filling her below. "Jesus, you're tight."

Carefully, he began to move, each thick, deliberate thrust followed by an achingly slow withdrawal. She clenched around him anxiously, hoping to help, trying to hurry him up, but he was too strong for her. Too much. His control was absolute. Indecent. Arousing. *I'll take care of you.* Slide and withdrawal, over and over, heavy and relentless. Until his rhythm caught and overtook hers like the rise and fall of his breath in the bakery. Until she moved to his tempo, until she pulsed to his beat, absorbing his cadence in very fiber and tissue. Until everything in her swelled and broke, and she came, again and again.

He turned his face into her neck and followed her into the depths.

JACK STARED UP at the twilight sky through the windows in the bow, his body heavy and replete. Satisfied. He stroked his free hand lazily down Lauren's back, and she made this little sound and burrowed against him, her head on his shoulder, her fingers exploring the hair on his chest like she was testing the curls for spring. His arm tightened around her reflexively.

She tilted her face up, her hair tickling his jaw. "You're smiling," she observed. "That's good, right? It was good."

He slanted a look down at her. He'd figured a woman like Lauren—smart, articulate, college educated—would be a talker during sex. Obviously, having skipped the play-by-play, she was ready for the post game analysis.

Her hair was mussed, her lips swollen. He wanted her all over again. *Wanted her hot and slippery, yielding under him . . .*

"There is no bad sex," he said. "But there are different kinds of good, you know?"

She nodded, her eyes dark and dilated like she could see inside his head. God, she was so fucking beautiful.

"Like sometimes you're hungry, you get a steak and a nice bottle of red," he explained. "And sometimes you're on the go, you grab a hamburger. Either way, you get fed, you're lucky."

Her expression shifted subtly, the warmth more projected, less personal. A therapist's face. "So, are you saying this was like fast-food sex for you?"

"No." He cupped her jaw. His thumb traced the arch of her eyebrow, skimmed the soft pout of her lower lip. "I'm saying that it's like all my life, I've been going to the wrong restaurants."

Her smile started in her eyes and grew.

Her glowing look kindled something inside him. Not only heat, but warmth. And what he thought was simple appetite became a hunger for something else, for her smiles and compassion, for her quick, questing intelligence, for the optimism and empathy that made her brave.

Something—pleasure, misgiving, a cop's instinct for

danger—raised the fine hair on the back of his neck, shivering over his skin. *Shit.* He could be in trouble here.

He pushed the thought away. It felt too good to lie here with her squashed and warm against his side.

Squashed and warm and naked. That was nice.

He ran a hand down her smooth, bare arm and patted her hip. In the evening glow of the skylights, the jewelry in her navel glittered like stars. He flicked the stones gently with his finger, making them dance against her skin, surprised by this unexpected kink in his psyche. It turned him on, how they made her tough and vulnerable at the same time, the contrast between the hard, polished metal and her sensitive skin. Like the ink on her back. Or the cuff in her ear. Or that tiny, winking nose stud.

He frowned, his detective's instincts stirred. As if he were staring at a big, fat clue and missing the vital information that would put the puzzle all together.

"When did you get this?" he asked.

"Hm?" She roused. "Oh. When I went away to college."

"And this?" His finger traced the scrolling tattoo on her back.

"I've had that for ages. After my dad died . . ." she said and stopped.

Jack's finger stilled. He studied her upturned face, her mouth closed on a secret, her eyes cloudy with memories.

And then she blinked at him and smiled. "How come you don't have any tattoos? I mean, you were in the Marines, right?"

She was deflecting again, the way she always did when the focus turned to her.

He didn't carry his memories on his body. He wanted to forget.

But he had buddies who wore their losses in their skin,

the wives and sweethearts they'd left behind, their comrades fallen on the battlefield.

"You got it to remember him," he guessed.

"Not really." Her smile quirked, full and infectious. "I mean, it's not like I got the date of his death tattooed on my arm or my ass or anything. I'm from the Midwest. The suburbs. When somebody dies, you send flowers and a nice covered dish. You don't get a tramp stamp."

She made him smile. But she made him wonder, too. He'd spent the past hour learning her body, deciphering her responses. There was more, for a man who cared to look for it.

"You can tell me," he said. Like they were in an interview room and he was asking her to confess to some crime. "Why did you get a tattoo after your father died?"

For a minute he thought she wasn't going to answer. But then she shrugged. "I didn't really have a chance to grieve, you know? My mom was falling apart, and Noah was flipping out, and somebody had to deal with shit, Dad's shop and the insurance and the funeral arrangements. Somebody had to be the calm, responsible one."

Jack thought of the girl he'd seen on TV, the one who kept her head in the face of threats and deprivation. Who'd bargained her own life to save others. "You shut down your feelings so you can get the job done."

Her glance was surprised and grateful.

"Like a sniper. Or a hostage negotiator. Emotion fucks things up," he said. He was living proof of that. "So you stay calm. You stay in control."

"Right." She tilted her head, studying his face with those too-aware eyes. "Except eventually you have to accept your emotions. You need to express them somehow."

Or you could hit a punching bag until they went away, Jack thought.

"You didn't have this on TV." He touched the tiny jewel, bright and defiant, on the side of her nose. "You call that self-expression? Or a disguise?"

Her humor lit her face. "Are you interrogating me, Detective?"

"No more than you're analyzing me. Doctor."

She smiled her crooked smile. "I'm not a doctor yet. Maybe . . . A little of both? I did want to change my appearance. I was so numb after everything happened. I needed to feel something. Even if it hurt, even if it was only temporary, at least I'd know I was alive."

Even if it hurt, even if it was only temporary.

"Is that what this is?" Jack asked suddenly. "You being with me?"

"Would that bother you?"

That she was using him to make herself feel something? To make herself feel better? "No."

He wanted her to use him. And then maybe it would be okay if he used her, too. If he let himself feel something, too.

Even if it was only temporary.

He grabbed another condom and rolled with her, pinning her to the mattress. "I feel something now."

Their bodies pressed together, length to length. There was no disguising what she did to him.

Lauren's breath caught as he rocked against her. Her eyes crinkled. God, he loved her smile. "Funny, I feel something, too."

He scowled down at her in mock outrage. "You think it's funny?"

She grinned up at him, twining her arms around his neck. "What I think is this isn't going to hurt at all."

Nine

"GOOD NIGHT, SLEEP tight," Jane said to Aidan. She ran her hand over her son's straight brown hair, already outgrowing its summer haircut. "Don't let the bedbugs bite."

"Mom." He rolled his head on the pillow, annoyed at her touch. Asserting his independence, protecting his male dignity. A six-and-a-half-year-old version of his grandfather. "There's no such thing as bedbugs."

She didn't correct him because she wanted it to be true. No bugs in the bed, no bumps in the night, no monsters in the closet in Aidan's world.

Not anymore.

"Well, sleep tight anyway," she said and bent to kiss him.

He rewarded her as he did most of the time, flinging one skinny arm around her neck in a brief hug. She gave herself a moment to savor his unique little boy smell, baby shampoo and Aidan, before she straightened and turned out the light.

"Mom." His voice caught her at the door. "Can I go to Christopher's tomorrow after camp?"

Jane swallowed. "Tomorrow's Thursday, buddy," she reminded him gently. "You come to the bakery on Thursdays."

"But Christopher's mom is taking him to the water park."

Christopher had two working parents. His mom, Gail Peele, was wonderful about including Aidan in her family's plans. But with only a single salary and no benefits, there was no money in Jane's budget for weekly visits to the water park.

"How about when I finish at the shop tomorrow, we go to the beach?" Jane suggested.

"The beach is too sandy. And I won't have anybody to play with."

His whining drove her to distraction and made her want to laugh at the same time. "Maybe one of the many, many children whose families brought them to the beach on vacation might want to play with you," Jane said. "What do you think?"

Aidan sank under his covers, defeated. "Maybe."

She smiled. "Night, buddy. God bless. I love you."

She left the door open exactly two inches, enough that she could hear him in the night, not enough for the light from the bathroom to disturb him. She was almost at the top of the stairs before she heard his muttered reply.

"Love you, too."

Like a whispered absolution, the words eased the muscles in her shoulders, the anxious ache of her heart.

Seven hours before she had to get up and go to work again, she calculated. She started down the stairs. Nothing left tonight but to ready Aidan's cooler for camp tomorrow, move the laundry to the dryer, wipe down the kitchen, check her phone messages, and go to bed.

She walked past the living room, where her father sat every night after dinner in the flickering glow of TV. *Twenty years in the same recliner.*

When she was nine, twelve, fourteen, sometimes she would sit with him, hoping he would look over and . . . What? Talk to her?

Now she was relieved when he turned away, thankful not to see the disappointment in his eyes.

In the kitchen, while she waited for the water in the sink to run hot, she checked her cell phone. Four calls in the time it took to shepherd Aidan through his shower and into bed. Jane scrolled through them. The dairy, confirming tomorrow's milk order. One CALLER UNKNOWN. And . . .

Her heart slammed. Two calls from Island Security Systems. *Oh, God. Travis*, she thought. But no. He'd said—he'd *promised*—he was on his way to Florida. But her fingers trembled as she pressed the contact button.

Please, please, please, she thought as the phone rang on the other end, but what she was praying for, she couldn't say.

"Island Security."

"This is Jane Clark?" She hated the way her voice rose at the end like a question. Like her identity was suddenly in doubt. *Jane Tillett.* "You called me?"

"Hey, Ms. Clark. Can I have your password, please?"

"My password." Her mind blanked. What was her password? "Cupcakes. Is there a problem at the bakery?"

"Thank you. Don't worry, everything's fine."

She could barely hear him, she couldn't think, over the water rushing in the sink and the pounding in her head. She shut off the faucet.

". . . false alarm," he was saying. "But since she didn't

have the code and we couldn't reach you, we had to notify the police."

"The police." Thank God her father wasn't on duty tonight.

"Yes, ma'am."

There was more, but in her relief, she hardly cared. Something about resetting the alarm and a nuisance charge because Jack Rossi had to respond to the call. She missed some details because her father chose that moment to walk into the kitchen.

"Yes, yes, I understand," she answered distractedly as he opened the refrigerator and pulled out the pitcher of water. "Thank you. I will. Good night."

She disconnected the call.

Hank stood watching her, clutching his glass. "That the security company?"

She pulled herself together. Of course he would have heard her mention the police. At fifty-eight, there was nothing wrong with his hearing. Or his understanding. "Yes. Lauren—my new hire?—went back to the shop to get her laptop and set off the alarm by accident."

His deep brown eyes remained fixed on her face. "So everything's all right, then."

For one wild moment she was tempted to tell him everything, to throw her fears and troubles on her father's broad chest and beg him to take care of her.

But he'd already done so much, taking them in after the wreck of her marriage. She'd already let him down so badly. Let herself down.

She couldn't ask him to do more.

She found a smile somewhere and pasted it on. "Everything's fine."

He nodded, accepting her assurance as he always did,

relieved to be spared the necessity of dealing with her feelings. She listened to his footsteps in the hall, waiting until she was sure he was settled in his recliner before she checked her phone again.

CALLER UNKNOWN. A wrong number, maybe. Yet a whisper ran like a spider over her nape, all the little hairs rising in its wake, stirred by the call from the security company, teased by an instinct. Something left over from her marriage, like the queen-sized sheets or the scar on the back of her head.

Travis. She felt it in her bones, a remembered ache. If she ignored him, would he call again? And again. Or maybe he wouldn't call. Maybe he'd drop by at the bakery, at her house. *You want to have this discussion in front of Aidan and your daddy? Or we settle things now.*

He picked up after the first ring. She recognized his voice, a sense of inevitability sinking her stomach.

"Janey, Janey." His drawl was reproachful. Familiar. "Took you long enough to get back to me."

She resisted the urge to apologize. She grabbed the trash bag from the kitchen garbage can, carrying it outside, where there was no risk her father would overhear her call. "What do you want, Travis?"

"Maybe I just want to see my wife. My family."

Standing by the Dumpster, she let the trash bag slide to her feet; clutched the phone tighter. "I thought you were on your way to Florida. You had a job, you said."

"Yeah, about that . . ." A pause, while she felt sicker and sicker to her stomach. "I need some traveling money to get down there."

"I gave you money already."

"Enough to get on. Not enough to get gone."

"It's all I can afford."

"I seen your place. You're doing all right."

"I have . . ." A child to provide for. *No, don't say that, don't remind him of Aidan.* "Expenses."

"New security system."

"How did you hear about that?"

"New air conditioner, too."

"The insurance paid for that," she said, hating the defensive note that crept into her voice.

"Maybe you need more insurance."

Her heart pushed into her throat. The old, remembered helplessness rose, threatening to choke her. "What are you talking about?"

"Just saying. It's cheaper to pay for things up front than worry about what could go wrong down the road."

"You stay away from us," she said, as if he'd ever listened to her.

"Or what? You'll call the cops?" He laughed softly. "Janey, Janey. You really gonna lock up your baby's daddy? How you going to explain that to Aidan?"

"I won't have to explain anything. He doesn't know . . . He doesn't need to know anything about you."

"He'll learn," Travis said. "If I stick around. You think about that."

The connection cut off.

"Travis? *Travis!*"

No answer.

She leaned against the Dumpster, folding her arms over her waist like a woman protecting her stomach. He'd always known what buttons to push.

He'll learn . . . You think about that.

She wouldn't think of anything else now.

Ten

LAUREN WAS AN expert on morning afters. The trick was to manage expectations from the start.

She generally provided couch crashers and other overnight guests with a toothbrush (disposable), coffee (optional), and sometimes her phone number (assuming either party had a repeat performance in mind). But spending the night was not like checking into a bed-and-breakfast. When she slept over at a guy's place, she had learned not to overstay her welcome. No leisurely checkouts, no experimenting with bath products, no hanging around waiting for an invitation to return.

Hit it and quit it, as one memorable guy-in-a-band explained crudely the next morning.

So she was a long way from confusing sex with commitment.

But Jack confused her.

He kissed her good morning, for starters. And then, while

she was still weak with lust and wrecked from lack of sleep, before she had a chance to worry about morning breath or think about the places she was sore, he used his mouth and hands to arouse her, making her sigh and reach for him, making her arch and moan. Filling her, possessing her, body and heart, while the soft pearl light slipped through the windows.

After which, she'd slept. Peacefully. Without nightmares.

When she opened her eyes again, Jack was looming over her, showered and fresh and in uniform.

Heat flooded from her breasts to her hairline. It wasn't like he hadn't seen her naked before. He was now intimately familiar with every square inch of her body. But he'd never seen her with pillow creases and beard burn and hair that looked like she'd brushed it with a whisk.

He, of course, looked amazing, closely shaved, completely in control.

He watched her grab for the sheet and raised one dark, sexy brow. But all he said was, "Head's free, if you want to use it."

Head? Oh, the bathroom.

"Thanks." She cleared her throat. What exactly did you say to a man who'd given you four earth-shattering orgasms the night before? *Thank you? Way to go? Let's do this again sometime?* "What time is it?"

"Almost seven. I'll drop you on my way to work."

Guy code for *Please leave now.*

Her stomach sank. She should have snuck out while he was in the shower. Although, sneak how? There were no cabs on Dare Island, only the senior shuttle service. And she very much doubted they would appreciate being called out at seven in the morning to spare her the walk of shame.

She scrambled for her bra. "Right. Just give me a second,

I'll . . ." *Pull myself together.* Where were her panties, damn it?

"Lauren."

She stopped.

Jack swooped and kissed her hard, like he wasn't finished with her yet. He smelled so good, like toothpaste and clean male skin. Her toes curled under the covers.

Before she could wrap her brain or her arms around him, he straightened. "You're fine. Coffee'll be ready when you get out."

She watched, confounded, as he strolled through the narrow door.

Coffee.

Galvanized, she threw back the covers. A corner of the blanket swept the built-in storage unit on the other side of the bed, knocking something to the floor. A book. She flopped across the mattress to retrieve it, fingers stretching, naked butt in the air.

Her own face—younger, smoother, under a blond pixie cut—smiled up at her from the carpet. Her publicity photo, on the back cover jacket of her book.

Her breath backed up in her lungs. Jack was reading her book, *Hostage Girl: My Story.*

She sat back on her heels on the bed, the book in her hand. Lots of people read her book. *Forty-eight weeks on the* Times *list.*

But knowing Jack was reading up on her, investigating her like one of his cases, made her feel exposed. At a disadvantage. Vulnerable. It was a degree of intimacy she wasn't prepared for. Like the bed-head-and-pillow-crease moment all over again.

She could still smell him on her skin. Still feel the imprint of him deep in her body, every breath, every movement, a reminder of last night and those four devastating orgasms.

Positive thoughts, she told herself. Constructive action. What she needed was a shower.

So she took one, standing under the lukewarm spray before dressing hastily in last night's rumpled clothes.

When she went out on deck, Jack was squatting by the animal trap, talking in a calm, soothing voice to the kitten pressed against the bars. So he was kind to animals, too.

Lauren sighed. Like he wasn't irresistible enough already.

At the sound of her footsteps, he straightened, all muscled competence and controlled male grace. For a moment, she let herself drink in the scene: the hazy sunlight, the golden sea, the scent of the breeze off the water. The man, unwrinkled, unwilted, his strong Roman features gilded by the sun, his smile a miracle of disciplined beauty.

Why spoil the moment? Why not just, well, *live* in it and keep her mouth shut for once? She could pretend she hadn't seen anything.

But she was really sick of pretending.

"I wasn't snooping," she said.

Jack's lips did that unbelievably sexy quirk thing. Her breath caught. The man should really smile more often. "So you didn't find the stack of *Playboy*s under the bed."

"No. Thank you." She accepted the coffee he handed her and took a careful sip. Hot and bitter. "I found . . ." Her throat closed. *Oh, crap. Just do it.* Wordlessly, she held out the book.

His gaze dropped to the cover; rose to her face, his dark eyes alert. Assessing. He didn't say anything.

She swallowed. "When did you . . ."

"Buy it?" He shrugged. "A couple days ago."

The same time he'd bought the condoms? "Why?"

"I was interested in you."

"In me? Or in Hostage Girl?"

"That's pretty insulting," Jack said quietly. "To both of us."

She closed her eyes. "I'm sorry. I don't mean to be."

Silence. Onshore, a chorus of birds tuned up for the day, their calls sharp and sweet against the whisper of the water.

"Look, I get it," Jack said slowly. "You're on tour, you get hit on by guys trying to tap a celebrity. That's not me."

"I know. I said I'm sorry." She opened her eyes, looking at him directly. She had to make this right. And the only way she knew to do that was to tell the truth. "This isn't about you. I'm trying to tell you something about me."

"Go on."

Her courage faltered. Her throat felt like she'd swallowed broken glass. *Not everybody wants to relive your fifteen minutes of fame over and over . . .*

"Don't you have to get to work?"

"I will. Tell me about you."

She'd spent six months trying to write a book, talking about what happened, but never about herself. Never about how it made her feel. *My Life After Crisis.*

"It isn't only guys who hit on you," she said, forcing the words out her shredded throat. "It's everybody. Like, people would see me on TV or they'd read part of an article online, and they'd think they knew me. Like they had the facts to judge. The right to comment. To me personally, sometimes, but online, too. God, they'll say anything online." The words, once started, trickled through her crumbling defenses like water through a dam. "Twitter's the worst. And yeah, okay, there were guys who got off on the whole hostage thing in a really creepy way, who thought I got Ben to give himself up because I was giving him blow jobs out of sight of the security cameras. But it wasn't like that with him and me. It was never like that."

"What was it like?"

"It's in the book."

"I'll read the book later. I'm talking to you now."

He was so calm. So unmoving. Like she could pour herself out in drabs and spurts and wild torrential bursts, all her guilt and grief and regret, and he'd never flinch.

"He had a brother." The words spilled out, widening the crack in her chest. "Joel. It wasn't supposed to be Ben who did the job that day. Their uncle George planned it. He wanted to take Ben's brother Joel, because Joel was still a juvie, and he figured the DA would go easier on Joel if he got caught."

"So what happened?" Jack prompted, smooth as a priest in a confessional.

"Ben found out. He told their uncle he'd take Joel's place, that it was him or nobody. They needed the money, their mom has diabetes, he figured he was the responsible one. The interviewers, they kept saying I was so brave, and the comments, they made it out like I manipulated him, but I didn't. It's just . . . I kept thinking about my brother, Noah, and how we were alike, really, Ben and me. We were both so scared. He was just trying to take care of his family. And now he's in jail, his mom's still sick, his family's still broke, and I have all this money from my book deal. It's not fair."

"You're not the same. You didn't try to support your family by holding up a bank and taking people hostage."

"You do what you can, what you know how to do. Ben didn't have my options. He didn't know any better."

"Don't kid yourself. He knew and he chose to do the wrong thing. Just like you chose to do the right one. I was a sniper. SWAT and Afghanistan. I don't take out a target, maybe he kills twenty other people. Sometimes you have to make the tough call."

Oh, he was good. Like a detective extracting a confession,

he offered just enough of himself to keep the conversation going without ever truly laying himself open. Without ever making any promises.

"The situations aren't the same. You don't understand."

"Try me."

His words set up echoes in her flesh. This was an intimacy more seductive, more dangerous, than sex. All the vulnerable places in her body clenched.

"Ben *trusted* me." She made herself say it. "I promised I would help him. And instead, his uncle George was killed when he surrendered to the authorities."

"Some surrender. The guy resisted."

Her brows tweaked together. "I don't say that in the book."

His gaze met hers. Flat, black, unreadable. "I watched the entry go down. On TV."

That made sense. He was a cop. On a SWAT team, he'd said. He might have followed the situation out of professional interest. But she was missing something. She watched his hands ball in his pockets, making the fabric of his uniform slacks stretch across his thighs. Hands betrayed emotion when the face did not. "The tapes don't show everything," she said. "Some people say the SWAT team overreacted."

"That's on them, not on you."

She knew that. She'd talked about survivor guilt with her therapist. But . . .

"Ben's mother blames me. Her brother is dead, her son is in jail, because they listened to me."

"Bullshit. That day at the bank, you did everything you could. You kept your head. You got three thugs with guns focused on you. You talked them into letting seven other people go. You put yourself out there for some strangers, even though it meant your brother, your mother, might not see you again."

"You're making me sound brave. I'm not. There just wasn't anybody else who could talk to them. Who was trained at talking with people."

"Well, you are good at that," he said very dryly.

She laughed shakily, the sound scraping through the ground glass in her throat. "I'm sorry. I'm talking too much."

He smiled slightly. "It's all good. You got something to say, you say it."

"I wish. I haven't been able to talk about my feelings or write about them or anything else in months."

"Talk about your feelings," he repeated without expression.

"Yes." She expelled her breath, a huff of amusement and frustration. "I've been on a book tour. I'm supposed to be connecting with people, inspiring them, and I've been reading off a script for so long I can't remember what my feelings even are anymore. I'm numb. All I can manage is sound bites."

All the same questions, over and over, scraping her nerves, probing barely healed wounds. *Tell me how it felt . . . Were you close . . . I've heard you write to him in prison . . .*

"So? You don't owe a pound of flesh every time somebody asks you a question. You give them the answer that takes off the least amount of skin. Otherwise you bleed to death."

Oh, God. She stared at him, stricken. That was it exactly. "Or you cauterize your emotions until you can't feel anything anymore."

"That's not you."

She wanted desperately to believe him. "How do you know? Trauma *changes* you." From someone who wanted to make a difference in the world to someone who couldn't bring herself to leave her hotel room.

"It can," Jack agreed calmly, his gaze steady on hers. "Or it can show you who you really are."

She winced. "Hostage Girl." Captive to her fears.

He shook his head. "That's not who I see." His fingers traced the silver coil of her ear cuff; traveled her jaw to the point of her chin. The solid heat of his body tugged at her like gravity. His pupils were wide and dark. She swayed, lost in their darkness.

"You're not afraid to get involved. You're not afraid to get hurt. All those feelings you say you don't feel? They're all in there."

"In my book."

"In you. You've got something inside you," he murmured. "A spark. A heart. You care in an uncaring world. That takes a kind of courage most people will never have."

The look on his face tightened her heart in her chest. She struggled to speak. To breathe.

He released her chin, stepping back. "You need more coffee?"

She blinked, rocked off balance. "Um. No. Thanks."

"Because I'm going in for a minute." He picked up the trap with the tabby kitten inside, the muscles in his arm flexing. "I can get you some."

"What about . . ." She waved her hand around.

"Should be fine. I don't have time to get to the shelter this morning, but the cabin's cool enough. I'll leave food and water."

Her jaw jarred open. He thought she was talking about the *cat*?

But no. Lauren's eyes narrowed. This was a pattern. Intimacy and retreat. He'd done it before.

The kitten lurched as the trap swung, pressing its skinny gray body against the wire. Separated from its—*litter? nest? colony?*—the poor little thing was frantic for contact. Even human contact.

Jack reached through the bars, rubbing the scruffy head with one broad finger, and Lauren's heart turned into this gooey mass in her chest that *hurt*.

She cleared her throat. "Will I see you later?"

"Probably." He set the cage on some newspaper inside the cabin door. "Unless Marta's made coffee for the staff meeting."

"Who's Marta?"

"New dispatcher," he said as he went inside.

She watched the shadow of his head, the silhouette of his shoulders, as he moved efficiently in the small galley. Getting food and water, she guessed, for the cat.

She gulped her cooling coffee. She'd only known Jack a week. She'd only slept with him once. (*Four orgasms*, her body whispered.) Pride, practicality, and hookup etiquette all demanded that she let it go. Let him go.

But wasn't the whole hookup thing a retreat from intimacy, too? To accept sexual pleasure while ignoring any emotional connection. To pretend she didn't care.

You care in an uncaring world, Jack had said. *That takes a kind of courage most people will never have.*

He came out on deck, buttoned up and beautiful in that controlled masculine way, and she took one ragged breath for courage and said, "I meant tonight. We could do dinner or something."

"Can't." At least he had the manners to look briefly regretful. "I'm tied up. Matt Fletcher's throwing some kind of bachelor party for Luke tonight."

"Oh." She exhaled, deflated. Well, she couldn't argue with that.

"Things should wind down on the early side. I'd like to stop by. Or call." Jack's eyes met hers, and her heart betrayed her by skipping a beat and then rushing to make up for lost time. "If it's not too late for you."

Her smile started in her chest and radiated outward, a big goofy glow that spread all over her face. She was getting mushy over a booty call. But she was so glad she got to see him again that she mostly didn't care. "Not too late at all."

"LAUREN, DO YOU know where the other sugar dispenser is?" Jane asked as Lauren moved through the tables, cleaning up after the lunch crowd.

Sugar dispenser? Lauren tried to focus. It was like there were two Laurens today, Lauren the stirred-up mind and Lauren the thoroughly satisfied body, both absorbed in remembering and processing the unfamiliar events of last night. Neither focused on the bakery at all. Every breath, every stretch, every thought recalled Jack.

She struggled to keep herself together. "Yeah, sure, it's in the . . . It's not on the coffee station?"

"You put it in the refrigerator," Thalia said. She took out the dispenser and grinned. "Right next to the milk."

"Oops." Lauren smiled apologetically. "I guess I'm a little distracted today." An understatement.

"I'm really sorry," Jane said. "It's my fault."

Lauren blinked. *Concentrate.* "Why?"

"I should have given you the passcode. You must have totally freaked when the alarm went off."

Sirens blaring, stabbing, vibrating through her like electric shocks . . . Lauren took a careful breath. "Why should you? You had absolutely no reason to think I would need to be in the bakery after hours."

"Besides," Thalia said cheerfully, "she got rescued by Hot Cop Rossi."

Jane's distressed frown stayed in place. "I still should have warned you. I'm so sorry."

"Jane, it really is all right. He was very . . ." *Professional?* "Reassuring."

"Is that all? Because when he came in this morning?" Thalia put her hand on her chest and mimed a thumping heart. "Major vibes. I thought he was going to order coffee to go and you on the side."

Heat swept through Lauren. He'd already had her on her side. And on her back. And . . .

"Oh, wow, he did, didn't he?" Thalia asked in an awed voice. "You and Chief Rossi? Seriously?"

"Thalia, that's none of our business," Jane said firmly.

"I think it's great," Thalia said. "I mean, you're both single, healthy adults."

"Which doesn't make her private life a suitable topic of discussion for you. You're sixteen."

"Mom says adolescence is a modern invention of wealthy industrial societies, and that I've been a woman since menses," Thalia said. "She feels I should be free to explore my natural sexual impulses before deciding if a monogamous heteronormative relationship would be personally fulfilling."

"Bless her heart," Jane said.

Which Lauren had learned could mean anything from *You poor thing* to *Your mama is an idiot.* She bit down on a laugh. "Did she also talk to you about the importance of using protection while you're, um, exploring?"

Thalia grinned, apparently unfazed by a relative stranger quizzing her on birth control. She was a *very* self-possessed sixteen. "No, that was my dad. He told me the frontal lobes of boys my age aren't fully connected yet, and I shouldn't waste my time on them."

"And what do you think?" Lauren asked, falling into counselor-speak.

"I'm going to college—Chapel Hill—in another year. I don't really want to get serious about anybody yet."

"What about Josh Fletcher?" Jane asked.

Matt Fletcher's son, Lauren thought. Meg's nephew. Meg had mentioned the two were dating. Lauren had seen the teen around the Pirates' Rest, a handsome boy with broad shoulders and big hands and a mop of tawny hair.

A cloud passed over Thalia's round, sunny face. "He understands. We're friends."

"'Friends' is good," Lauren said gently. And probably hard to pull off when you were sixteen years old and spending time with a boy who could have modeled for Michelangelo's *David*.

"Yeah." Thalia wiped her hands on her apron, looked at Jane. "Would it be okay if I took off now? Camille wants some Mommy-and-me time with Océane, and I told her I'd take Chloe to the pool."

"That would be fine. Thalia works for a French family in one of the big houses on the beach," Jane explained to Lauren.

"It's not *work* work. I'm babysitting."

"Still . . . Two jobs," Lauren said.

Thalia shrugged. "More money for college. Anyway, I like kids. I've got four younger brothers and sisters." She hesitated. "I can watch Aidan, too, if you want. Camille won't mind. She wants Chloe to practice her English."

"Oh, that's sweet of you, both of you, honey, but Aidan's got camp 'til five. Anyway, I'm taking him to the beach later."

"Mommy-and-Aidan time," Thalia said.

Jane smiled. "Something like that."

Thalia left. Customers came in, three laughing, chatting women who settled at a table, a couple who took coffee and pastries outside, a family picking up a cake. Lauren pulled shots and watched as Jane expertly boxed a Chocolate Seduction with Bavarian cream for the young mother's birthday.

Jane was a mother. How could she have missed this important piece of personal information? But Jane never talked about herself.

"So, Aidan is your son?" Lauren asked when the shop was quiet again.

Jane nodded.

"How old is he?"

"Almost seven."

"So . . . starting second grade?"

"First." Jane wiped unnecessarily at a spot on the counter, as if disclosing even that much information made her uncomfortable. "His birthday's in October."

"How long have you and his father been . . ." She trailed off deliberately, leaving a space for Jane to define any way she wanted.

"Separated?" Jane asked.

Lauren nodded.

"Forever. He took off right after Aidan was born."

Lauren winced in sympathy. "Ouch."

"Yeah. I was stupid." Jane shrugged. "I've always been stupid about men."

"When I first got here, I thought maybe you and Jack Rossi . . ." Another pause Lauren wasn't sure how to fill. A space she hoped would stay empty.

Jane shook her head. "I would never marry a cop. My

dad's a cop. If I ever take a chance on another guy, it won't be somebody who always puts his job ahead of me."

Lauren drew a relieved breath. So, no romantic attachment on either side. That was good news.

She should drop the whole subject right there, Lauren thought. She and Jane worked well together, but the other woman had no particular need or reason to trust her. To confide in her. Jane had lived on Dare Island all her life. For all Lauren knew, she could have this great, giant support system of friends to laugh and talk with, to cry and confide in.

Or not. Maybe familiarity carried the same cost as fame. Maybe a small town was like the online community, everybody thinking they knew you, that they had the facts to judge, the right to comment . . . Hard to sustain friendships when every move was under the microscope. When every neighbor remembered your mistakes. Maybe Jane needed a friend.

Maybe Lauren was ready to be a friend again. "It's tough," she said. "Raising a son and running a business on your own."

"We do all right," Jane said.

"You do a great job. I'm impressed. When my dad died . . ." Lauren's chest tightened. *Positive thoughts.* But being friends wasn't about having all the answers or even asking the right questions. Friendship required making yourself vulnerable. Admitting weakness. Opening yourself to the possibility of loss.

Jack's words glowed inside her. *You're not afraid to get involved. You're not afraid to get hurt. That takes a kind of courage most people will never have.*

"My mom had a lot of trouble coping. I had to leave school to look after things for a while."

Jane's smooth face creased in sympathy. "I'm sorry."

"Thanks. Shit happens, right? I'm just saying, if you ever need someone to talk to . . ."

"Thank you." Jane's gaze met hers. "I mean that. But it's not the same. Aidan's father isn't dead."

Lauren leaned against the counter, refusing to be turned away. "Maybe it would be easier if he was."

A shocked laugh broke from Jane. "Maybe."

"That guy who came in last week," Lauren said. "Was that him? Aidan's dad?"

"Travis is incapable of being anybody's dad."

"Oh." Okay. She hadn't seen that coming.

Jane slid her a sideways glance. "It's not what you're thinking. What I mean is, Travis doesn't care about Aidan. He never has. Leaving was the best thing he could have done, for Aidan and for me. Anyway, Travis has some job lined up in Florida. He just needs a stake to get down there."

A stake? The errand at the bank, Lauren thought. "So basically you're paying him off."

Jane bit her lip. Nodded. "I don't want him to have any contact with Aidan. I don't even want Aidan to know that he's here. Especially now that Aidan's old enough to ask questions."

"He's going to ask anyway," Lauren felt compelled to point out. "Or his friends at school will."

"I know. But they'll be easier to answer when Travis is gone."

"Jane." Lauren searched for the right words. "You can't pay to make your problems go away."

"How do you know?"

Because I've tried. The thought caught her under the ribs like a missed breath. Every month, a check to Ben's mother. Every week, a letter to Ben with a credit to the prison commissary for pens, for paper, for candy bars and shaving supplies. *How is Joel? Did you read the book I sent? Have you forgiven me yet?*

"I'm just saying money doesn't solve your underlying issues. You still have to deal with your feelings." *The guilt.*

Jane smiled wryly. "I have a six-year-old depending on me. My feelings are the last thing I'm worried about."

Lauren inhaled slowly. "Okay."

"So you won't say anything to Aidan?"

"Of course not."

Jane relaxed. "Thanks. That's all right, then."

But it wasn't. Not really. And Lauren didn't know what she could do to help.

Eleven

THE LAST BACHELOR party Jack attended, a twenty-year-old stripper named Brandi ground on the bridegroom's lap—big Mike Malone from Vice—while a bunch of wasted cops stuffed bills into her G-string.

Jack was no Boy Scout. But he was too old for that shit.

Marriage was enough of a crapshoot. A guy who kicked off the whole I-Do deal by getting high, drunk, and laid days before his wedding was just worsening the odds.

But for Luke, Jack could put up with the ritual boobs-and-booze fest. Sam Grady had offered his family's restaurant, the Fish House, for the party. Jack figured he'd sip a beer for a couple of hours and then play cabbie before giving Lauren a call. He walked into the bar's back room feeling pretty good about life in general and positively optimistic about the way his night would end.

He hadn't counted on Luke's dad, Tom, being there, tall, weathered, and tough as a telephone pole. Or Luke's seventeen-year-old nephew Josh, nursing a Coke at the poker table. Jack had routed the town's teens out from under the pier enough times to guess the boy had snuck a few beers before. But at Luke's party, in Sam's bar, everybody was on their best behavior.

The only bills seeing any action tonight were in the pot in the center of the table.

Jack's muscles relaxed. He was glad he wouldn't be breaking up a bar fight tonight. Or talking the groom back into his pants.

Luke introduced him to some guys from his old squad who had made the trek from Camp Lejeune and a couple of buddies from boot camp. There was talk of a third, Gabe Somebody, who had left the Corps and couldn't be reached. But all in all, a nice group. Nice guys.

It seemed almost a shame to take their money.

"Seven-card stud," Matt said, shuffling the deck in his work-hardened hands.

"What's wild?" Josh asked.

His grandfather, Tom, snorted.

One of the Marines smothered a grin.

"Seven-card stud," Matt repeated quietly. "No wilds."

"Unless I get trash all night," Sam said. "Then it's deuces, eights, and one-eyed Jacks."

Josh shot him a grateful look.

Jack sat with his back to the wall, angling his chair to keep an eye on the entrance. Like a cop. Or, he thought, looking around the table, a guy recently returned from a war zone. Luke and his Marine pals had already commandeered the chairs on the other side, facing the door. Guarding their backs, watching the entrance. Clearly, they'd had the same idea. The same training.

Matt dealt the cards.

Sam, Jack thought as the game progressed, was his only competition, the only one watching as the others picked up their cards, the one who understood that you played your opponents and not your hand.

Matt was shrewd but conservative, betting the cards he was dealt, never taking the big risks that rake in the pot. Tom's expression never changed, but he had a significant tell, glancing at his stack of chips on every strong hand. Josh threw everything he had into the game, betting, bluffing, and losing with boyish enthusiasm. The Marines had skills. In a Muslim country, cards were pretty much the only acceptable vice to while away the long hours of tension and boredom. But they drank more than the others, and young Danny Hill kept texting his wife.

"Sorry," he said, looking up. "This is the first night I've been away since we got back."

Luke was a fine player, alert and careful, but his heart wasn't really in the game.

When Jack bluffed him with a pair of threes, Tom rolled his eyes to the ceiling. "Shit, son, didn't I teach you better than that?"

Luke grinned, unapologetic. "Guess I've got other things on my mind."

Matt smiled. "Understandable."

Sam, who was sitting out this hand, set another plate of sandwiches on the table. "I've got orders to keep you away from the inn until eleven. Deal."

Eleven, Jack thought. He'd told Lauren it would be an early night. But *eleven*?

Get over it, Rossi. You're not in Philly anymore.

Not too late at all, Lauren said in his head, her warm

eyes glowing, her lips curving, and his dick surged behind his fly. Like he was Josh's age again, when every random thought gave him a hard-on.

Jack dropped his gaze to his cards, shifting in his chair, giving himself a moment to recover.

"You betting? Or playing with yourself?" Tom wanted to know.

Jack grinned and tossed the required bid into the pot.

Rafe Slater, one of the Marines, reached a long arm for another beer from the bar, offered a bottle to Luke.

Luke gave a quick shake of his head. "I'm good for now."

"Jesus, pal, you're getting married in four days. You can't be whipped already. Gotta drink up while you can."

Jack knew, because Luke had told him, that Kate Dolan's old man was a hard-drinking Marine who took his career frustrations out on his wife and daughter until he died. Obviously Luke didn't intend to provoke bad memories in his bride by stumbling home to her reeking of alcohol.

But this was his bachelor party. It wouldn't hurt to keep an eye out.

The last hand ended near midnight when every man but Jack and Sam was out. Jack got a queen on the final deal and won with an ace-high straight.

Sam shrugged philosophically as he turned over his two pair. "You got lucky tonight, pal."

That was the plan.

Jack smiled and pushed the pot across the table.

Luke looked down at Jack's winnings and raised his eyebrows. "What's this?"

"Wedding present," Jack said and stood. "Who needs a ride?"

"We're good," Matt said.

Josh grinned. "I'm designated driver."

Tom winked at his grandson. "God help us."

Jack looked at the four Marines. "How about you?"

"We've got an empty rental," Sam said. "Sudden cancellation. I can put them up there tonight, see them on their way in the morning."

Jack doubted Grady Real Estate had a cancellation at the height of the rental season. But Sam was generous that way. As long as the impaired Marines stayed off the road tonight, Jack was happy.

"Great. Let's get you home then," he said to Luke.

He waited patiently while the groom said good-bye to his buddies with as much sentiment as if they were all going off to war again. Matt caught his brother in a fierce, short hug. Backs were slapped, arms punched.

Seventeen-year-old Josh collared his uncle with one arm around his neck. Something about the way they stood together, almost the same height, Luke's blond head against Josh's tawny mop, grabbed Jack's throat and wouldn't let go.

"Unc Luke." Josh's voice was muffled against Luke's shoulder. "I hope you'll be as happy as my dad."

Ah, Christ. Jack's eyes stung.

It should have been corny.

But seeing their closeness reminded him of what he'd left behind, his father, his brothers, his nephews and nieces.

And it recalled in a worse way the things he'd once counted on and never really had at all. His hand curled in his pocket as if he could hold on to his illusions.

He missed Frank. Not the partner who had betrayed him, but the friendship he'd thought they had. The trust.

He missed the life he had planned with Renee, back when he'd believed they could make it. The Sunday dinners, the baptisms and first communions, surrounded by her family and his.

If she'd gotten pregnant on their honeymoon, the way she'd feared, their oldest kid would have been a few years younger than Josh by now.

Moving forward? Or running away?

He had moved out. He'd moved on.

But tonight, watching Luke with his family, he felt his foot caught in the door of the life he'd left behind.

LAUREN SAT WITH her back to the headboard, surrounded by the story of her life—*okay, the last eleven months*—in the form of two hundred and eighty printed manuscript pages.

Reading over the hard copy helped her evaluate the work differently. Or maybe she was responding to the memory of Jack's voice echoing in her head like a drumbeat, like a call to action, encouraging her heart to a fresh cadence, rousing her to life. *All those feelings you say you don't feel? They're all in there.*

But she hadn't put them on the page. She turned down a corner to come back to later, frowned, read some more. The structure was good. *If I move this bit here . . .* The events were all there. *That part with the therapist . . . The visit to the prison to see Ben . . .*

Only the emotion, the way those events made her *feel*, was missing.

And the emotion was everything.

Her pulse quickened. She started to make notes, slowly at first and then with confidence, scribbling in the margins, jotting on the backs of pages, inserting more sheets when she ran out of room. Writing as if she had nobody to offend and nothing to lose.

She worked until the words streaming across the page blended with the paper in shades of gray.

She blinked, distracted, and looked up. The light was gone. The sky outside her windows was dark. She took a deep breath. Good heavens, it must be . . . Her glance fell on the clock. *Nine?*

Shifting the piles of paper, she uncurled from the bed. Her legs trembled under her as she stretched her back and her fingers. Her stomach growled. She'd been up here for *hours.*

Writing.

She smiled.

Noises drifted up the stairs. Women's voices. Meg, she wondered, come to visit her mother?

Lauren took another look at the notes spread out over the white duvet cover. Her grin broadened. She could tell Meg. She was *writing.* She couldn't wait to tell Meg.

She stumbled to the bathroom and then downstairs. She felt tired and shaky, cramped and . . . Well, pretty fabulous, actually. But she needed a brain break. And carbs. She was starving.

More voices, more noise as she rounded the beautifully restored banister. The hundred-year-old inn had been painstakingly restored with natural wood and warm, rich colors. But Tess Fletcher had a knack for the kind of homey touches that kept the Pirates' Rest from feeling too much like a museum or another hotel. A sea grass basket filled with shells stood by the door; a vase of big yellow sunflowers nodded on the table; a stack of colorful towels under the stairs waited for guests going to or coming from the beach.

A burst of laughter penetrated from the kitchen. Lauren smiled at the sound and then hesitated outside the swinging door. *Homey,* but not *her* home. She didn't want to intrude on the Fletchers' family space or Meg's time.

But the prospect of creeping quietly back to her room,

away from the laughter, away from the *food*, was remarkably unappealing. She knocked once and nudged open the door.

"Oh."

The kitchen was a rainbow of summer dresses and flowers and candles and food. A party.

Lauren stopped on the threshold, abruptly aware of her jeans, tank top, and outsider status. "I'm so sorry, I just . . ."

Meg, in bright red, came forward, champagne glass in hand. "Lauren! Is everything all right?"

"Fine," Lauren assured her.

Meg's eyes narrowed.

Lauren held up her hand in I-swear fashion. "Honest. I, um, kind of lost track of the time. Working."

Meg's smile flashed. "Well, that deserves a celebration. Come have cake. I'll introduce you around."

She wanted to. The warmth of the room tugged her forward. The smells were amazing. On the table behind Meg, the cake, already sliced, shared pride of place with a loose arrangement of black-eyed Susans and fat orange roses. Lauren's stomach rumbled.

"Is that Jane's lemon mascarpone five-layer cake?"

"Nothing but the best."

"Maybe I could take a slice upstairs? I don't want to crash your party."

A pretty woman with coppery hair came over. "It's my party, and I'd love for you to join us. Kate Dolan." She held out her hand, her grin as wide and shiny as the sea at dawn. "I'm getting married on Monday."

Her joy was irresistible. Contagious. Lauren smiled back. "I heard. To Luke Fletcher. Congratulations."

"Thank you. And this is Taylor," Kate said, drawing the girl to her side.

"Yeah, we've met." Lauren smiled at Meg's eleven-year-old niece. "I like your dress."

"Thanks. I have to wear one for the wedding, too. Do you want a sandwich?"

"I would, but—"

"Please stay. We have more than enough," Tess said.

"Well . . ." She was engulfed by their kindness, swept up by their welcome.

"We're going to watch a movie," Taylor said. "I picked it out."

"What did you pick?" Not *The Hangover*. Taylor was only eleven. *Bridesmaids?*

"*Princess Bride.*"

Lauren's confusion must have shown on her face.

" 'Mawwiage'!" Meg explained. " 'Mawwiage is what bwings us togethew.' "

" 'And wuv,' " Kate said.

" 'Twu wuv,' " caroled Taylor.

Lauren grinned in appreciation. "Got it. Excellent choice."

"They're all nuts." A young black woman in an orchid-colored dress smiled at Lauren. "Hi. Alisha Douglas."

"And I'm Allison." A long-stemmed blonde introduced herself. "Matt's wife. I married into this madness."

"Nice to meet you both." Lauren took a breath. She could do this. She wasn't in disguise anymore. "Lauren Patterson."

Alisha's brows rose. "Yeah? Like that hostage girl."

"Not 'like,' " Meg said. "She is."

"Have a plate," Tess said to Lauren.

"Thanks." She began to load up, aware of Alisha's warm brown eyes watching her across the table.

"I saw you on *Dr. Phil*. You look different."

Lauren took a breath. *Trauma changes you*, she'd told Jack.

Or it can show you who you really are.

"It's the hair." Lauren added a cookie to her plate. "What do you do, Alisha?"

"Social worker. Child Protective Services."

"That's how we met," Kate explained. "I'm a family lawyer."

Blond Allison looked around the table. "Wow. It's like a family intervention meeting."

"Excuse me?" Lauren asked.

"High school teacher." Allison pointed to herself and then began going around the table. "Lawyer, social worker, psychologist . . . We're like a family crisis team."

"I don't actually have my doctorate yet," Lauren said.

"Don't need one to be a counselor in North Carolina. Just a license," Alisha said.

"Are we talking shop?" Meg said. "Because if we are, I need more champagne."

Allison laughed. "Says the workaholic."

"I'll get it," Kate said.

"You go sit," Tess said. "You're the bride."

"I can help," Lauren said.

And with her offer, she slipped into the gathering like a fish into a stream. Despite her initial introduction, she found it remarkably easy to be herself with the other women, to be accepted as someone other than Hostage Girl. Plates were emptied. Glasses refilled. Conversation bubbled and flowed. Lauren liked listening to them, enjoyed unwinding in their company.

All accomplished women, in their different ways. Tess, running her inn with ease and authority; Meg, quick and dark, vibrating with energy; coolly pretty schoolteacher Allison; lawyer Kate, with her vibrant hair and shadowed hazel eyes.

But for all their differences, they were bound together. By the child Taylor, threading her way between them. By a hundred tiny words and gestures, a quick hug, a laughing glance, a sly tease.

Family.

"They all seem so sure of themselves," she murmured to Alisha. "Confident."

"Lucky. They've all got good men."

Lauren quirked an eyebrow. "Not to get all feminist in your face, but I don't think you have to be part of a couple to feel confident."

"Amen. What I meant was, I did the home evaluation for Taylor after Luke got back from Afghanistan. And one of the things I saw right away is those Fletcher men stand behind their women. Her daddy will help that child be whatever she wants or needs to be. He's the same with Kate, and she didn't always make that easy for him. He sees her. He gets her. That's powerful, when a man can do that for a woman."

Yearning flooded Lauren's chest. Her father had been the owner of a small-town shoe store, a soft-spoken, quietly affectionate man who never made much noise in life or around the house.

But when he died, the silence he left behind was devastating.

The emptiness had echoed inside her for years. The bank robbery—the shattering of security, the loss of privacy, that sense of being helpless, powerless—had only increased her personal void.

But when Jack looked at her, he didn't see someone who was empty.

You've got something inside you, he'd murmured. *A spark. A heart.*

She drew a shaky breath.

Alisha leaned forward and tucked a cocktail napkin in her hand. "I'm sorry. I didn't mean to upset you."

Lauren blotted her eyes. Managed a smile. "No. Thanks. It's just . . ."

Alisha nodded. "I know. It's the whole wedding thing gets us stirred up. Almost makes me want to take the risk on an actual relationship instead of flirting online with my Soul Mate in a Box. Assuming, of course, I could find an actual, real live man who isn't a player."

"Or a musician," Lauren said, thinking of the couch crashers.

"Or lives with his mama."

Meg, overhearing, grinned. "Maybe you're too picky. You've just eliminated both my brothers from your list of possibles."

"Easy to be smug when you're engaged to Sam Grady. Anyway, your brothers are off the market," Alisha said.

"And Luke doesn't live with his mother," Kate, the lawyer, said with precision. "He rents a cottage out back."

"Matt paid rent, too," Allison said loyally.

"So, where will you live after the wedding?" Lauren asked politely.

"We're looking for a house nearby," Kate said. "We want Taylor to stay in the same school. And the commute to my office isn't bad. Forty-five minutes or so."

Sometime during the conversation, Tess had slipped away. She returned now, a smile on her face and a small, beribboned box in her hands.

"I know you said no shower presents," she said to Kate, handing her the box. "But I wanted to give you this before the wedding."

"But you've already given us so much. The dishes . . ."

Tess waved a dismissive hand. "For the house. This is for you."

Kate's face opened like a flower. "Oh, Tess."

"Just a little something."

They all watched as she tugged at the pale yellow ribbon, working it off the corners of the box.

"What is it?" Alisha asked.

"Let me see," Taylor said.

With trembling hands, Kate lifted a white square from the creamy tissue, the cloth delicately embroidered all over with tiny blue flowers.

"It's a handkerchief," Tess said unnecessarily. She cleared her throat. "My mother-in-law gave it to me to carry on my wedding day. I thought . . . Something old?"

"And borrowed," Meg said.

"And blue!" Taylor bounded on the couch cushions.

Kate raised her face, her eyes bright with unshed tears. "I love it. I love you."

Tess caught her in a warm embrace. "We love you, too, sweetheart. Welcome to the family."

"Where is Kate's mother?" Lauren murmured to Alisha.

Alisha rolled her eyes. "Don't ask."

My mother would be here. The thought was oddly comforting.

After that, there were more tears, more laughter, more champagne.

Marriage, Lauren thought later as they all snuggled on the couch, on the floor, to watch the movie. *Is what brings us together.*

Alisha was right. It was almost enough to make her want to take the risk on an actual relationship.

Lauren hugged a sofa pillow to her empty chest. But was Jack interested in taking a risk on her?

Twelve

LAUREN SNUGGLED INTO the couch cushions. The movie was almost over. She should go upstairs and work. For the first time in months, the thought didn't bring the hot tightening in her chest, the greasy ball of panic in her stomach.

She *wanted* to work. Recharged by her break, she could feel her energy returning, her thoughts mustering, like static electricity buzzing against her skin.

In the hall, the grandfather clock struck midnight. The chimes mingled with the noise from the TV, the sound of running footsteps as Inigo Montoya chased the six-fingered man through the halls of the castle.

Taylor hugged Kate's arm against her chest. "I love this part," she whispered.

"Was that the door?" Tess asked.

Lauren blinked, confused. On TV? Or . . .

Meg stirred from the couch. "I'll get it."

Voices rumbled from the kitchen. Kate kissed the top of Taylor's head—such a sweet and natural gesture, such a mom thing to do, that Lauren's heartstrings twanged—and got up.

Lauren rolled her head on the back of the couch to watch Kate cross the kitchen.

Two men stood at the back door, the first tall and blond and muscular, as if Westley the Farm Boy had done serious gym time. Lauren watched Kate go up on tiptoe to kiss him. This must be the bridegroom, then. Luke Fletcher.

The other . . . Lauren's heart beat a quick tattoo.

If Luke was the classic movie hero, Jack was . . . Well, he was no Prince Charming. Against Luke's tall, golden, easy gorgeousness, he looked dark, compact, and dangerous, a star collapsed upon itself, a black hole exuding stunning gravity. The pleasant buzz of the evening transmuted to a different kind of excitement, electrifying all her limbs, running through her veins like quicksilver.

She met his gaze. Connection arced and sparked in the space between them. Her fingertips tingled. She wanted to jump off the sofa and fly to him.

Like a bug to a bug zapper.

She shivered. Not a reassuring image.

His dark eyes flared. But his voice as he spoke to Kate was calm and reassuring, the voice of a man used to taking charge, to taking care of things. A man who could be trusted.

"Get his ass to bed soon," he was saying. "I need him on shift at seven tomorrow morning."

"I'll be there," Luke assured him earnestly.

Jack's mouth curled. "I know you will. Great party, Luke. Your friends are good guys."

He nodded. "The best. Best guys. Best time. Thanks, Jack."

"Anytime, buddy."

Kate slipped an arm around Luke's waist. "I've got him from here."

His deep blue eyes focused on her carefully. "I didn't have that much to drink."

Meg rolled her eyes.

Kate laid her free hand gently on Luke's cheek. "Not too much. Did you have a good time?"

He turned his head, pressed a kiss to her palm. "Yeah. Thank you."

Not simply for inquiring about his evening, Lauren thought, picking up on the current between them. Something else was going on, another question being asked and answered, another trust being given. For some reason, for no reason at all, her eyes pricked with tears.

Taylor paused the movie. "Did you win the poker game?"

Luke grinned. "Jack won. But he said I should take all his money and buy you girls presents."

Lauren looked at Jack, who shrugged.

"Cool." Taylor's smile shed sunshine on them both. "You want to watch the movie with us?"

"I wish I could." Jack's gaze flicked briefly to Lauren. "I've got to go on a call."

Disappointment and concern lurched inside her. "Nothing serious, I hope."

"Nope. Alarm call at Evans Tackle Store. Owner's already on the scene. But Hank's got his hands full with some teenagers partying in one of the rentals, so I have to take the report."

Lauren got her legs under her. "I'll see you out."

Taylor switched those huge blue eyes on Luke. "Can you watch the movie with us, Daddy?"

Luke's arm tightened around Kate's waist. He smiled down at his daughter. "As you wish."

LAUREN WALKED WITH Jack along the deck that ran the length of the house to the trellis-covered patio. The sky was like velvet, the stars scattered over it like a jeweler's diamond display. The brutal sun slept. The close, sticky air of the day had lifted. A freshening breeze rose off the water, teasing the scents from the summer garden.

Jack turned to face her, his back to the house, a shadow against the deeper shadows of the porch. Tiny white flowers starred the vines behind his head.

Lauren took a deep breath of jasmine-scented air and thought, *Take me*.

"You're missing the end of the movie," he said.

She shrugged, trying to speak lightly. "I'm not really into revenge scenarios."

He frowned at her.

"What?"

"Your pal in jail, the bank robber—"

"Ben." He had a name, just like she did.

"Yeah. He ever talk about revenge? Threaten you in any way?"

"No. *No*." She was genuinely horrified she'd given him that impression. "Nothing like that. Ben always says he knows I did my best. He *thanks* me. All the time." His mother wanted her dead, but Ben was grateful.

"For getting him to give himself up."

"Well, that," Lauren said. "But mostly I think for the money."

Jack went very still, a black granite garden sculpture. "What money?"

Crap. "It doesn't matter. Don't you have to go? I thought you had to take a report."

"It can wait." Jack stuck his thumbs into his pockets, watching her. "Do you send that guy money, Lauren?"

"Not him. Well, only a little. If it weren't for Ben . . . Okay, that's a little weird. But if it weren't for what happened,

I wouldn't have any money. Did you know in prison they don't even supply you with a full-size bar of soap?"

Jack was silent.

Lauren swallowed. "Mostly, I send it to Ben's mother," she offered.

All around them the night pulsed with life, cicadas and tree frogs merrily getting it on in the dark.

Lauren drew a shaky breath. This evening was *so* not going as planned. "What are you thinking?" she whispered.

He shot her a dark look. "As a cop? Or as the guy who took you to bed?"

"Are you ever *not* a cop?"

"I wasn't a cop last night," he said, and she deflated, her frustration leaking away.

"I'm sorry." She hung her head. "I just . . ." *Want you. I don't want to fight.*

Jack wrapped his arms around her, his legs bracketing hers, his body solid and warm and right against her. With a sigh, she laid her head on his chest. Gradually, her tension drained away from her muscles and the back of her neck.

"Let's try this again." His voice rumbled under her ear. "Hello, Lauren."

She smiled against his shirt, everything in her softening. Relaxing. "Hello, Jack."

He caught a strand of her hair between two fingers and pulled it carefully out of her face, stroking it back to blend with the rest of her hair. His hand lingered, cradling her skull against him. "Sorry I have to go."

She swallowed an unexpected lump in her throat. "Me, too."

"So, I'll see you."

"Okay," she whispered.

"Tomorrow."

She nodded, pushing down her disappointment. Obviously, he couldn't see her in the dark. But he could feel her head moving against his chest. And she could feel him, his hard man's body, the muscles of his abdomen. "That would be good."

"Hell." He exhaled against her hair. "Tomorrow's Friday."

She raised her head. "Is that a problem?"

"Weekend in a resort town, that's all. It's a full day. I probably can't get away until late."

If I ever take a chance on another guy, Jane had said, *it won't be somebody who always puts his job ahead of me.*

That guy wasn't Jack. That would never be Jack.

But Lauren wasn't Jane, either. She wasn't struggling to balance her needs with the demands of a six-year-old child. She wasn't living with her father. She didn't need Jack to save her or to take care of her or to put her first.

She was his rebound relationship, that's all. Sure, he was a terrific guy. Yes, he'd come through for her last night. But she knew better than to put long-term expectations on a short-term relationship. They'd only known each other a week.

He was simply a very pleasant detour on her way to someplace else.

The thought was vaguely depressing.

"Lauren?"

She pulled herself together. "Late works for me," she said. "I've got to work tomorrow anyway."

He raised an eyebrow. "Long bakery hours."

"Actually"—she lifted her chin—"I'm writing."

He smiled that little half smile that caused a warm, liquid rush in her knees. "Good for you."

She swallowed. "I don't know if it's good or not," she confessed. "But at least I'm not standing around waiting for inspiration to strike."

He tilted his head to one side, considering her.

All her doubts flamed into her face in one giant blush. She moistened her lips. "What?"

He took her by the arms, his hands hard and just the right amount of rough, hauled her up onto her toes, and took her mouth with his.

Her brain melted. Her heart pounded, shaking her from the inside. He was hot and hard and solid against her, and her body, already primed, fused against him like wax. Her nails dug into him as he gave and took and took some more.

And then he let her go.

His chest moved up and down. Her breathing was loud in the stillness.

"What was that?" she asked when she could speak.

His mouth quirked. "Inspiration?"

She laughed shakily. His teasing felt warm and intimate as a kiss. She had the impression he didn't joke very often. "Am I supposed to thank you now?"

"Thank me tomorrow."

Anticipation swelled, a big, shiny soap bubble in her chest. "All right, I will."

She was still smiling as she went into the house.

THE NEXT DAY, Jack worked from an hour before sunrise until damn near sunset. Nothing like the job to put things in perspective.

Four commercial alarms in the past five days had spooked the normally stolid islanders. His biggest challenge, as the new police chief, was to convince the residents to reach for the phone instead of a shotgun at the threat of an intruder. He spent several hours checking locks, doing drive-bys, and reassuring older residents like Dora Abrams that, yes, they were safe in their homes.

Small-town police work was mostly a matter of learning patterns and routines, putting together a picture of the community that would tip you off when a piece was out of place or missing. So today he took his coffee breaks with the guys at Evans Tackle Store, chatting with the watermen in the predawn as they prepared to go out with their boats.

"How's that new dispatcher working out for you?" old Walt Rogers on the town board wanted to know.

"Good, thanks."

"Marta? She sure is a looker," Evans said.

One of the other fishermen standing around the coffeepot chuckled knowingly. "I hear old Carl was sorry to see her go."

At ten o'clock, the retirees moved in to talk about the weather and their neighbors, who had money or needed some, whose kids were in trouble, who had a grudge or a wandering eye. Jack sipped his coffee, listened, volunteered the occasional comment or reassurance.

He wasn't avoiding Lauren, he told himself as he said his good-byes and headed back to his marked SUV.

But maybe the interruption last night had been a good thing.

He drove back to the station house. The coffee in his to-go cup left a bitter taste in his mouth.

In the heat of the moment—*Lauren, hot and slippery under him, wet and tight, gasping his name*—a guy could be forgiven for losing his head. Especially when he hadn't gotten laid in . . . He calculated the months. *Way too long.*

Being married to another cop, he'd tried to preserve some semblance of a regular personal life, to compartmentalize work and home, to separate sex and the job. And on the island, he was never off the job.

Jack knew cops who turned every call into a fucking

opportunity. Badge bunnies, hot for anybody packing, druggies desperate to escape a charge, bored stay-at-homes who answered the door in nighties or nothing at all . . . There were guys who sampled whatever was on offer and bragged about it after.

Not Jack. He was traditional, like his pop. *Old-fashioned*, Renee had called him, first affectionately and finally . . . Well, there hadn't been much affection there at the end.

So this thing with Lauren, this, what had she called it, rebound relationship, this singeing hot, rock-his-fucking-world sex with a woman he'd met a week ago, wasn't him.

But, Jesus, when he was with her, when he was in her, when she looked up at him with those dark, perceptive eyes and yielded and trembled and came, again and again, it sure felt like him.

He shook his head. Shook himself. So, yeah. Time to take a step back. Slow things down.

The rest of his day was taken up with the usual end-of-week hassles, fender benders, lost dogs, lost keys, an altercation at the water park, a complaint about parked cars blocking a beach access.

Marta, the new dispatcher, logged the complaints, soothed the callers, handled permits for parties and fires on the beach. He was glad he'd hired her, despite the fact that she and Hank had taken to bickering in the office like an old married couple.

By the time Jack hunt-and-pecked his way through the last report, set calls to go to his cell phone, and got back to his boat, the sky over the water was turning pink.

He needed a long hot shower and a tall cold beer to rinse away the stink of the day. Then maybe he'd have the distance he needed to deal with Lauren. *Job here, sex there, everything in place, everything under control.*

Or almost under control.

He opened the cabin door. The gray tabby cat shot from the galley counter, claws scrambling on the laminate, and dived under the table.

Jack sighed. At least it hadn't peed everywhere. The shelter volunteer had explained that the kitten would use the litter box instinctively to hide its scent from other predators. She hadn't warned him about the climbing. Or told him that his new boat companion would scuttle under the furniture like a cockroach every time Jack walked into a room.

Ignoring the cat, he stripped off his shirt and secured his weapon and utility belt in the onboard locker.

The water beating on his neck relaxed him. It didn't take much imagination to summon Lauren into the shower with him, her dark hair wet around her shoulders, her pretty breasts pebbled with drops, that intriguing sparkle against her bare belly . . .

By the time he strode naked out of the shower and found his phone lit up like a Christmas tree, he was ready for her. Smiling, he picked up his cell phone, prepared to call her back.

CALLER UNKNOWN, read the screen.

And the area code was familiar. He frowned. Very familiar. He pressed to return the call, a funny feeling in the pit of his stomach. His cop's instincts kicking in.

"Jack?" said Renee's voice.

Too late.

"How'd you get this number?" Jack said and then kicked himself for asking. Renee was a high-ranking police officer on a special security task force. She could get any number she wanted.

"Your mother gave it to my mother."

That was worse. Ma had vehemently taken her son's

side over that cheating *puttana* he'd married. But their families had grown up together. Their mothers had served together on the parish altar guild for twenty years. If Renee's mother had asked his mother . . . Yeah, Ma would have a hard time saying no. But it still stung.

"What do you want?"

"Jesus, Jack. I have to want something to give you a call?"

"That's usually how it works," he said.

She laughed. "How well you know me." Her voice softened. "Maybe I just want to hear how you're doing."

He waited for the familiar rush of anger. She had betrayed him. With his partner. And then used her connections to encourage him to resign. But the anger, once so dark and hot, felt pale and cold. Mostly he felt tired. Tired and very, very cautious.

"Fine."

"Come on, Jack. I know you, too. I know that nothing-bothers-me voice. Tell me about the new job."

"It's fine."

"That's all? 'Fine'? You used to be a little more enthusiastic about your work, Jack."

He used to be more enthusiastic about a lot of adrenaline-charged, high-risk behaviors. SWAT team. Detective squad. Marriage to Renee.

"It suits me."

"Writing traffic tickets and busting underage parties in Mayberry? I find that hard to believe."

"Believe what you want," he said. "I gotta go."

"Hot date?" she teased. Because, yeah, she did know him.

"Yeah."

"Oh." For the first time, she sounded uncertain.

In the twelve years they were together, he'd never made a big deal out of Friday night. Dinner out on her birthday and their anniversary, weekends with her family or his . . . He'd assumed that was enough. Before the fights over dishes, laundry, having kids, before Frank, maybe that had been the problem—him assuming things.

The thought made him uncomfortable.

"You take care of yourself," he said gently, and got off the phone.

Maybe he should take Lauren out to dinner, he thought. *On a Friday night? Good luck with that, pal.* The local restaurants would all be slammed with vacationers out for one more seafood dinner before their rentals ended tomorrow. Even the pricey Brunswick wasn't likely to have a table on such short notice.

Though they'd probably make room for the chief of police. He could call.

Jack paused with his shirt half over his head. What did it mean, that after one time with Lauren he was thinking of taking her to a candles-and-white-tablecloths kind of place?

Nothing, he decided, and yanked the shirt on.

He was hungry, that's all.

He stuffed his phone into his pocket, snagged a beer from the galley. The gray kitten crept from under the table and crouched by the door.

Jack lowered the bottle. "I'm supposed to keep you in an enclosed space," he told it. "Until you get used to me."

The cat fixed him with huge green-blue eyes and emitted a piercing mew.

"You want to go outside, I have to hold you," he warned. "You hate that."

A blink.

"Yeah, that's what you say now. Let's see what you do when I try it."

He put down his beer. Crossed the salon. The little cat

froze at the sound of his footsteps, cringed from the approach of his hand. He scooped it up anyway. It twisted— one second of clawing panic—and then, much to his surprise, collapsed bonelessly against him. Like a lapdog.

Or a baby.

He rubbed its chin with his thumb, undeniably flattered when a rusty purr vibrated from its throat. Jesus, he was pathetic. If he wasn't careful, he was going to end up like one of those old ladies, living alone with thirty or forty cats for company.

Maybe he should move back north, like his ma wanted him to do, take a job in security somewhere, let one of his sisters-in-law fix him up with one of her single friends, a nice Catholic girl from the neighborhood.

He wasn't looking for true love. Just somebody to share the loneliness and maybe raise a family with. He was thirty-eight years old, for Christ's sake. He didn't want to turn into one of those doddering dads on the sidelines, too old to teach his kids to throw a ball or ride a bike. Too out of it to know when they were screwing up.

He grabbed his beer and carried the cat out on deck.

Somebody was biking along the wharf on one of the heavy tourist bikes. A woman. Lauren, wobbling along on big fat tires with a bright pink basket, her skirt working its way up her thighs as she pumped along.

She had great legs, firm and smooth and lightly golden, and her dark hair lifted in the breeze from the sea, and everything inside him lifted, too.

She skidded to a halt at the edge of the dock, bracing herself with both feet, trying to balance the weight of her basket. What the hell did she have in there?

She tilted her head, studying his face, like she wasn't sure of her welcome. "Hi."

He was so glad to see her that his throat constricted. He unglued his tongue from the roof of his mouth. "Hi."

Those wide, dark eyes narrowed a fraction. "Everything all right?"

My ex-wife called, he thought of saying, but that seemed like a lousy opening to an evening that suddenly looked much better. Especially when Lauren had biked all the way out here to see him. Why ruin the mood? "Fine."

Her look said she wasn't buying his answer, not completely, but instead of challenging him, she smiled. "I brought dinner. Mind if I come aboard?"

He set down his beer. "Let me give you a hand."

"I've got it." Her gaze dropped to where he cradled the cat with one hand against his chest. Her face got all soft. "Aw. You still have the kitty."

He nodded.

She unstraddled the bike—her skirt hiked up even more, very nice—and kicked at the stand. "I thought you were giving it to someone to take to the shelter."

He shrugged, embarrassed. "Yeah, well, the volunteer was busy, so . . ."

"So you had no choice. You *had* to adopt it." Her tone was teasing, but her eyes were warm. "What a—"

"Sucker?" he suggested.

"I was going to say nice guy, but I know you don't like that word."

He looked away, a smile tugging the corners of his mouth.

She hauled two bags from the bike basket and approached the boat. The plastic handles fluttered in the wind, startling the kitten, who squirmed.

Jack adjusted his hold. "Easy, tiger."

Lauren smiled. "That's her name? Tiger?"

He hesitated. Glanced down at the stripes, gray on gray. *Sure, why not?* "His name." He'd checked. "Yeah."

She arched a brow. "Big name for a little cat."

"A guy's gotta dream."

He took the bags from her with one hand, setting them on deck, and then helped her aboard. Her hand was warm and firm in his. She smelled good, sun-warmed and sexy. There was a moment when he held her hand and her gaze met his, when he could have kissed her.

And then she bent to fuss with the bags at her feet, and the moment was lost. When she straightened, her face was pink and she didn't quite meet his eyes. *Damn.*

"Let me put Tiger here in the cabin," he said. "What can I get you to drink?"

"I brought wine." She glanced at the Carolina Lager on the table. "But if you'd rather have beer—"

"Wine's good," he said firmly. "I'll get glasses."

It took him a minute or five to settle the cat. When he came out, Lauren had everything set up on some kind of picnic cloth she must have borrowed from Tess: a couple cheeses from the pricey shop in the harbor, bread from the bakery, a fat bunch of grapes, containers of olives and shrimp salad.

He looked at the trouble she'd gone to, the cloth napkins, the bottle of wine and felt a pinch of something. Regret, maybe. He needed to step up his game. Next time he would make reservations.

"I was going to call you," he said.

She anchored the lid from the olives under the plastic container. "You don't have my number. Hard to booty text without a number."

"Booty text," he repeated slowly.

"Or booty call. Whatever." She didn't sound mad. Although with women, you never knew.

Jack frowned. She wasn't a booty call to him. She was . . .

He covered both her busy hands with one of his. She looked up in surprise, glowing and exotic in the setting sun, the tiny jewel winking. He leaned forward and kissed her, long and soft and slow, until her eyelids fluttered closed and her hands flexed under his.

He raised his head. "Hello, Lauren."

Her lips curved. "Hello, Jack." She opened her eyes. Exhaled. "We keep screwing up, don't we?"

He checked her expression. Definitely not mad, he saw with relief. "I'm willing to practice with you," he offered, straight-faced. "Until we get it right."

She grinned, widening her eyes in mock concern. "If we get any better, we'll kill each other."

She was talking about sex. He laughed, as she obviously intended him to, and reached for the wine. She'd even packed a corkscrew.

"This looks great," he said, nodding at the spread. She'd transformed his deck to someplace he wanted to be.

"I'm glad you like it. I owed you for last night."

His brows twitched together. Last night he'd walked out on her to take a call.

"Last night," she prompted. "The inspiration?"

He thought back. They'd been saying good night, talking about her writing, and then he'd kissed her.

Inspiration, he'd teased.

Her eyes had gleamed with humor, her smile rueful in the moonlight. *Am I supposed to thank you now?*

Thank me tomorrow.

He shook his head. "You didn't have to do all this."

"I wanted to."

He stared at her, oddly humbled. Shaken.

In the past year, he'd gotten used to doing for himself.

Cooking for himself. Caring for himself. He'd almost forgotten how it felt to have someone do for him. Freely. Because she *wanted* to. Renee always had a hidden agenda, a secret scorecard on which he always lost.

He cleared his throat. "Guess that makes me a lucky guy."

Her grin flashed. "Lucky comes later. Pour the wine, will you?"

He filled her glass. "How'd the writing go today?"

She paused cutting the bread, like he'd surprised her. "It's going."

"That's good, right?"

"Yes." She picked up the bunch of grapes. Put it down. "I had . . . I guess you'd call it a breakthrough," she confessed, almost shyly.

"What sort of breakthrough?"

She looked at him doubtfully. "We don't have to talk about my work. Most of what I do, writing . . . It's kind of boring if you're not another writer. You don't have to be polite with me."

Yeah, he did. He was sleeping with her. That entitled her to be treated with respect. But more than that, he was genuinely interested. He'd read her book—her first book—but he still didn't know what made her tick. She was a puzzle to him.

He'd always liked puzzles.

He put some cheese on some bread and offered it to her. "If you were a cop," he said, "and you told me you caught a break in a case, I would know what that meant. But I don't know what a breakthrough is for a writer."

"Well." She swallowed. "I don't see the end yet. But for the first time, I can see how I might get there."

He frowned. "How do you know you're on the right road if you can't see the destination?"

He wasn't talking about her book anymore. Not entirely.

And she knew it, too. She smiled her funny smile. "I guess we'll find out."

"Life's about the journey, not the destination?" he asked with heavy irony.

"Since we're all headed to the grave, then, yes. 'Thus, though we cannot make our sun stand still, yet we will make him run.'"

He liked the way she talked, her attitude, her optimism. Maybe he liked them all a little too much. "What is that, poetry?"

She nodded. "Andrew Marvell, 'To His Coy Mistress.'"

"Yeah?" He grinned sharply to cover a sudden sense of inadequacy. "You know the one about the girl from Nantucket?"

She didn't get pissy. She laughed. "All I'm saying is, life's too short. When you're not sure of your destination, you might as well enjoy the trip."

He didn't entirely agree, but he liked talking to her. He couldn't imagine having this conversation with the guys back home. Or Renee. *Marvell. Jesus.* "You religious, Lauren?"

"I believe that what we do in this life, the choices we make, matter," she said carefully. "But whether they matter to some afterlife . . . I don't know."

Not Ma's Catholic girl.

"So how does this thing with us fit into your travel plans? You're a pretty girl. Smart. Well educated. A couple of book deals under your belt. What are you doing with a thirty-eight-year-old divorced cop from Philly?"

"Well, if I'd known you were *that* old . . ." She trailed off teasingly, trying to make a joke.

He didn't smile. He didn't know what he was asking. Why he was pushing her the way he'd push a suspect in an interrogation, trying to get her to confess . . . What?

Her big, dark eyes fixed on him. Her take-no-shit therapist's look, shrewd and warm at the same time. "I want to be with you, Jack. Don't you think you deserve that? To be wanted? Desired? Loved?"

O-kay.

She'd turned the tables on him, turned the interrogation on its head. The talking portion of the evening was over.

He took the wineglass out of her hand, moved the container of dip out of the way, and kissed her. Because he wanted to kiss her and also to shut her up.

Her mouth was sweet and cool from the wine and hot, with a taste that was purely Lauren. She kissed him back eagerly, meeting his tongue with her own.

Renee had always liked sex, but she was stingy with her mouth, like kisses were unsanitary or something. Lauren kissed with her whole heart, like she loved kisses, his kisses, exploring his mouth greedily, experimenting with different depths and tempos. Like being back in high school, when long, drowning-in-you make-out sessions were all there was, were everything, when a girl might let you touch her breasts but never past her panties.

Kissing Lauren, he could almost believe she was right. *Life's about the journey, not the destination.*

Until she reached down and put her hand on his dick and squeezed.

All the blood abandoned his head.

He slid his hands up from her waist, taking her shirt with them, and pulled down her bra. The elastic caught under her breasts, shoving them up and together. Her nipples tightened under the kiss of cool air. *Beautiful.* He licked her nipple, sucking it into his mouth. She grabbed his head like she needed something to hold on to, like she wanted him to go on. So he did, using his tongue and the edge of his teeth, and instead of complaining or resisting or fighting him for control, she made this gratifying little noise, her hands moving down to his shoulders, rubbing him, patting him. He couldn't remember the last time someone had touched him with eagerness. With affection.

He pushed her down and spread her wide. So pink. So beautiful. His stomach sucked in, like he'd been punched in the gut. She lay back in the middle of the picnic things and closed her eyes and let him do whatever he wanted. He worked her until he couldn't stand it, until he couldn't stand not being in her one minute more. Rising to his knees, he yanked at his belt.

She half rolled away from him, reaching across the blanket.

He grabbed her back, crazy-man possessive. "I'm not finished with you yet."

She grinned up at him. "Good." Pulling her hand out of her bag, she slapped a condom in his palm.

She was killing him. He was dying here, dying to have her moving and under him, dying to feel her around him. He covered himself and fell on her, kissing her hard and fierce and deep, finding his place between her thighs.

He rammed home, filling her in one slick thrust. God, she felt good. So good. He gritted his teeth and began to move in and out, his breath coming in ragged pants, all his frustration and longing for her surging against his control.

She planted her feet flat on the deck and arched to take him. He felt the tremors start deep in her body, moving through her, moving through him. He couldn't breathe.

"Jack." She came around him, his name on her lips, her fingers digging into his butt.

He buried his head in the warm curve of her neck and lost himself in her arms.

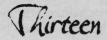

Thirteen

THE LAST RAYS of the setting sun glowed behind Lauren's closed lids. She sprawled amid the ruins of their picnic, sweaty, sore, and slightly sticky, as if she'd lain out at the beach too long. Jack lay over her, heavy and golden and warm. She stroked his back, raking her nails lightly over the cotton of his shirt, and he shivered in reaction.

"I've never made love outdoors before," she said dreamily.

He made a noncommittal noise into her neck, and she sucked in her breath as all the nerves there vibrated in pleasure.

"Did you? Ever make love outside before?" she asked, seeking . . . More than sex. Emotional connection. Reassurance, maybe. *That was amazing. Was it as good for you as it was for me?*

"Does the backseat of a car count?"

Another little flutter of humor or doubt. "I don't think . . . No."

"Then, nope." He levered off her, their bodies separating by slow, near painful degrees. Her skin protested the loss of his heat. "This was a first for me."

She nodded, her chest uncomfortably full, her throat unaccountably tight.

He looked down at her, his dark eyes unreadable. "Are you all right?"

A flush swept from her chest to her hairline. Her bra was still twisted under her breasts, her skirt around her waist, leaving her feeling more naked than if she wore nothing at all. "Fine."

She struggled to sit. He allowed that, but when she started tugging at her clothes, he covered her hand with his until she looked at him.

"Are you sure?" he asked quietly. "I was pretty . . . aggressive there. Rough."

Everything in her melted and surrendered at the concern in his voice and his eyes. "I liked it," she answered honestly. Her flush deepened. "How . . . How are you?"

That little half smile played around his mouth. "Never better."

She glowed from the inside out.

"You've got dip on your, uh . . ." He gestured.

"Oh." She wiped it from her hip. "Thanks."

She tucked her boobs back into her bra.

"Luke's wedding is Monday," Jack said.

"Yes, I know. Kate—well, Meg, really—invited me. Isn't that sweet?" She adjusted her bra straps, glancing at the deserted shoreline. "You don't think anybody saw us, do you?"

"Not unless they were spying from a low-flying aircraft," Jack said dryly. "Your reputation is safe."

"I was thinking about your reputation, Chief." She rolled to her knees to wriggle her skirt back over her butt.

"You wouldn't want it getting around town that you were performing lewd acts in public."

"I don't think the fish will report us. So, Monday . . . You need a ride to the church?"

Her heart stumbled. She stopped fussing with her clothes to stare at him. "Are you asking me to be your date to the wedding?"

Another quirk of his lips. "You got a dress?"

His teasing made her feel warm all over. "Do you have a tie? Or do you go everywhere in uniform?"

"I own a tie."

"I can find a dress."

Their gazes met. Held. *Oh, brother.* Her breath went and her pulse quickened and little spots danced in front of her eyes. Like a panic attack, only better. Worse.

Jack cleared his throat. "So, I'll pick you up at four," he said, his voice husky.

Do not read too much into this. Rebound relationship, remember?

"Do you dance?" she asked. "Or are you strictly a prop-up-the-wall-with a beer kind of guy?"

"I dance. But I don't shag."

She laughed. "I think we've just established that you do."

"Not Austin Powers shagging. It's a Carolina thing. A dance."

"Never heard of it," she said cheerfully.

"Good. Then you don't know what you're missing."

"You could teach me."

He shook his head. "I'm too old to learn new tricks."

She smiled up at him, big and dependable and dark against the sunset, and all the soft places in her body reminded her that this was a man who Knew Things. "It's never too late to try something new."

His gaze met hers, and the earth moved. Or maybe that was the boat rocking. "I'll remind you of that later."

She forced herself to speak lightly. "Lucky for you, I'm a big fan of wedding sex."

Another of those contained, heart-stopping smiles. "Then it's a date."

"Gee, it's like prom. Not that I went to my prom."

"I'll bring you a corsage," Jack said dryly. "What color is your dress?"

"That would depend on what Meg has in her closet that will fit me."

"You'll be beautiful whatever you wear."

She swallowed. "Now you're making me nervous."

"It's an island wedding. Friends and family. No big deal."

"Right." Only a public date in a sanctioned setting among people he cared about. Only an opportunity to be part of his life on the island.

"I can't wait," she said.

"I HAVE BOOBS!" Lauren exclaimed, turning from the standing mirror in Meg's room with a little flourish.

"You do," Meg agreed. "And legs. Long legs. I'm trying not to be annoyed that you look better in my dress than I do. It's because you're taller and have bigger tits than me."

"Not better." Lauren swiveled back to face her reflection. "Different."

On Meg, the bold red sheath dress projected confidence and class. On Lauren, the same dress screamed, well, sex. Classy, appropriate-for-a-guest-at-a-wedding sex, but still . . .

She frowned, smoothing the fabric over her hips. "You sure it's not too tight?"

"Absolutely not. You look amazing."

Lauren grinned. "Thanks. And thanks for letting me borrow it."

"What are friends for? Jack is going to swallow his tongue."

"I hope not."

Meg raised her eyebrows in question.

Lauren's grin broadened. "He's very good with his tongue."

Meg picked one of the discarded dresses from the bed and slid it onto a hanger. "Hm. Not that it's any of my business, but Mom says you haven't slept at the inn the last two nights."

Lauren glanced over her shoulder. "I'm sorry, should I have said something to her? Does she need the room? I know you have out-of-town guests for the wedding."

"Don't be silly. There aren't that many, they're only here for a few days, and Sam put most of them up in Grady rental properties. No, I was just wondering how things were going."

"The writing's going great."

"You're not too . . ." Meg paused.

"Distracted?"

"I was going to say too busy going at it like rabbits, but *distracted* is a good word, too."

Lauren laughed. "I'm a writer. I know lots of good words." She reached between her shoulder blades for the dress zipper.

"Let me give you a hand."

"Thanks." She presented her back, pulling her hair over her shoulder.

"So, how long until you finish the book?" Meg asked.

"Another couple weeks, I think." Lauren stepped carefully

out of the dress. "It's the same basic outline, I'm just trying to dig a little deeper into how I felt. Feel. To be more honest."

Meg gave an encouraging nod in the mirror. "Sounds wonderful."

"It's . . . cathartic," Lauren told her. "Like a good cry. Or a cleanse."

Meg laughed. "I'm sure your work is not a pile of crap."

"Actually, I feel good about the work. About the changes," Lauren confessed. "I just wish I had the resolution figured out."

"You mean, like a happy ending?"

"Not exactly. I'm not writing fiction."

"You know, happy endings aren't only in fairy tales. It's just that in real life, they take hard work. And time." Meg smiled crookedly. "And sometimes they don't look the way you expect them to look."

Of course Meg believed in happy endings. Her parents had been married for forty years. Meg had recently reinvented her career to make a life with her longtime love, Sam. And her brother's wedding was tomorrow. Lauren wasn't going to rain on that parade.

"I believe in happy moments," she said. "In enjoying as many moments as you can make in the time that you have. What I'm really looking for, though, is meaning. Something that would take all the loose ends and tie them together in a neat little bow." She slid the dress onto a padded hanger. She'd never stayed in a house with padded hangers before. Her mother would be so impressed. "But maybe the message of the book is that not everything in life is resolved. Not everybody finds closure."

"Speaking of closure . . . What happens in a couple of weeks when you finish the book and it's time to go home?"

Lauren didn't question Meg's genuine concern . . . or

resent her interest. Meg had brought her here, bought her the time and space she needed to finish her book. But as Lauren's publicist, Meg naturally wanted to know that Lauren was going to meet her obligations.

"That depends. I need to meet with Eleanor—my faculty advisor."

"I thought you were on leave. You don't have to go back to school this fall, do you?"

Lauren shook her head. "I'm pretty much done with my course work. Clinic work, too. Which is a good thing, since I'm sure the department has already made all the teaching and clinic assignments for fall. But I still have to finish my dissertation. I'm way behind there."

"What about Jack?"

Lauren's heart took flight like a startled bird, beating, beating against the walls of her chest. What about Jack? Jack, with his good cop/bad cop vibe, his dark, intense eyes, and unbearably sweet half smile.

"Jack's a great guy," she said, which was such a lame understatement that it felt like a betrayal. Of him. Of her feelings.

Meg arched an eyebrow. "Not a fixer-upper?"

Her own words came back to taunt her. *Nice guys, but not long-term relationship material. So they stay with me until I can fix them.*

And then, when they don't need me anymore, they move on.

Lauren cleared her throat. "I'd say we both need a little fixing. We're good for each other. At least for now."

"Listen, you can tell me to butt out of your business. But I care about you as a client and as a friend. And I care about Jack. What about when you leave here? Will you try to see him again?"

"We haven't talked about it. We've known each other less than two weeks. It's a little early to be throwing words like *commitment* around."

"Absolutely." Meg smoothed another dress onto a hanger. "I just don't want to see you get hurt. Either of you. In the long term, Jack strikes me as a more traditional kind of guy."

"He is. We're very different. That's one reason I'm not going to risk what we have now by projecting too far into the future."

"And what you have now is . . . sex?"

"Great sex."

She had never craved another man the way she hungered for Jack. Never known another man who loved sex so much, who was so creative, so intense. She wanted him all the time. She spent her days churning inside with anticipation, lust, and happiness. And the nights . . . They'd made love on every horizontal surface of the boat and a few vertical ones. Rolling across his bed. On all fours on the floor of his salon. Pressed close together in the cramped shower, his hands tight on her butt. Propped on the galley counter, her legs around his waist.

She couldn't get enough of him. Even when they'd finished making love, when she'd moved past desire into sleepy, sore satiation, she wanted to pull him inside her again and again. She found herself reaching for him across the mattress at night, the warmth of his hard-planed body, the texture of his skin.

They really were going to kill each other.

And yet all Jack had to do was look at her a certain way or smile that half smile or move or breathe and she was lost. Awash in lust.

"I never knew it could be like this," she admitted. "That I could have all these feelings inside. Jack makes me feel . . ." *Cherished. Desired. Safe.* "Alive."

"Now you're just bragging, you lucky bitch."

Lauren returned Meg's grin. "Well, yeah. But you've got Sam."

"I do," Meg said with deep satisfaction. "Which is the only reason I'm not jealous. I won't tell you not to be happy. But be careful, okay?"

Too late, Lauren thought.

"You bet," she said.

YOU COULD TAKE the cop out of Philly. You couldn't take the Philly out of the cop. Weddings, funerals, Christmas Eve, Easter, Jack dressed like every other male member of his tribe. White dress shirt, dark suit, subdued tie. The uniform varied only slightly—a pinkie ring for Grandpa Joe, a gold chain on Cousin Pete, a black-on-black shirt for Maria's boy, Eddie, who was too young to know any better. *It's like a wake at the fucking Corleones*, Jack's sister-in-law Tricia (red haired, Irish, and outnumbered) liked to say.

He wondered what Tricia would say about Lauren. What they all would make of Lauren.

Looking at himself in the mirror, seeing his father's face above the crisp white collar, his father's hands at the end of his starched white cuffs, Jack wondered if it was time for a change. Island weddings tended to be casual affairs.

But when he saw Lauren coming down the stairs at the Pirates' Rest, he was glad he had the suit.

Because she looked amazing.

She glowed in eye-popping red that hugged her curves

and glossed her lips. Her eyes were smudged and sultry. Her hair looked like she'd tumbled out of bed, an effect he'd learned women only achieved with a curling iron and serious effort. She wore a tiny diamond in her nose and sparkly earrings. Everything about her was sparkly and shiny and hot. Even her sandals, made of gold leather straps that wrapped around her toes and ankles. He wanted to bundle her back up the stairs and onto the nearest bed. Or over a chair. Against the wall.

Yeah, and ruin her makeup and probably piss her off. Not to mention make both of them late for Luke's wedding.

That was another thing marriage had taught him. Women didn't get all dressed up for men. They got dressed up to be seen by other women.

Her eyes widened and took him in. "Wow. Hello, Jack."

"Hello, Lauren. You look good."

Her smile increased her glow by another hundred watts. "Thank you. I like your suit."

"I like your dress."

"And your shoes."

Not cop shoes, the standard-issue black shit kickers he wore every day of his working life.

He smiled faintly. "Thanks. My ma used to say you should spend money on your eyes, your teeth, and your feet, because they have to last you all your life."

"Your mother sounds like a wise woman." Her smile turned wistful. "My dad would have liked that saying. He used to tell customers, 'Take care of your feet and they'll take care of you.'"

Her dad used to own a shoe store, he remembered. It was in her book.

"Here. For you." He produced the single long-stemmed rose from behind his back, red, fresh, and full, if a little wilted from its brief stint on the front seat of the SUV. He'd bought the flower on impulse, a sentimental gesture. Or a joke.

Her face went blank.

Hell.

You didn't give a woman a single flower, Renee had taught him. Or a stupid cellophane-wrapped bouquet from the grocery store. You bought a damn dozen roses from the florist or none at all. But then Lauren had made that comment about prom, and Jack had thought . . . he'd thought . . .

"I can't believe you brought me a rose," she said. "It's . . ."

Too much. Too little. Not right.

"It's so pretty." Her eyes sparkled as she held the single bloom against her chest, framed by the soft curves of her breasts. "My corsage."

She remembered.

Muscles he didn't know had tensed relaxed. He smiled. "You want to put it in your room? I'll wait."

Or you could invite me up to your room. Invite me up.

All the Fletchers were already at the church, the caterers busy in the kitchen. He had a brief, sexual fantasy in which he and Lauren were late to the wedding after all before she shook her head.

"I want to carry it. Is that all right? Or will I look like a flower girl?"

Her face was shining. You'd think no guy had ever brought her flowers before. Next time he would do better, Jack thought. She deserved better.

And didn't question how easy it was to think *next time*, to imagine a week, a month, a year ahead with her.

"You don't look like any flower girl I ever saw," he said. "You can do what you want."

A LARGE EXTENDED Catholic family had made Jack something of an expert on weddings.

The wedding of former Staff Sergeant Luke Fletcher, USMC, to Katherine Dolan, attorney, was damn near perfect.

The tiny chapel at the Franciscan retreat house was flooded with sunshine, family, friends, and flowers. The Fletchers filled the front pews. Luke's brother Matt stood with him, shoulder to shoulder. Luke's eleven-year-old daughter, walking carefully in her high-heeled shoes, preceded Kate down the aisle. The sun, striking through the stained glass windows, fired the bride's coppery hair to gold. And the look on Luke's face when he saw Kate walking toward him, a smile on her face and love in her eyes . . .

"They look perfect together, don't they?" Lauren whispered, echoing his thought.

You and Renee make the perfect couple, everybody used to say. And on the surface, everybody was right. Same neighborhood, same schools, same job.

Until she missed going out with her friends on a Saturday night and he worked late and forgot to call. Until arguments over paying the bills or who took out the trash scraped all the shiny off their life together.

But watching Luke take Kate's hand at the front of the church, listening to the strength of his voice and the faith in her responses, Jack was tempted to believe it wouldn't be like that for them.

"They've had some rough times," he murmured. "Let's hope they make it work."

" 'The triumph of hope over experience,' " Lauren said softly.

He slanted a look down at her, warm and round and glowing in her red dress. "What?"

"Samuel Johnson, on second marriages. But it applies to love generally, I think. Love is always a leap of faith. We all have barriers to overcome."

Shrink talk. College girl talk. But, God, he liked the sound of her voice. He liked the way she looked for the best in everything. In everyone.

She wasn't one of them. Not a Fletcher, not an islander. A last-minute addition to the guest list. But at the reception at the Pirates' Rest, she slipped into the gathering like a fish into water.

The Dare Island community was like the sea, all calm and welcoming on the surface, with unexpected depths and currents. It had taken Jack months to navigate with ease. Assimilation was not his thing. He was marked as an outsider before he even opened his mouth.

But Lauren's warmth, her genuine interest, made her welcome. She circulated like a champ, naturally seeking out and drawing in the outliers.

A tent with a dance floor filled the garden, edged with rosebushes and daylilies. Tables dotted the grass under pink blooming crepe myrtles. The wedding party was announced. The bridal couple danced slowly together to Vince Gill singing "Look at Us."

From the setup, it was clear that the mother of the bride had a place of honor near the head table, but at the moment, she sat all alone.

Brenda Dolan was a washed-out version of her daughter, the coppery hair faded to peach, her figure rigidly maintained, her face nipped, tucked, and Botoxed free of any expression beyond mild distaste. She looked as if she would rather be waiting for a pap smear than sitting in a sunny summer garden watching her daughter circle in her new husband's arms.

Jack gave a mental shrug. Not his problem. From the little Luke let drop, Brenda Dolan had never been much of a mother.

The servers were busy passing hors d'oeuvres, mini crab cakes and prosciutto-wrapped asparagus, cold jumbo shrimp and tiny stuffed cherry tomatoes.

Jack touched Lauren's arm. "Get you another drink?"

She smiled. "That would be great. Thanks."

He strolled the long ramp to the deck, where a bar had been set up next to the deejay. Hank Clark was already there, clutching a beer and staring morosely through the kitchen windows at Jane.

"She's a guest, right?" Hank asked Jack. "Not a damn waitress."

Jack followed his gaze through the glass, where Jane appeared to be giving the caterers a hand. "She's dressed like a guest. Champagne and a Newcastle, please," he told the bartender.

Hank grunted. "Right. So why isn't she out here dancing and enjoying herself instead of inside working her ass off?"

"I don't know, Hank. Why don't you ask her?"

"She won't talk to me."

"Ask her to *dance*," Jack said and collected his drinks and went back to Lauren.

Who was not standing where he had left her.

He looked around and spotted her at the table with Brenda Dolan.

". . . must be very happy," Lauren was saying as Jack approached.

"Obviously you don't have children," Brenda said bitterly. "I've lost her. I had nothing to do with this wedding."

Lauren met Jack's gaze and gave a barely perceptible shake of her head. He stopped.

She patted Brenda's thin arm consolingly. "Kate will always be your daughter," she said in her warm, soothing voice. "This is your celebration, too."

"I lost her years ago. And now, seeing her like this, seeing her with them . . ." Brenda shredded her pretty paper napkin. "The Fletchers are all the family she wants now. She doesn't want me."

"She invited you."

"Because she had to. It wouldn't look good if she didn't invite her own mother to her wedding."

"Would you say appearances are important to her?" Lauren asked quietly.

Brenda sniffed. "Not to her. Never to her."

"Then she must really want you here."

Brenda's eyes brightened. Her lips trembled. "She doesn't know how hard I tried . . . I did the best that I could."

Maybe, Jack thought cynically. And maybe her best wasn't enough to protect her daughter.

But Lauren's face revealed nothing but patience and sympathy. "Obviously, things have been a little strained between you. But it's never too late to start over."

Brenda dabbed at her face with the ruins of the napkin. "What do you know?"

"I know a daughter wants her mother's blessing on her wedding day. Why don't we walk over there right now and see her?"

Brenda's shoulders drew up to her ears. Jack expected her to refuse.

But Lauren already had an arm around her, urging her

from her chair, supporting her around the edge of the dance floor. As Jack watched, Lauren brought her to Kate.

Jack couldn't hear what was said over the flow of the music, the buzz and hum of laughter and conversation. But he saw Kate's face, naked and vulnerable, and he saw Lauren's nod before she literally pushed Brenda into her daughter's arms, and then Brenda was crying and the two women were hugging and Luke was running his finger under his collar and looking relieved.

"Well done," Jack said softly to Lauren when she came back to him. He offered the glass of champagne.

"Thanks." She sipped. Shrugged. "It's not hard to get people to do what they really, secretly want to do."

He gave her a slow smile. "I'll have to try that."

She beamed back at him. "You won't have to try very hard. I already told you I like wedding sex."

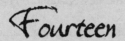

Fourteen

Jane took one last careful survey of the dessert table and tugged off her apron. Nothing more to do until it was time to cut the cake.

Across the sunlit yard, the mother of the bride hugged her daughter tight. Even as Jane smiled at the picture, her eyes stung. The summer garden blurred.

There had been no mother-daughter moments at Jane's wedding. No contact at all.

But Jane was glad for Kate.

When Jane met the bride for her cake tasting, Kate had Luke and his little girl along to gobble up samples and offer their opinions. Tess Fletcher, Luke's mom, had accompanied Kate to the final consultation, approving the bride's choice of round tiers over square, of fondant over buttercream, of gum paste seashells over real or sugar flowers. Clearly, the Fletchers had welcomed her warmly into their family.

But no one took the place of a mother.

Jane curled her toes inside her sandals, trying to ignore the straps cutting into her arches. She'd been on her feet since four this morning.

"Wow." Lauren stopped beside the dessert table. "That cake looks amazing."

Jane blinked away her tears and the pang that came with them, turning her attention to her work instead.

The cake design was one of her favorites, each tier decorated with a piping of lace coral, white on cream. Delicate shells, starfish, and flowers in various shapes and sizes tumbled over the edges. Cookies, in the same shapes and iced with the bride and groom's initials in yellow, surrounded the base.

Jane smiled. "Thanks." She was good at giving expression to other people's dreams.

"You must have been up early this morning," Lauren said. "To get all this done."

Jane was up early every morning. But she smiled and said, "I finished the cake last night, to give it time to set. And I'm taking the afternoon off."

"You should be dancing, then."

"My feet hurt."

"So take off your shoes."

"And I don't have a date."

"You don't need a date. I bet you know everybody here."

Jane smiled ruefully. "That's part of the problem."

The dating population in a small town was limited to the people you grew up with. Most couples had been together since they were, like, twelve. And if they ever did break up, and you got over the awkwardness of dating a guy you basically regarded as a brother, you still ran the risk of running into his ex every time you left the house.

Not that she was looking for romance anyway.

Lauren grinned. "Well, then, you can hook up with an attractive stranger. Lots of hunky Marines around."

"I don't do strangers, either." *Not since Travis.* "And I'm definitely not interested in some gung ho guy with a gun."

Oh, dear. Jane winced. She sounded as sulky as six-year-old Aidan when he didn't want to do something.

But Lauren, bless her heart, never lost her smile or her patience. "I'm not saying you should marry one of them. Or even have wild wedding hookup sex. But it's a party. You should enjoy yourself. Live in the moment."

Jane admired Lauren's attitude. Her daring. Of course, Lauren didn't have a child at home, dependent on every decision. Or an ex, threatening to bring her carefully constructed life down around her ears.

"I'll think about it," Jane promised.

"Think about what?" her father asked.

Wild heat stormed Jane's face. *Please, please don't let him have heard the part about wild hookup sex.*

"Dancing," she said.

Hank scowled. "Well, how about it, then?"

Jane resisted the urge to fidget. "How about what?"

"You want to dance with your dad?"

She blinked. "I . . . Yes." Something expanded in her chest, warm and light as rising bread. "Yes, I'd like to very much."

She took his hand. He pulled her close, his muscles hard and sinewy as a ship's rope. He smelled familiar, of laundry detergent, bay rum, and tobacco, and just for a moment she was transported back to the days before her mother left them, when her daddy waltzed her around the living room while she stood on his shoes.

They never had been any good at talking.

Sometimes it was better to communicate without words.

LAUREN WATCHED THEM go with a lump in her throat.

I'll never dance with my dad. The thought nicked her heart, a tiny, unexpected slice as sharp as a paper cut.

"You all right?" Jack asked behind her.

She resisted the urge to turn and throw herself against his chest.

Hastily, she pulled herself together. It was good to remember and to feel, even to feel pain. But to wallow in it . . . Not so good.

She turned and smiled at him. *Live in the moment.* "I am now."

He didn't say anything. He stood there, solid, self-contained, and imperturbable, regarding her with those dark, watchful eyes.

"Do you ever miss your family?" she asked abruptly.

He took her right hand in his and set his arm around her waist. "You're doing it again."

He pulled her forward, stepped back. She followed automatically, distracted by the brush of their legs, the clasp of his hand. "What?"

"Answering a question with another question."

She nodded. "Deflecting."

"Dodging."

She widened her eyes and batted her lashes, hoping to make him smile. "Maybe I simply find you fascinating."

A corner of his mouth ticked up.

Encouraged, she asked, "Do you?"

His arm tightened around her as he turned. Her breasts brushed his chest. "Ask questions? What do you think?"

She grinned. Talking with him was like dancing or sex, each of them alert to the other's moves. "Miss your family."

"Yeah. Some."

She waited. She didn't recognize the music, something smooth and slow and country. When he didn't say anything more, she asked, "Do you ever think about going back?"

What did she want him to say? That he was staying on the island? She wasn't staying. What did it matter?

His shoulder bunched and flexed under her hand. "For the holidays, maybe. Sure. My folks are still there. But longer than that, I've got to ask myself, what for? Am I going back to be with them? Or am I trying to get back to the way things used to be? Because if it's the second thing, it's not going to happen. That boat's already sailed."

She almost lost a step.

He gathered her in. "What?"

"You're not . . ." She shook her head. "Every time I think I have you figured out, you surprise me. You're nothing like what I expected."

He raised an eyebrow, his black eyes impenetrable. "You're not what I was expecting, either."

Hostage Girl. He'd seen her on TV. He'd read her book. Reality couldn't live up to that.

She stuck out her chin. "Disappointed?"

"No. Not at all."

She flushed with pleasure.

He held her close, not grinding, but apparently the past five days had sensitized her to sex or something. She was constantly aware of him, the strength of his arms, the solid muscles of his chest and belly. His animal heat, rising through his civilized clothes.

The afternoon whirled like a kaleidoscope toward evening, the action breaking and shifting, falling into bright, glowing patters. Sunshine, flowers, music.

Moments.

Tom and Tess Fletcher, married forty years, cheek to cheek on the dance floor. Meg, flirting outrageously with Sam. Taylor, grinning up at her uncle Matt. Love, radiating from the bride and groom, all around.

Thalia, glowing and grown up, danced by in Josh's arms. Lauren's heart clutched at the sight of them, clumsy and happy as puppies, full of hope and hormones.

"They're so cute together."

Jack followed her gaze. "Teenagers. That won't last."

She frowned, feeling out of step. Statistically, of course, he was right. "I don't think it matters. Love doesn't have to last to be real."

"You're talking about puppy love."

"First love," she corrected. "It's formative. The first—maybe the only—relationship where you haven't had your heart broken yet. The novelty of the experience creates a chemical rush that makes it memorable. It's the lens through which you see all future relationships."

"What about parents?"

She beamed at him as if he were a particularly bright student. "Your parents' example is significant, too," she said in her classroom voice. "And of course, early loss of a parent can cripple your ability to form attachments, to trust yourself completely to another relationship."

Another dark, unreadable look. "So where does that leave us?"

"Us?" she repeated uncertainly.

"Yeah. Basically you're saying that since I got dumped and your dad died on you, we're screwed."

Oh God. The sunny wedding scene shifted and re-formed again into a picture she did not want to see. "I did not say that."

"Pretty damn close."

"I just meant . . ." Her brain scrambled. "A negative first relationship can set up an expectation of failure, make it more difficult to build intimacy."

He slanted a glance down at her. "Or it can teach you what you really want."

She nodded. "Your first love is like a starting point. It dictates where you are. But you decide how to go on."

"Moving forward."

"Yes."

"Good." He held her tighter. "Because I'm in this thing, all right? I'm in this thing with you, whether it fits your theories or not."

Her heart jumped. Her feet stopped moving. She couldn't keep up with him, in the dance or in the conversation. *I'm in this thing with you . . .*

That didn't sound like a hookup. Or even a rebound relationship.

Breathe. "That doesn't . . . We haven't . . ."

" 'Enjoy the trip,' " he said softly, and she realized he was quoting.

Is that what she'd said? It sounded like her. "Yes."

His hand on the small of her back urged her closer into the warmth of his body, the hard planes of his torso, the ridge of his erection.

She sucked in her breath.

He kissed her hair. "So let's enjoy."

Live in the moment. Savor the moment. Store up as many moments as you can, a bright and shining hoard against the time when you are gone.

Resting her head against his chest, she closed her eyes and let him lead her where she wanted to go.

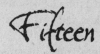
Fifteen

THE ISLAND SPARKLED in the wake of a summer squall. High piled clouds, the color of a bruise, swept west over the mainland, dragging a thin curtain of rain behind them. The water had the dull gleam of tarnished silver.

Lauren walked from the bakery to the Pirates' Rest, the wind tugging at her hair, her laptop bumping at her hip. When her pocket buzzed, she grabbed her phone and looked at the number on the display.

PATRICIA BROWN. Her agent.

Lauren sucked in her breath.

Two days ago, shaking with nerves and bravado, she had e-mailed the first seventeen chapters of her book to her editor and her agent.

Now . . . She fumbled with the phone, cupping the device against her ear to block the rustle of the wind. "Patricia?"

"Lauren, darling. I just got off the phone with Colleen." Her editor.

Lauren's heart slammed against her ribs. "And?"

"Well, she loves it, of course. We both just love it."

The horizon blurred, soft and bright. She'd been braced so long under the pressing burden of failure. Now, with that weight lifted, she felt ridiculously light, her head like a balloon, her legs wobbly. Her chest inflated with air.

"Really?" Her voice squeaked as if she'd inhaled helium.

"Absolutely. I laughed, I cried," Patricia said. "Colleen is thrilled."

Lauren pressed a hand to her chest. After so many months of churning panic, of feeling like a fraud, of being unable to write, she couldn't quite take it in. Her agent's reassurance felt almost surreal. "That's . . . great. So great. Thank you."

Jack. Her heart swelled.

She had to tell Jack. She was seeing him again tonight. *Every night.* The thought brought another rush of pleasure.

". . . very emotional, very powerful," Patricia was saying. "All those memories of your father, the reactions of your friends . . . I had no idea. And Colleen and I loved the way you used Ben's letters from jail to talk about what you were both going through."

"I'm so glad," Lauren said. Maybe they should go out tonight. To celebrate. She could buy.

"She did mention that the story feels a little . . . unfinished," Patricia said.

Lauren jerked her mind back to the present. "Maybe because it is?" she suggested.

"Don't get me wrong, we both think it's terrific. But Colleen was hoping for some sort of blockbuster happy ending."

Blockbuster?

"I was thinking a car chase," Lauren said. "Or me standing on a fire escape and Richard Gere driving up in a big white limo." *Jack climbing toward her, a whole bouquet of roses in his teeth. Save me.*

"Excuse me?" Patricia said.

Lauren shook her head. Clearly, Mom should never have let her watch *Pretty Woman* at that sleepover when she was twelve.

"A happy ending," she repeated. "You bet." Meg had said the same thing.

"Just a little kick," Patricia said. "A little oomph. Your readers want that big emotional payoff. They want to be *inspired.*"

"Sure."

But all she could think of was Jack, cooking her dinner on his boat while the sun sank into the sea. Jack in his uniform, talking softly to the cat. Jack, smiling at her with that crooked half smile, making her laugh. Making her come.

"Lauren? Did you hear what I said?"

Lauren blew out her breath. Not the kind of inspiration her editor was looking for.

"I'll work on it," she promised.

"Of course you will. I have total faith in you."

Given that her agent had just read—in raw, real, irreverent detail—Lauren's struggles with anxiety on the road, Lauren appreciated her confidence very much. "Thanks, Patricia."

"You are better now, right? No more problems?" her agent asked.

Lauren heard the concern in her voice. "Much better, thanks."

Sex was a proven stress reliever. But it wasn't only the orgasms. She felt safe around Jack. Free from danger, yes, but also free to be herself. She hadn't had a panic attack since she'd set off the alarm at Jane's more than three weeks ago.

Of course, nothing had happened recently that would trigger her symptoms.

But she was well enough to finish her book.

She shivered despite the bright sunshine, goose bumps breaking out on her skin.

"Wonderful," Patricia said. "Let me know if there's anything you need. And tell Meg to copy me on your speaking schedule. When do you get back?"

"I don't know." Out in the harbor, a seagull hung suspended in midair, making no headway at all against the wind. "I might . . . I was thinking of staying awhile after the book is finished."

Where had that come from?

"Smart girl. You deserve a break. I would kill to get out of the city right now. Well, listen, darling, you finish up and copy me when you send the final manuscript to Colleen, all right?"

"I will," Lauren promised. "Thanks so much, Patricia."

"Don't thank me. It's a wonderful story. I can't wait to read the ending."

They said the usual things and hung up.

Lauren floated up the hill from the harbor, buoyed by the wind at her back, almost giddy with relief.

Her editor liked—her editor *loved*—her book.

Her agent loved her book.

All Lauren needed now was a blockbuster ending.

A bubble of panic rose under her breastbone. Her story had no end.

She swallowed hard. *One step at a time.* A month ago, she couldn't have imagined getting this far. *Enjoy the trip.*

The pitched roof of the Pirates' Rest rose above the

trees. Lauren lengthened her stride. She and Jack weren't at the keep-my-toothbrush-at-your-place stage. She still needed to pull some things together before he picked her up.

The puddles by the side of the road reflected back the windswept sky. Raindrops glittered from the blooming branches of crepe myrtle by the fence, the heavy clusters scattering pink petals on the wet grass.

Lauren pushed open the front gate.

A man waited in the shadows of the porch, sheltered by the eaves from the rain and the heat. A young man in military fatigues. A young, sunburned man with familiar features beneath his buzz cut, standing as she came up the walk.

Her heart pounded. The swing swayed gently back and forth.

Her past, waiting for her.

Lauren stopped, her lungs constricting. "Joel?" she whispered.

UP NORTH, JACK was known as a by-the-book cop. But he was slowly learning that if he enforced every ordinance on Dare Island, he'd have to lock up half the tourists and a quarter of the town into two little jail cells.

The native islanders figured that since they were here before everybody else, including the chief of police, whatever laws they didn't agree with did not apply to them. The dingbatters moved here because they loved the idea of living at the beach and then complained about the resort town regulations. The tourists believed that their money entitled them to a good time.

Jack figured as long as he kept the peace and no one got hurt, he was doing his job.

But today dealing with one more bored rich kid rebelling

against too much family vacation kept him at the station almost an hour past his scheduled shift.

"The merchants don't want to press charges," Jack said to the bored rich kid's dad. "But they don't want to pay the town for every time the police have been called to respond to a false alarm at their businesses. Marta, here, can give you a total of the fines."

The father scowled. "That's extortion."

"Restitution," Jack said calmly. "Seems to me you'd want your boy here to take some responsibility for his actions."

"You can't prove Cliff set off all those alarms."

"Yeah, that's probably what a lawyer would say," Jack agreed. "The good news is, Cliff won't be sixteen for another couple weeks, so he can't be charged as an adult. If you want to go the juvenile court route, there's just a little paperwork and then I can release him into your custody. Or we can handle things here."

"You'll pay for this," Cliff's dad said, but he was looking at his son.

Jack left them settling the tab with Marta and drove to the Pirates' Rest.

He couldn't say when seeing Lauren at the end of the day became a necessary part of his routine. Forward his calls, drive patrol, feed the cat, sit on his boat as the sun went down, and listen to Lauren talk about her day. Unlike a lot of people, she always had something interesting to say.

Plus . . . sex. With no trouble at all, he could picture Lauren, hot and glowing, naked and coming, in his bed. In his life.

At least until she left.

The thought caused a twinge. More than a twinge, if he was honest.

But he knew better than to try and kid himself. He wasn't seventeen anymore, clinging to a summer romance when summer was over, making stupid promises that he wouldn't keep. *I'll call. I'll write. I'll visit.*

Not going to happen. When Lauren was gone, she was gone.

But maybe he could talk to her about leaving a toothbrush or something at his place.

Wet asphalt hissed under his tires as he turned onto the inn road, lined with gnarled oaks and tall pine.

Lauren was standing on the front porch of the Pirates' Rest deep in conversation with some guy in camouflage. Army, not Marines, Jack saw as he parked by the gate.

Which meant the guy, whoever he was, wasn't a buddy of Luke's.

Jack got out of the SUV just as Lauren threw herself into the guy's arms.

What the hell?

The soldier grinned and patted her back awkwardly.

Young guy, Jack observed. Seventeen? Eighteen? Not much older than the bored rich kid he'd left sitting at the station.

Jack stopped at the bottom of the porch steps—*See? Nothing to prove*—and caught the kid's eye.

The soldier dropped his arms in a hurry.

Lauren turned, her face shining. "Jack!"

That glowing look made him feel better. Not that he was suspicious or anything.

"Lauren," he acknowledged. He looked at the soldier. "Who's your friend?"

"This is Joel. Private Joel Johnson," she said, patting him on the arm with as much pride as if she were the kid's mother. "Joel, Chief Jack Rossi."

Johnson. Jack's shoulder blades tightened. He kept his face impassive. That was the name of the bank robber. The one whose family she was sending money to. And wasn't Joel the kid who'd been pulled in on the job by their uncle in the first place?

"What brings you to Dare Island, soldier?" he asked.

"Just finished Basic at Fort Jackson, sir. I'm on my way to Virginia to start AIT and stopped by to see Lauren."

Advanced Individual Training.

Jack narrowed his eyes. "A little out of your way, isn't it?"

"Yes, sir. Five and a half hours. My mom drove us up."

Lauren started. "Your mother's here?"

Ben's mother blames me, she'd said to Jack that first morning on his boat. Because the woman's brother was dead and her older son was in jail and she had to blame somebody.

A deeper color swept under the boy's sunburn. "Not here. She's waiting at the restaurant. The Fish House. I walked up from there. But she brought me, all the way from South Carolina. That says . . . That means a lot. She knows what we owe you."

Lauren shook her head. "You don't owe me a thing."

The young soldier's jaw set. "Beg pardon, ma'am, but I figure we do. I talked to Ben. He told me what you've been doing for him. For us. That's why I'm here, to thank you."

"I don't need thanks. I want to help."

"No more," Joel said. "That's the other reason I came, to tell you face-to-face. My family is my responsibility now. We don't need your money anymore."

Which sounded good to Jack, but he was watching Lauren's face. She looked like his sister-in-law Tricia watching his nephew get on the school bus the first time, like Ma the day Jack left for Basic, and for one bad moment he was afraid she was going to talk to this kid, this soldier, like he was five years old.

But she didn't.

Her mouth wobbled briefly before she bent it into a smile. "I always felt . . . I told Ben it's only fair that some of the money from the book goes to your family."

"I appreciate that, ma'am. I know you made him a promise to look out for us. But I figure that's my job now."

Silence fell.

The kid had said his say. And Lauren, who always knew the right words to smooth an awkward situation, looked lost.

Shit.

Jack cleared his throat. "Where are you staying tonight?"

"We're heading out after dinner. I report tomorrow."

"Don't you get time off to be with your mother?" Lauren asked.

"Thirty-six hours." Joel met Jack's eyes. "We wouldn't even have that if I took the Army bus."

And in return for her son's company, Jack guessed, his mother was willing to give at least her partial blessing to his mission. "Semper fi, soldier."

Joel grinned. "I'll take that in the spirit it was offered, sir."

"Will you . . . You'll at least let me buy you dinner," Lauren said.

Joel hesitated.

Jack remembered what it was like making ends meet on an E-1's pay. But having steeled himself to make the big gesture, to take responsibility for his family and himself, the new soldier's dignity would make it hard for him to accept charity.

"Hop in," Jack said easily. "I'll run you back to the Fish House. Unless you need the exercise."

Joel smiled. "No, sir. I mean, yes, sir. Thank you, sir."

Jack stood back while the two of them said good-bye, Lauren's face wavering between smiles and tears.

He met her gaze, thinking, *I've got this, don't worry*, and maybe she read his eyes or his mind because the smiles seemed to win.

"I'll be back," he said.

She nodded. "I'll be waiting."

The moment seemed to call for something more, but he didn't know what. Even if he'd been able to think of something, Joel was watching them.

He brushed his lips over hers. "Pack a toothbrush," he said and left her.

AFTER DINNER, LAUREN sat with Jack on his boat, leaning against him as the sun went down. "Thank you for taking care of Joel and his mother."

Jack shrugged, making her head rock against his shoulder. "No big deal. I bought them dinner. You took care of them."

"I tried." Had she done enough?

"Hey." Jack's arms were warm around her. "You saved that kid."

She pressed closer, grateful for his reassurance. "Ben saved him. And now he's saved himself."

"Because you bought him time to grow up."

"Joel did all the work." She tilted her face to smile at him. "You know how many therapists it takes to change a lightbulb?"

Jack arched an eyebrow.

"Only one," she said, straight-faced. "But the lightbulb has to want to change."

His lips twitched.

Satisfied, she settled against him, letting herself sink into the solid rightness of the moment. To the west, the sky flamed and the water blazed and the clouds sank down to purple haze. "I heard from my agent today."

His arms tightened around her, but his voice was as calm as ever. "How'd that go?"

"Good." She smiled over his arm at the setting sun. "Really good. She likes the chapters."

"That's terrific." He kissed the top of her head. "Congratulations."

"Thanks. I need a blockbuster ending, though. A happy one."

"Well, that's easy," Jack said.

She twisted to look at him again.

"Joel," Jack said. "The story starts with him, right? With him wanting to do the bank job with his uncle."

She nodded. "And Ben taking his place." The idea sparked. *Okay, yeah, that could work.* She sat up, wiggling around to face Jack. "And Ben and I bonded because we were both trying to take care of our brothers."

Jack was watching her, his dark eyes alert. "There you go. So if his brother's taking care of himself now . . ."

"Then the story comes full circle." She beamed at him, feeling that dizzy lightness return. "You're brilliant."

Another half smile. "I'm not the one writing a book."

"I'm not writing tonight, either. I'm taking the night off." She spread her arms wide. "To celebrate."

"There's an idea."

"I have many ideas," she said grandly.

"Do they involve you getting naked? Because those are the kind of ideas you should share with me."

She grinned. "You share first."

"Okay. I think about you naked all the time."

"No, I meant . . ." She expelled her breath, caught

between laughter and lust. "We should talk about you. How was your day?"

"It was a day."

She waited, giving him space to talk, her heart beating as if she had something at stake here, something more than conversation, something more than sex. Good communication was important for developing intimacy in a relationship. And they were in a relationship, even if she didn't change her Facebook status anytime soon.

I'm in this thing with you, whether it fits your theories or not.

She really needed to start leaving a toothbrush here.

And he needed to talk.

"A long day," she said, to help him out.

"Yeah."

She narrowed her eyes.

Amusement gleamed in his. But then he said, "I had this kid in with his dad this afternoon. Summer people."

She nodded encouragingly. *Go on.*

"Turns out there's not enough for the kid to do on the island, so he decided to make his own excitement. He set off a bunch of alarms around town."

Lauren thought of the blaring sirens at the bakery and shuddered. "Well, that's a cry for attention. What did you do?"

"Collected the fines and let him go. You can't get too tough on tourists' kids in a resort town. It's not good for business. But maybe I wasn't doing him any favors."

"Would the outcome have been any different if he went to court?"

"Not really. But it might have been a wake-up call for him. Or his folks."

He was such a good man, she thought. Careful. Conscientious.

"I don't think there's one right answer," she said. "What do you want? What's the behavior that's going to get you what you want?"

He smiled faintly.

"What?"

"You sound like a therapist."

"Is that bad?"

He shook his head. "It's who you are."

Which didn't quite answer her question. "Did you ever see a therapist?" she asked curiously. At thirty-eight, a cop, divorced . . . It was a reasonable assumption.

"I'm looking at one now."

"To talk to, I mean."

His dark eyes turned opaque. "The department back home had a shrink on call for intervention, fitness for duty evaluations, stuff like that."

She waited, but that was apparently as much as he was ready to share. "What about down here?"

"You looking for a job after graduation?"

Answering a question with a question, she thought. Deflecting. No, *dodging.*

But she didn't want to spoil the mood by calling him on it. She wasn't *his* therapist. Only his . . . girlfriend? Lover? Fuck buddy?

She sighed. The problem with living in the moment was it didn't help you talk about the future.

"I don't need my doctorate to work as a therapist," she said. "Although it would certainly give me more choices. Once I finish my dissertation, I'll probably look around for a postdoc fellowship—a research position. We say, psychiatrists write prescriptions, psychologists do testing, and counselors talk. But there are a lot of mediocre counselors out there. I don't want to be mediocre."

"You're not mediocre."

"But people don't know that."

"When did you start caring what people think? I thought you just wanted to help."

"I'd still be helping people. Research on psychological models is necessary to developing effective therapies."

"But you're not on the front lines."

"No," she admitted. "But I'd be doing important work."

"If that's what you want. Is that what you want?"

His words struck at her heart. She hadn't bothered to ask herself that question in a very long time. She'd been so focused on getting through each day, one task, one step at a time, that she never lifted her head to see where she was going.

Was she lost?

Or had she simply changed direction?

"Now who sounds like a therapist?" she asked breathlessly. *Covering.*

He shrugged. "I'm a cop."

She arched her eyebrows. " 'We have ways of making you talk'?"

"You got a problem with that?"

"No. No, how could I? I'm the same way."

He got her meaning immediately. "Cops and shrinks. Both observers."

She nodded. "Listening for hidden meanings, watching for nonverbal clues." *Trying to get confessions.*

His eyes were almost black. She could not read his thoughts. "So you're saying we both play mind games."

"That's not a bad thing," she said. "Exactly. Not as long as we understand each other."

"And don't get stuck in our heads."

She smiled ruefully. "I do have a tendency to overthink things."

He put his hand on her ankle. Warmth stole upward, traveling along her veins. "I have a cure for that."

Her pulse fluttered. Her smile spread. "I'm in your hands."

"That's the idea."

Holding her gaze, he slid his hand up her calf to her knee. His palm was warm and calloused, scraping her nerves to life. She opened her mouth to breathe, and he leaned in to kiss her, taking her mouth in soft, greedy bites that raised the fine hair on the back of her neck and tightened the tips of her breasts. She wanted to rub over him like a cat.

She twined her arms around his neck, scooting closer, and he kissed her again, lazy and deep, taking full possession of her mouth as his finger traced tiny circles on the inside of her knee, the curve of her thigh. Sliding under the hem of her skirt, moving higher. Her excitement rose with each small incursion, every warm advance, until she made a sound in her throat, and he reached under her with both hands and gripped her bottom. He half pulled, half lifted her toward him, astride him, her legs straddling his thighs on the padded bench seat. His hands stroked down her back, fitting her curves against his lean, tough body, breasts to chest, sex to sex.

This. Liquid desire. Here, now, only this. Only him. She shivered, overwhelmed by the delicious contrast between the cool breeze on her bare arms and the solid heat between her thighs, by the scent of salt and man.

"What are you thinking now?" A breath against her lips.

She blinked. "What?"

She felt his chuckle warm against her cheek, deep in her belly. She ground against the hard bulge of his erection, loving the way he felt, the way he made her feel, aching and trembling and hot. He inhaled sharply, his fingers curving, pressing in her flesh, moving down, delving into her ready sex. Her flesh swelled. She trembled, hiding her face against his hot throat, rising on her knees as he thrust one big finger inside her. Two. She gasped.

He released her. She cried out in disappointment, raising her head.

But he was yanking at his buckle, button, zipper, pants, digging in his pocket for a condom. *Yes. This.* She reached for him—stiff and hot—as his hips arched off the seat. He covered himself with quick, jerky movements. She stretched her panties out of the way. Grasping her hips, he positioned her above him. His dark gaze, heavy-lidded and intent, caught hers. He pulled her down and impaled her, filling her in one heavy, upward thrust. *Oh, hell, yes.* Her body closed around him, milking the sensation of him deep inside her, solid and thick inside her.

They were locked and moving together, fused with sweat and heat. She pulsed and steamed. He pumped and thrust, working her with short, strong digs, push and retreat, push and retreat, bringing her to the edge again and again. Her breath sobbed. She labored to rise. Fought to fall. And still he never quite let her go over, holding her off, catching her back, pressing, always pressing.

Until the question he was asking with his body pounded through her, the demand he was making imprinted on her brain, the admission wrung from her flesh.

"I love you."

And that must have been the confession he wanted, the words he was waiting for.

He slid and held inside her hard, and the echo of her words, the shock of him at the center of her, was enough, was everything. She shuddered and came so hard she saw stars. He held her through the spasms of her release and then took his own while the night tumbled down around them.

Sixteen

LAUREN WASN'T LOOKING for commitment. Not after three weeks. But reassurance? Yeah, she could use some of that.

Especially after her blurted admission last night. *I love you.* She winced.

Especially since Jack hadn't said it back.

That was okay, she told herself the next morning. She was in touch with her emotions. She'd been honest about her feelings. She wouldn't take the words back if she could.

But she had never before said them to anyone outside her immediate family. She was having enough trouble processing her own feelings.

Maybe it was a good thing she didn't have to deal with Jack's.

At least silence was better than some of the things he could have said. Like *Don't.* Or *Thank you.* Or *I love you, too.*

She sucked in her breath, suddenly light-headed. Her insides churned. Okay, she definitely wasn't ready to cope with the implications of *I love you, too.*

And Jack had been very solicitous this morning, waking her with a kiss when he got out of the shower, bringing her coffee in bed.

Tiger trotted at his ankles, tail in the air, a bend in the tip making a fuzzy question mark. *What are you doing here? What are you doing?*

Jack, already in uniform, handed her a mug.

She seized it gratefully. "Thanks."

He straightened at the foot of the bed, in the center of the room, the only place he could stand fully upright. Looming over her. Her insides clenched and relaxed helplessly.

It wasn't just the sex and the sunset, she realized with a tremor. Even in the cold light of morning, she was in love with this guarded, principled, complex man with his sharp-edged face and eyes like knives.

His black gaze sought hers. "How are you doing?"

"Great," she said heartily. At least they'd reached the stage where she packed an overnight bag. "Give me ten minutes, and I'll be ready to go."

"You could stay."

She burned her mouth. Gulped. "Excuse me?"

"You're not due at the bakery until, what, ten? Eleven? Why don't you take your time this morning? I can swing by later to drive you to work."

The hot coffee seared its way down. She cleared her throat painfully. "Actually, I asked Jane for the day off so I could work on my book. She's got one of the catering gals covering for me."

"You've got your laptop with you."

"Ye-es." She curled her hands around the warm mug. Where was he going with this?

"So, stay."

Her heart beat faster. "For how long?"

A corner of his mouth kicked up. "As long as you want."

She couldn't read his eyes. *What do you want? Do you want me to stay?*

"Okay," she whispered.

He regarded her solemnly. "You want to go out for dinner tonight or should I bring something home for us?"

"Home sounds wonderful."

A blush raced over her face. They were not playing house. A day on his boat did not equal an invitation to move in. Still, she was here, wasn't she? On his boat. In his home. In his space.

"I'll pick something up, then."

He leaned forward. Cupping her jaw, he kissed her, a long, sweet, simmering kiss that brought her fully awake. Her blood hummed.

"Is that what you're bringing home?" she asked breathlessly when he raised his head. "Because, yum."

His smile kindled deep in his eyes. "It's on the menu."

"I can't wait."

Enjoy the moment, she told herself after he left. Because, really, the moment was kind of perfect.

She pulled on her clothes and went out on deck with her cup of coffee. Tiger mewed to join her.

She eyed the kitten uncertainly. "Okay, but if you look like you're making a break for it, it's the cabin for you," she warned.

Released into the sunlight, Tiger sniffed around before jumping to curl on the padded bench.

So he'd done this before, Lauren thought, reassured.

But for her, this was all new. The setting. The feelings. She filled her lungs with the ocean-scented air. She loved the Pirates' Rest, with its glimpses of sea and sound, the deep, wraparound porch, the sheltering garden. But this . . .

A bird, its black-tipped wings as sharp as the angles of a kite, darted over the water, blazing in the sunlight. Atop the dunes, the tall sea grass plumes swayed and bowed like dancers in the breeze. The world around her teemed with life, the sky flushed with promise, the sea sparkling with possibilities as far as the horizon.

She got her laptop and a second cup of coffee, setting up for the day. Settling in.

Bring on the happy ending, she thought, and began to type.

The sound of an engine roused her minutes—hours?—later. A car, low-slung, sleek, and white, purring down the unfinished road.

Lauren raised her head as the car parked at the edge of the dock. A woman got out, greyhound thin and graceful in white jeans and a black T-shirt, her hair caught back in a sleek, dark ponytail, huge sunglasses flashing on her face. She marched toward the dock as if she knew where she was going. As if she had every right to be here.

Maybe she did. But from what Jack had said, this was development property, not yet open to the public.

Lauren slid her laptop to the bench and stood, shading her eyes against the sun. "Can I help you?" she called.

The woman stopped. Angled her head. "I'm looking for Jack Rossi."

She had a husky, well-modulated voice, with a hint of accent—the swallowed *L*, the long *aw* in place of the *o*—that was somehow familiar.

Lauren's nerves prickled. "I'm sorry, he's not here right now," she said politely. "Can I take a message?"

"Where is he?" Answering a question with another question.

Lauren's breath caught. "He's at work. If you give me your name, I can tell him you stopped by."

"Sure." The woman pushed her sunglasses on top of her head, revealing eyes like gold coins, hard and bright, in her honey-toned face. Her smile curved, shiny and sharp as a knife. "I'm Renee. His wife."

JACK LEFT HIS office to pour himself another cup of coffee from Marta's pot, Lauren's words replaying in his head like a summer song on the radio.

I love you, she'd said.

Which was the sort of thing men said before sex and women said after. Even when they were sincere, you couldn't always trust words said in the heat of the moment.

They were still damn good to hear.

"You are in a good mood this morning," Marta said.

Probably because he couldn't stop smiling.

"Nothing makes my day like filling out grant applications," he joked.

"He's in a good mood every morning," Hank said. "Now that he's getting some."

Jack gave him a bland stare. He'd figured that once he hired a dispatcher, Hank would spend less time in the office. Especially since he and Marta couldn't be in the same room without sniping at each other. But it seemed the retired sheriff's deputy was around more than ever before.

"Then you should try it," Marta said. "Maybe sex would improve your attitude."

Hank grinned. "How do you know I'm not getting any?"

"Please." Marta snapped a file drawer shut. "I know everything."

"How are you coming with that monthly report?" Jack asked, changing the subject.

"Finished," Marta said. "I e-mailed it to you for your review. I read her book, you know."

"Thanks. I'll take a look at it," Jack said, preparing to escape into his office.

Marta arched her brows. "You haven't read her book yet? But you are together."

Hank snorted. "He doesn't have to read her book to sleep with her."

"Okay, we're done here," Jack said.

"You should show more respect," Marta said to Hank. She smiled at Jack. "She seems like a very interesting young woman. I'm sorry she is leaving so soon."

"Janey said she was staying through the summer," Hank said.

Marta raised her brows. "Which is how long, another week? Two weeks before the kids go back to school. I talked to Tess Fletcher this morning. Meg is already scheduling Miss Patterson's next book tour."

Two weeks?

Jack forced himself to ignore the jolt to his system, the tiny clutch at his gut.

With Renee, he'd been so damn sure he knew where they were going all the time. It wasn't until she had betrayed him with his partner that he'd finally admitted he didn't have a clue. He'd been wrong about her, wrong about them, wrong about everything all along.

He didn't know—he couldn't know—where this thing

with Lauren was heading. But everything suddenly felt all right.

I love you, she'd said.

Whatever the hell she'd meant by that, wherever they were going, they were together now. At the end of the day, she would be waiting for him on his boat.

It was enough for him. For now. He had a grant application to write. The town council had found the funds for the dispatcher's position, but they'd balked at buying the dashboard security cams he'd requested for the patrol vehicles. So he was stuck begging for money from the feds.

The outer door opened and a woman walked in.

He almost dropped his mug.

She pushed her sunglasses up and smiled. "Hi, lover."

Renee. He waited for a blast of something—gladness, fury, resentment—and couldn't find anything. "This is a surprise."

His voice was calm. Good.

"Right? Of all the gin joints in all the world . . ." She grinned, inviting him to smile back, but he couldn't find that, either.

"What do you want?" he asked evenly.

"Since you won't talk to me on the phone, I decided to see for myself how you're doing. What you're doing with yourself these days." She propped a hip on the edge of Marta's desk, angling her body to best advantage. "Why don't you show me around?"

"I'm busy."

"Come on, Jack." She swept a look around. For a moment, he saw the department through her eyes: three desks jammed close together, the cheap veneer door to his office with the premade POLICE CHIEF sign, the narrow hallway that led to the cramped back rooms, the gun closet, and two small holding cells. "It's not like it will take very long."

"We only give tours to the kiddies on Tuesdays," Hank drawled.

Renee glanced in his direction, her smile sharpening. "You must be Barney Fife."

Jack sighed. Renee didn't take anybody's shit. Ever. He used to admire the way she always brought a gun to a knife fight. Now it just made him tired. And wary. "Hank Clark, Marta Lopez, this is Renee Mancuso."

She angled her chin. "Six months ago, it was Renee Rossi."

"Except at work," he said.

Renee had never used his name professionally. *There are too many damn Rossis on the job in this town*, she'd said when they were married. *It's confusing.*

And he, poor sap, had gone along with whatever she wanted, determined not to act like the knuckle dragger she'd sometimes accused him of being.

His coffee was suddenly bitter in his mouth. *Whoops.* Seemed like he had some lingering resentment after all.

He set down his mug. He couldn't imagine his family sending his ex-wife to find him. Especially Ma. Still . . . "Everybody okay back home?"

"They're fine. They miss you." She laid her perfectly manicured hand on his arm. Looked up into his eyes. "I miss you."

"Good to know." He realized how that sounded and winced internally. Not so calm, either. *Shit.* "I mean, I'm glad that everything's okay. We really have to get back to work here, Renee."

"Of course." She stood. "I can wait for you. On your boat?"

Ah, shit. He kept his face impassive.

"Or you could let me buy you a drink. Unless . . ." She widened those big golden eyes at him. "I'm sorry, I didn't think. Maybe you don't drink anymore."

She could have been concerned or testing or digging at him. With Renee, it could be all three.

That had been the last straw, the final incident that cost him his cool and his reputation.

All cops drank, coming off shift at four in the afternoon, at two in the morning, taking the edge off, diluting the stress of the job before they went home to their three-bedroom suburban houses, to their bills and their lawns and their dogs and their wives.

The brass didn't give a damn if you drank.

But if you looked up from your beer and saw your bastard partner with your cheating wife sitting together at the bar, if you saw her hand move up his thigh and his hand close around her nape, if you hauled off and slugged him in a public place, precipitating a bar fight . . . Yeah, they cared about that.

Particularly if your wife outranked you in the department.

"Not at ten thirty in the morning," he said dryly.

"Coffee, then. Come on, Jack." She leaned forward, exposing taut, tanned cleavage, shifting position and strategy with ease. "I drove eight hours to see you. Aren't you the slightest bit curious to hear why?"

Not particularly, he realized. But it seemed unkind to say so, especially with Hank and Marta listening. In fact, if there was going to be a discussion, he'd rather have it where no one was listening in.

Which ruled out Jane's.

Gossip traveled fast on the island. If you sneezed before

driving the length of the island, somebody at the other end would say "Bless you" as soon as you stepped out of your car.

Maybe the Fish House, where the high-backed booths provided a little privacy. Somewhere quiet, somewhere dark, where Renee could say her piece and be gone.

"I'll buy you coffee," he said.

"My treat." Renee hopped off the desk, her smile almost conciliatory. "Consider it a peace offering."

MATURE ADULTS IN committed relationships did not freak out when one of their exes drove into town.

She could be mature, Lauren told herself as she closed her laptop, as she fed the cat, as she checked her phone for the twelfth—or was it the twentieth?—time. Onshore, the shadows lengthened. A flock of pelicans sailed by, low against the golden sky.

She'd told Jack she loved him. Love involved trust.

Of course, he hadn't said it back. But he was committed to her. Wasn't he? *I'm in this thing with you, whether it fits your theories or not*, he'd said.

Stay . . . As long as you want, he'd said.

Lauren wandered back on deck, restless. The fact that he was also at least an hour late wasn't a particular source of concern. Okay, maybe it was. A little. Only because he hadn't called.

She stared up the empty road, willing his cruiser into sight. Was he all right?

Tiger mewed at her feet. Lauren scooped up the kitten, cuddling its soft fur against her cheek. *Don't overthink this. Don't get stuck in your own head.*

Headlights flashed, pale against the fading sun.

Her heartbeat quickened. She watched as the black-and-white SUV drew up to the end of the dock and Jack got out, moving stiffly.

"Sorry I'm late," he said as he came aboard.

She leaned in to kiss him, a soft brush of lips. Stepped back to scan his face, the tension bracketing his mouth, the lines of tiredness around his eyes. "That's okay. Bad day?"

"Accident out on the highway. Bunch of kids going to the beach. Teenagers, three girls, two boys. The driver was texting, hit the median, and flipped."

Her heart squeezed. "Oh, Jack."

"Looks like we're going out tonight after all. I didn't have a chance to pick up dinner."

"Of course. I'm so sorry."

"It's okay." He scratched Tiger briefly behind the ears. "It's over."

"I'm glad you were there to help them."

His hand dropped. "Yeah."

He walked past her toward the galley.

She trailed after him. "How . . . how are they?"

He bent to get a beer from the fridge. "Nobody died. Bumps and bruises mostly. Lucky for them, they were all wearing seat belts. The driver got it the worst when she hit the steering wheel. I had to stay with them 'til the paramedics got there."

"And how are you?" Lauren asked softly.

He popped the cap. "Fine."

No, she thought, *you're not*. Frustration and concern roiled inside her. "You had an exciting day all around," she observed.

He swigged his beer. "I've had better."

Lauren took a deep breath. Say something now? Or say nothing and let the silence eat at both of them?

Say something, she decided. "Renee came by this morning looking for you."

"She found me."

Lauren waited. "Do you want to talk about it?"

"No."

"We can discuss it later."

He lowered the bottle. "There's nothing to discuss. She came. I dealt with it."

"That's very reassuring. But it's not enough."

His eyes were very dark. "You don't trust me."

"Of course I trust you. But you have to trust me, too. You should be able to share with me how you're feeling."

"I just had to tell some parents their sixteen-year-old daughter is on her way to intensive care. I can't be feeling the feelings all the time the way you do."

Ouch.

"So you're going to close down and keep everything to yourself."

He didn't say anything.

He was a guy, she reminded herself. Guys had a tendency to compartmentalize. She needed to be patient.

"I understand you need to separate your emotions in order to do your job," she said, choosing her words with care. "But a visit from your ex-wife . . . You need to talk to me about things that affect you personally."

"I didn't say anything about Renee's visit because it doesn't have anything to do with you."

The words slapped, stinging color to her cheeks. Her mouth jarred open.

Jack dragged a hand through his hair. "Oh, Christ. I meant, it doesn't make any difference to me. To us."

"Wow." She shut her mouth to swallow. Opened it to

say, "We are now dealing with textbook levels of denial and compartmentalization."

"I'm not some patient you're seeing at the free clinic, sweetheart. I don't need you analyzing me. I don't need fixing."

Heat and hurt swarmed to her face. Maybe she'd been guilty in the past of treating lovers like clients. *Fixer-uppers*. But not Jack.

"I'm not trying to fix you. I'm trying to know you. I'm trying to be supportive."

"If you don't know me well enough to believe I wouldn't run around on you with my ex-wife, I don't see much point to this conversation."

She had obviously hurt his pride. Trust, she thought. It was clearly a hot-button topic. "I'm not accusing you of sleeping with her."

"Good."

But she couldn't stop trying, couldn't stop digging. "Was that an issue for you before? In your marriage, I mean?"

"You could say that." He sipped his beer. "She slept with my partner."

"Oh." For a man like Jack, loyal and principled, the combination of physical and emotional infidelity, the betrayal of friendship, vows, and honor, would be unthinkable, unanswerable. The worst kind of blow. Her heart hurt for him. "Oh, Jack."

He set down his bottle, the glass clicking precisely against the countertop. "I need a shower before we go out."

Running away, she thought. "I can wait."

He tugged at his buttons, a black glint in his eyes. "You're not going to offer to scrub my back?"

Hurt and helplessness roiled around inside her. "Normally, I would love to scrub your back. Since I'm not really into sex being used as a diversionary tactic, I think I'll pass."

"Fuck," he said tiredly. "What do you want from me?"

"I just want you to talk to me. Could we talk, please?"

"Fine." He leaned against the counter again, arms crossed over his chest. "What do you want to know?"

Her chest ached. *Tell me you love me. Tell me everything's going to be okay.*

"You could start by telling me why Renee was looking for you."

"She wanted to let me know there was a job opening in my old department. Detective squad with a chance to get back onto the tactical response team."

"She didn't have to come down here to tell you that."

He was silent, giving her time to work it out.

Lauren moistened her lips. "I suppose the job comes with . . . special compensation."

"She mentioned perks, yeah."

She nodded, unsure how to respond.

"I'd be living near my family again, for one," he said, watching her closely.

She struggled to contain her reaction. This wasn't about her. This was about Jack, what he needed, what he wanted. "Is that what you want?"

"All other things being equal?" He shrugged. "Sure. But I like it here. I like small-town policing. I like being able to follow every case from beginning to end. I've got no plans to leave."

"Well, that's good," she said, relieved. "That's good to know."

"Unlike you."

"What?"

"Marta told me you have a book tour coming up. When is that, a couple weeks, a couple months away? Funny how we never talk about that."

She gaped at the unexpected attack. "It's not like I've been keeping secrets. I've been totally honest with you. You've always known I was leaving."

But he was right, too, she thought guiltily. They never talked about it. Because that was a need she preferred not to acknowledge, one pain she didn't want to feel.

"Yeah, I've always known." He stuck his thumbs in his pockets, those black, alert eyes fixed on her face. "So what do you care what I do or where I go after you're gone?"

The blood drained from her face, from her brain, leaving her light-headed. Her lips felt numb.

Jack swore again. "Fuck, I'm sorry. Look, we're both tired. This is stupid. Let me get cleaned up and I'll take you out to dinner."

"You're right. We are both tired." There was a band around her chest, cutting off her air, making it hard to breathe. She inhaled carefully, painfully, holding the boiling hurt inside so it wouldn't spill out and scald them both. "It's been a long day. Why don't you take me home instead?"

Seventeen

SHE'D BEEN STRAIGHT with him, and he'd cut her off at the knees, Jack thought as he dragged his sorry ass on board the *Wreck* the following night.

Three six-minute sets on the heavy bag in the back room after work, fighting an invisible opponent, hadn't knocked out the voices in his head. But maybe the exercise had exhausted him to the point where he could sleep tonight.

Alone.

Alone and fucking miserable.

His own fault.

He dropped into a deck chair and propped his feet on the rail, but for once the rocking boat, the coastal breeze, the deep, bright water, didn't ease his piss-poor mood.

He closed his eyes. He'd pressed too hard.

Or she had, with her questions and concern. She was always nudging, pushing, prodding, trying to get inside his head, to poke around in his heart. She uncovered pieces of him he'd thought were buried, brought feelings into the light. He'd shared things with her he didn't talk about with anybody else.

They were a match in so many ways he'd lost sight of the fact that they were fundamentally different people.

Or he hadn't wanted to see.

Could be their differences made them work. He admired her loyalty to her family, her determination to make a difference in the world. He appreciated her quick observations, her bright, curious mind. Her willingness to see the best in others, her courage in putting everything out there.

Her heart.

I love you, she'd said.

But the words didn't matter. Because at the end of the day, at the end of two weeks, she was gone.

He wanted her. Fine.

He could respect her, admire her, enjoy her. But *need* her? Not smart. Not when she was on her way out of town.

Better for both of them, maybe, to get used to the idea, to get a taste of what life would be like when she was gone.

Hell. It was going to be hell.

He dropped his head back against the chair, willing away the pain pounding at the base of his skull, the tiredness dogging his body, the whisper of his heart telling him he was a fool.

He'd give her one more day to cool off, he decided. Give them both a chance to step back, simmer down. Take stock.

And then . . .

"I hear you and Pookie had a fight," said his ex-wife's voice.

His eyes snapped open.

Renee was standing on the dock beside the *Wreck*, holding a pizza box and a bottle of wine.

He lowered his feet from the ship's rail and stood cautiously. "I thought you left. Yesterday."

She bared her teeth in a smile. "You know me better than that. I won't go until I've got what I came for."

"Not from me." *Not ever again.*

"I brought pizza." She lifted the box, offering it like a bribe or a . . . What had she said the other day? A peace offering. *Sorry I fucked your partner. Have a pie.* "Bacon and garlic. Your favorite."

He could smell it, garlic, grease, and tomato sauce, drifting over the diesel-scented water. His stomach rumbled. He wanted dinner out with Lauren and got pizza in with Renee. It had been that kind of fucked-up day.

Renee tilted her head. "You going to make me eat this by myself?"

He should tell her to go. But he was hungry and feeling sorry for himself and too tired to go to the effort of making a meal. She was here. The pizza was here.

He shrugged. "Suit yourself."

So she came aboard.

The habits of marriage died hard. How many times over the years had they come home at the end of the day, too tired to cook, too exhausted for sex, and split a pizza or an order of Chinese from the take-out place around the corner? They slipped without discussion into the familiar division of labor, *You get the napkins, I'll open the wine.* Maybe that's what Renee was counting on, that he would fall without thinking into the old routines.

They carried the glasses out on deck.

The kitten followed, drawn by loneliness or maybe the

smell of bacon. He wove around Jack's ankles when he sat, head-butting his shins for attention.

Renee tucked her feet under her chair. "You got a pet rat. How cute."

"This is Tiger," Jack said, reaching down to scratch behind the cat's ears.

"Jesus, Jack, if I'd known you were this hard up for company, I would have come down sooner." Renee blotted the grease from her pizza with a napkin. "So, what did you and Pookie fight about?"

"We didn't fight."

Fighting involved yelling. He and Renee had fought, simmering resentments exploding into anger and bitter, hurtful words. Renee had always known what buttons to push, how to turn him from a decent guy trying to do his best into an angry asshole. Even when they hadn't connected emotionally any other way, they'd known how to fight.

Lauren hadn't yelled. She'd been caring and concerned, patient and dignified. And hurt.

He'd seen her face go white, heard that distressed little hitch in her breath when he went after her.

He'd hurt her. Damn it.

He took a bite of pizza he didn't want and put the slice down.

Renee looked from his plate to his face and raised her eyebrows. "Want to talk about it?"

He gave her a flat look.

She laughed. "Okay, not our style. But if you want to tell me how she makes you miserable, I'm happy to listen."

Reluctantly, his lips twitched. "I'm good, thanks."

"Yeah, you are. Too good for me, everybody always said. Saint Jack, the cool and incorruptible." She licked her fingers. "Except with me."

He heard her satisfaction. Was that what she was after? The anger that would turn him back into the man that she remembered, the rage that would give her power over him again.

"I'm no saint."

"I know that. But it got kind of old, listening to them go on all the time about what a great guy you are."

"You mean, my mother," he said dryly.

"Your mother, my mother, all of them. Frank."

He stilled. "I'm not talking with you about Frank."

"Suits me." Renee swallowed. "Bastard dumped me, you know. Couldn't get over what he did to you."

"He didn't do it alone," Jack said.

"Yeah, but what he did was worse."

He stared at her in heavy disbelief. "You were my wife."

"And he was your partner. Hey, I knew where I stood in the pecking order. The job came first with you. It always did." She slid him a sly look. "You ever think maybe I screwed Frank as a way to be closer to you?"

"Bullshit."

Renee grinned, not embarrassed at all at being called out. "Yeah, well, maybe not. It was worth a shot." Her smile faded. She leaned forward, putting her hand on his knee. "Come home, Jack. Come back to a real job. Back to your real life."

She was sincere. Looking down at her hand, he felt a flash of . . . Not regret. Not that. Remembered affection, maybe, the way he felt about his first bike or the car he'd sold when he joined the Marines, things he'd loved and outgrown.

Things he didn't need anymore, not worth the space they required.

"I have a job," he said. "I have a life. A home."

Renee rolled her eyes. "Jack, you're roughing it on a *boat*. Your uncles' old fishing boat. This isn't home. This was never meant to be anything more than temporary. You were never going to stay here."

Was she right? Maybe when he first came to the island, but now?

"Renee . . . I'm done," he said quietly. "I've moved on."

He wasn't sure when that had happened, or how, but . . . Yeah. Done with her, done with them, done holding on to his anger and the past.

You're ready for a rebound relationship, Lauren said in his head, and maybe it had started out that way, but it was more than that now. She was more than that.

"Moved on to what?" Renee's voice sharpened. "This job, that girl . . . They're like this pizza. Okay if you're starving, but you've had better. Sooner or later you're going to want the real thing again."

Real? Lauren was real, her open heart, her genuine smile, her lack of pretense. The shallow rise and fall of her belly as she slept, the warmth of her breath on his neck, her eyes reflecting back the moonlight in the darkened cabin.

"You're going to want me," Renee said. "Let me stay and I'll prove it to you."

He shook his head. "It's time for you to go."

"Seriously? After twelve years, you really going to tell me no? Where am I going to sleep tonight?"

"Wherever you stayed last night."

"They're full up. I don't have another reservation."

He stood. "You'll think of something. You always do. Plenty of places along the highway."

"Screw you, Jack. Just—" Renee broke off, searching his face. Her eyes glittered. With anger? Or tears? "You've changed."

He nodded slowly. "I guess I have."
He just hoped it wasn't too late.

LAUREN WAS GOOD at fixing things. But she didn't know how to fix this situation with Jack. Her failure poked at her as she tossed in bed that night, replaying their fight over and over in her head. Like the princess on the pea in that fairy tale, every remembered word a prod.

Should she apologize?

She didn't need to be right all the time. She didn't care about keeping score. In a relationship, it shouldn't matter who won or lost, only if you could find a solution that worked for both of you.

But if they were in a relationship, she should have the right to ask Jack questions. All her research, all her clinical practice, stressed the importance of healthy communication. She'd told him she *loved* him, for heaven's sake. And he'd said . . . He'd said . . .

I'm not some patient you're seeing at the free clinic, sweetheart. I don't need you analyzing me.

Her eyes burned. As if her interest somehow insulted him. As if his feelings were none of her business.

I didn't say anything about Renee's visit because it doesn't have anything to do with you.

So he "dealt with it." Full stop. He didn't need her help. He didn't want her interference. And the more she pushed him on a personal level, the more he clammed up and withdrew.

She rolled over and thumped her pillow.

Part of her appreciated that he was strong enough to handle things his own way. She admired his quiet confidence, his uncompromising principles, the matter-of-fact way he assumed responsibility not only for himself or with her but daily in his job.

But how could she be with someone who wouldn't be open with her, who wouldn't talk to her about what was important in his life? Who didn't value her thoughts and ideas.

Although . . . Another poke. Another toss. She hadn't been completely open with him, either.

She shot a look at the room's clock, the numbers glowing softly in the dark—3:00 A.M.

Well, that figured. After the robbery, this was the time when she would wake, heart pounding, mind racing with worry. In the quiet stretches of the night, with no outlet or distractions, her anxieties became overwhelming. Inescapable.

Except with Jack. She'd slept with Jack.

She flopped onto her back, staring up at the shadowed ceiling.

She couldn't, wouldn't, apologize for leaving, for going back to her real life. But Jack was right. She *had* avoided talking about it. She'd told herself she didn't want to spoil their remaining time together by focusing on its end.

But that was an excuse. The sneaky little truth, the one she hesitated to admit even to herself, was even more humiliating.

She didn't know what her leaving meant to Jack. *I love you*, she'd said.

And he hadn't said it back.

He acted like he loved her, at least in bed. He was a passionate, demanding, inventive lover. Outside of bed, well . . . He was guarded. Private. Cool.

But she knew he had the capacity to love. Underneath the expressionless face, his deceptively relaxed stance, he was decent and caring. She'd seen the way he did his job, the way he interacted with the Fletchers, his gentle courtesy with Tess, the smile he always had for Taylor. The way he made time and room for that skinny, affection-starved cat.

She was tempted to believe he could make room for her, too. On his boat, in his life, in his heart.

But then what?

The robbery had not broken her. But it had shattered her life in two, into Before and After. She'd put her plans, her career, her dissertation, on hold. She'd left her little student apartment and her family.

Caught up in the wave of fame and publicity, in the stress of writing another book, she'd nearly lost herself, her breath and her balance.

Dare Island had been her escape.

Jack had been her salvation.

He had kindled her heart again, given her the courage to love, to reach, to feel. To grow.

Writing the book had been another step in the healing process, a slender narrative bridge connecting her past and her future. But now she had to step onto that bridge. She needed to go back, to fit together the pieces of her old life with her new understanding. She was overdue for a meeting with her advisor. She missed her mom and Noah.

She wanted to go home.

She tossed and turned until dawn.

"DID YOU AND Jack have a fight?" Jane asked Lauren the next day.

The lunch rush was over, the bakery quiet as people took advantage of the glorious weather to hang out at the beach. Thalia worked the front of the shop. Jane was in the kitchen, putting the finishing touches on a duplicate of Kate and Luke's wedding cake for the display case.

Lauren flushed and finished reloading the tray of pastries for the front. "Why?" *Red-rimmed eyes? Puffy face?*

Jane tilted her head. "Maybe the way you're binge-eating chocolate chip cookies?"

Busted. Lauren smiled weakly. "It was that or self-medicate with ice cream out of the carton."

And she thought of Jack, smiling at her with that dark glint in his eyes. *Guess you don't worry about stereotypes, either.*

"I'm sorry." Jane rolled softened gum paste between her hands before pressing it into a shell mold. "I wondered when he didn't come in the past two days."

"We're sort of . . . taking a break," Lauren confessed. "We're not fighting, though."

You couldn't fight with somebody who didn't call.

"So it's not . . ." Jane broke off, focused on teasing the shell out of its mold with an X-Acto knife.

"What?"

Jane bit her lip. "It's gossip. It's nothing."

"Which only motivates me to badger you until you crack."

"Well . . ." Jane brushed the back of the shell with water. "Jack's wife was in Slice of Heaven last night."

The pizza place. "So?" There were lots of reasons Renee might have stuck around the island, Lauren told herself. Like . . . Like . . .

"She said she was picking up dinner for Jack." Jane focused on her delicate task as if she was afraid of making a mistake. Or wanted to avoid witnessing Lauren's pain. "And George Evans says somebody saw her leaving Jack's boat last night."

That jabbed, right at the heart.

Lauren ignored the pain, took a breath. Because she trusted Jack. She did. She believed in him, in the kind of man he was, even if at the moment he didn't have much faith in her. "His *ex*-wife," she muttered.

Jane slid her a cautious look. "Okay."

"Anyway, she's not the problem."

Jack was. The dummy.

"Exes are always a problem," Jane said.

Something in her tone pricked through Lauren's bubble of misery. "Jane? What's wrong?"

Jane pressed the paste shell gently to the fondant-covered model without answering.

"Is it Travis? Have you heard from him?"

Jane stepped back to assess the cake decorations, her face pale and stiff as a china doll's. "He didn't go to Florida."

"Oh, Jane. Is there anything I can do?"

"Like what?"

Good question. "You should talk to Jack."

"What can he do? It's not like Travis threatened me. At least . . ."

"Has he tried to contact Aidan?"

Jane's throat moved as she swallowed. Nodded.

"Then you should definitely tell Jack. As long as you have custody—"

"I don't," Jane whispered.

"What?"

"I got the divorce myself. Travis was away. He never signed a custody agreement. He has a right to see Aidan. He has a right to do anything he wants."

"Listen, it's not my job to tell you how to live your life," Lauren said gently. "But I think you should talk to some-body."

Jane looked doubtful. "You mean, like a therapist?"

That would help. But, "I was thinking more like a lawyer," Lauren said. "What about Luke Fletcher's wife?"

"Maybe."

"Think about it," Lauren urged.

"I will." Jane peeled another shell from the mold.

"I'm not trying to push you."

"Yes, you are." Jane smiled. "But only because you care."

Lauren laughed even as tears stung her eyes. "Thanks."

"Honey, don't cry," Jane said. "If it means that much to you . . . Of course I'll call Kate. I'll call her tomorrow."

"No, it's not that. I mean, yes, call her, you definitely need to talk to a lawyer, it's just . . ." Lauren laughed again shakily, blotting her eyes with her fingertips. "He didn't get it, you know?"

"Who didn't get what?"

"Jack. We were . . . discussing things, and I was pushing, I know I was pushing, but he won't let me in. I just wanted to help, I *care* about him, I love him, and he won't accept my help. He says he doesn't need my help."

"Or he doesn't want to need it," Jane said.

Lauren stared at her. "That's it. That's it exactly."

Jane nodded. "And then he went on the attack."

"No, actually, he was kind of sweet. He offered to take me to dinner." Lauren pulled a little face, ignoring the pang at her heart. "*After* he pointed out that I was the one who was leaving."

Jane winced in sympathy. "Oh, honey."

"At least he was honest." Lauren sighed and snagged another cookie. "And maybe a small part of me would like to believe he's bothered by my leaving and that's why he brought it up."

"Of course he's bothered." Jane hesitated. "I suppose you *have* to go?"

"I can't stay on vacation forever. Sooner or later, I have to face my dissertation committee. And I want to see my family before I go on tour again. I'll miss the island, though. I'll miss you." *And Jack. I'll really miss Jack.* She bit into her cookie.

Jane's face turned pink. "I'll miss you, too. I feel like everybody's leaving me."

Lauren nodded in understanding. "All the vacationers."

"The vacationers. You. Thalia."

"Jane?" Thalia stuck her head in the door. "I'm taking off now."

"Where are you going?" Lauren asked.

"To Camille's."

Oh, right. Her babysitting job.

"They want to take me back to France with them," Thalia volunteered suddenly. "Like study abroad, only they'd be my host family, and I'd help Camille with the kids."

"Wow. That's exciting," Lauren said.

"I know. I mean . . . France, right? I figured the farthest I'd ever get from home was Chapel Hill. I could never afford to go to Europe, and a whole year . . ." Her voice trailed off.

"How do your parents feel about this?" Lauren asked.

"They're all for it. Dad says it's a once-in-a-lifetime deal. And Mom's not really into the whole senior year, prom thing, so that's okay."

Mom isn't, Lauren thought. "How about you?" she asked gently.

"Oh, I've always wanted to get away. See the world. Only . . . I thought I'd have another year, you know? Before I had to say good-bye to everybody."

To Josh, Lauren thought.

"You'll figure it out," she said.

"She's so smart," Jane said after the girl left. "I hope she doesn't make a mistake."

Lauren looked at her quizzically. "You mean, stay? Or go?"

"That's the question, isn't it?" Jane sighed. "You don't realize when you're her age that you can make a decision that will totally screw up your life."

"Not just at her age," Lauren said wryly.

The front bell tinkled.

"I'll get that," she said.

A blond guy was standing by the cash register. A tall, blond guy in a stained T-shirt and ripped jeans. He looked up when Lauren walked in, and Lauren's back tightened. Her heart began to pound.

Travis Tillett. Jane's ex.

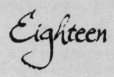

Eighteen

LAUREN'S PALMS WENT damp. "Can I help you?" she asked politely.

"Where's Janey?" Travis asked. A demand, not a question.

"She's busy at the moment."

"Travis?" Jane's voice rose sharply on the word. She came out of the kitchen, wiping her hands on her apron. "What are you doing here?"

"I want to make sure my boy is taken care of."

Jane's soft chin firmed. "I can take care of my son without any help from you."

"See, that's where you're wrong." Travis smiled, exposing too many yellowing teeth. "You can't do jack shit. Because I got him in my truck."

Every hair on Lauren's body stood at alert.

"Aidan?" Jane whispered.

"Yeah. Came along no trouble at all."

"You couldn't," Jane said. "He wouldn't. The camp

knows I never pick him up before five. Anyway, you're not on the list. They'd never release him to you."

That's right, Lauren thought. That had to be right. In these days of custody disputes and paranoid parents, schools and camps had to take precautions. Even on Dare Island.

"Didn't ask them, did I? Boy was standing around while the rest of them played ball. I called his name, told him you were expecting him."

"Aidan knows not to go with strangers."

But Lauren knew that to a six-year-old, "stranger" meant something different, someone scary, like a villain in a cartoon. If Travis smiled and called the child by name . . .

Travis grinned. "I'm not a stranger, am I? Anyway, he told me he gets rides all the time. You shouldn't have raised him to be so trusting, Janey."

Lauren's lungs emptied.

"Aidan!" Jane bolted for the door.

Travis grabbed her arm, wrenching a sound of pain from her throat.

Lauren couldn't move. Couldn't think. Couldn't breathe. The scene took on the flat, bright, jerky motion of a gif, playing over and over on her computer screen.

"I'm sick and tired of living out of my damn truck," Travis said. "You've got a house. You've got a business. Well, now, I've got our kid. What's he worth to you?"

"Anything. Everything," Jane said. "Just don't take Aidan."

Travis pushed her behind the counter. "I need cash."

Do something, Lauren thought. But her feet were glued to the floor, her mind frozen in fear. And maybe it would be all right, maybe he didn't have Aidan after all, maybe . . .

Jack. His name hit her brain like a jolt of pure oxygen. Jack would know what to do.

Her phone was in her purse under the counter, out of

reach. *Crap.* "This is obviously a family discussion," she said, slinking back toward the kitchen. "I'll just . . ."

"Cash," Travis snapped to Jane.

Jane fumbled with the register, her hands shaking. Lauren slid between the stainless counters of the work aisle toward the back door.

"Hey, you! Where the fuck do you think you're going?"

Lauren gasped and smacked her palm on the panic button of the alarm panel by the back door. There was a moment's silence, while her lungs seized and her blood drummed in her ears.

Then the alarm erupted.

"Fuck!" Travis screamed. "What the fuck did you do, bitch?"

The door. Lauren grabbed for the doorknob. The sirens blared. *Run, run . . .*

But Jane cried out behind her and she stopped, jerked back like a marionette by its strings.

"Get back here," Travis ordered.

Slowly, Lauren turned. Travis was holding Jane's arm in one hand, a stack of bills in the other.

He scowled. "All the way back. In here."

Lauren sidled forward, keeping out of his reach, out of his way.

The phone shrilled, jangling under the sirens.

He twitched. "Don't answer that."

"If I don't answer, the police will come," Jane said.

Lauren closed her eyes a moment. *Oh, Jane.*

But Travis only stuffed the bills into his jeans pocket. "Let 'em come. I'm out of here."

"What about Aidan?" Jane said. "Where's Aidan?"

"I'm taking him with me."

"No!" Jane cried. "I gave you the money."

"And you'll send me more after we're gone, right?" He grinned horribly. "Child support."

"Aidan!" She struggled against his hold.

Travis shoved her away from him, sending her sprawling onto the floor.

Lauren's lungs constricted. The sirens blared. *Save me*, she thought, but there wasn't time.

She would have to do the saving herself.

She scrambled through the tables and threw herself in front of the door.

"Move it, bitch."

She gulped for air. "You really don't want a child on the road with you," she said in the most conversational tone she could manage. "Think of the potty stops."

He gaped at her. *Good.* She'd broken his concentration. Now if she could only buy them time . . . "Have you thought about where the two of you will go?"

"I don't know. Florida." He reached past her for the door handle.

She flinched. "That's a really long drive," she said, pitching her voice low beneath the blasting sirens, using the smooth, soothing tone favored by psych staff and hostage negotiators everywhere. "Is that what you want? I hear that you're frustrated, but you have to think about what you want."

"I want you to get the *fuck* out of my *face*."

"Aidan's only six," she persisted. "That's a lot of responsibility for a—"

He seized her shoulder, his fingers digging in, and threw her out of his way. She flung out her arms to save herself and crashed into a table. She went down hard, the table on top. Her skull cracked against the floor. Her head rang.

After that, things got a little fuzzy.

There were sirens, more sirens, the thud of booted feet, raised male voices, the sounds of a scuffle. *Just like the bank*. But instead of terror, she felt gratitude. She'd done everything she could. *Now Jack could deal with it*.

She lay stunned, sprawled in an ungainly heap on the floor, her shoulder aching and her elbow throbbing and her head splitting with the scream of sirens. Her thoughts hovered and sparked like mosquitoes or fireflies in the dark. And then, blessedly, the alarm cut off.

"Oh, God, Lauren." Jane's voice. "Are you all right?"

"I've got her. Go with Hank." Jack's voice.

Lauren smiled and opened her eyes.

Jack stood looking down at her, face taut and pale, mouth grim, a line of sweat at his temples. His usually neat uniform was rumpled. But when her gaze met his, his lips curved in a faint half smile. "Hello, Lauren."

Her heart bloomed. Her smile spread. "Hello, Jack."

He squatted on the floor beside her. She struggled to lift her swimming head, battling the nausea that rose in her throat.

Jack put his hand on her chest. "Easy does it. Do you remember what happened?"

"Before or after I fell into the table?"

His lips twitched. "So, alertness, okay. How's your breathing?"

"I didn't have a panic attack."

"I almost did." He reached for his utility belt. "Took ten years off my life when I saw you on the floor."

"Aw." A bright light flashed briefly in her eyes. She moved her head restlessly. "Hey."

"Sorry. Pupils okay. How do you feel?"

"Okay." She tried again to sit up, and this time he helped her with an arm around her shoulders.

"Let's get you to the hospital."

"I'm fine," she protested.

"You need to get checked out."

She didn't want to argue. Her thoughts buzzed, a cloud of gnats in an empty jar. She touched her fingers gingerly to her forehead. "Aidan?"

"With Jane. They're both fine. Hank's taking a statement."

"He really was in the truck, then?"

"Yeah."

"Good. I'd hate to get pushed around for nothing."

His lips brushed her hair. "Nobody pushes you around, sweetheart. Jane said you got to the alarm."

"Thank you for coming." She turned her face into his shirt. He smelled like clean cotton and warm male. He smelled like safety. She wanted to crawl inside him and wrap him around her like a blanket. "I knew you'd come."

"Somebody needs to stay with you tonight," Jack said on the drive back from the hospital. "For observation."

Lauren turned her head—carefully, because of the ice pack—to smile at him. "Are you volunteering?"

His jaw set so hard, he thought it would crack. "I'm insisting."

"Protective custody?" she teased.

"Something like that."

He couldn't protect her all the time. He hadn't protected her today. She'd saved herself and six-year-old Aidan. All he'd done was provide backup. In a week or two he would be too far away for even that much. A phone call, a text, an e-mail, all he could do.

But tonight he could be there for her, could keep watch for any lingering effects of concussion.

Or fear. She'd held it together when she had to, for as long as she had something to do. But trauma was tricky. He wouldn't be surprised if the confrontation with Tillett triggered nightmares tonight.

It was probably a good thing that by the time Jack found Lauren, Tillett was already in cuffs. Because when he saw her lying bleeding on the floor, he'd wanted to kill the son of a bitch.

They'd shaved a tiny patch of her hair in the ER. Lauren, smiling, wincing, bloody, had joked that the two neat staples in her scalp were nothing compared to her other piercings.

Her guts, her heart, humbled him.

She was amazing. *Hostage Girl*. He could only guess at the courage it took for her to put herself out there again and again, knowing the risks, understanding the consequences. He could only admire her caring.

She put herself on the line like a cop. She was tough like a cop.

Or a cop's wife.

Don't go there, dumbshit. She was leaving.

He could never ask her to be less than what she was. Lauren wanted to matter, wanted to help people. He got that, because he did, too.

But she wanted to go back and finish her doctorate. *I don't want to be mediocre*, she'd said.

He didn't have anything to offer that would compete with her dreams.

And if he offered her everything and she said yes, he would live always knowing that he'd kept her from the future she'd worked for, from being the person she wanted to be.

Her father's death had robbed her of one chance at that life. The hostage situation had derailed her plans again. Jack wasn't going to take anything else from her by telling her he loved her.

Even if it was true.

They crossed the bridge from the mainland, suspended between the deep, sparkling water and the dark dome of the sky. He glanced at her profile, silver in the glow of the dashboard.

He cleared his throat. "I called the Fletchers from the hospital. Meg's waiting for you. She can tuck you in while I feed the cat and grab a change of clothes. I'll be back in no time."

"We're not going to the boat?"

"I thought you'd rather not rough it tonight."

"Since when is the boat roughing it?"

He shrugged, remembering Renee's scorn. *This isn't home*, she'd said. *This was never meant to be anything more than temporary.* But now didn't seem like a good time to bring up his ex-wife. "It's just temporary digs. I thought you might be more comfortable at the inn, that's all."

"Temporary? That boat is part of your family history. It's like you brought a piece of them down with you. That doesn't feel very temporary to me. You even have a cat, for heaven's sake. Besides . . ." The curve of her mouth slayed him. "I have very fond memories associated with that boat."

Yeah, so did he. He was never going to be able to sit on the deck at sunset without imagining her across from him. Never take a shower without hearing her soft, responsive cries echoing off the tile. Never again lie in bed with the moonlight streaming through the skylights without remembering her beside him, the curve of her shoulder, the warmth of her skin. "Sure, we can do that. You need anything from the inn?"

She shook her head. "I just want to go home," she said in a small voice.

Her words ripped him up. When she was gone . . . He shut that thought down fast.

"Whatever you want, sweetheart."

JACK DUCKED HIS head as he entered the stateroom. "You need another ice pack?"

Lauren eased back onto his pillows, feeling pampered and more than a little guilty. Maybe they should have spent the night at the inn. At least then Jack wouldn't be stuck waiting on her. "I'm good, thanks. Sorry I'm so useless."

"The doc said you should rest."

"I'll be able to do more tomorrow," she promised.

Jack arched an eyebrow. Began to unbutton his shirt. "Seems to me you did plenty today. You stopped Tillett."

She tore her attention from his chest to say, "I slowed him down. You stopped him."

"You got us there in time. If he managed to take Aidan out of state, there's not much Jane could do to get her son back."

"Wouldn't that be kidnapping?"

Jack shucked his pants, leaving on navy boxer briefs. He had a beautiful body. "Not in North Carolina. Aidan's his kid."

"Was that why Travis was able to pick him up from camp?"

Jack scowled. "No, that was some seventeen-year-old

counselor paying more attention to the kid on third base than the real threat in the outfield. I talked to the camp director. That won't happen again. But, bottom line, Jane never got Tillett to sign a custody agreement. Without that piece of paper, possession is everything. The presumption of the court is equal custody. Tillett didn't have a gun, so we can't get him for armed robbery. He's claiming Jane gave him the money in lieu of child support. The DA will prosecute for common-law robbery, but at this point the only charges I'm sure will stick are resisting arrest and assault."

He slid into bed beside her.

"So my head bump was good for something," she joked.

Jack gave her a hard, flat look. His cop look.

She tried again. "At least I didn't hurt my book-signing arm."

He didn't seem to find that funny, either.

Frankly, neither did she.

A depressed silence fell.

"When do you leave?" Jack asked.

Not, *Why don't you stay?*

She swallowed a lump in her throat. "I told my agent I was taking a little time off. I still need to go back and meet with my advisor, but I thought . . . two weeks?"

Two weeks. Two short, bleak words that dropped like stones into the silence.

"We could keep in touch," he said. "After you go."

She felt a ripple that might have been hope. "Are we talking about exchanging Christmas cards?" she asked cautiously. "Or something more?"

Something flickered in those dark, dark eyes. His lips curved just a little. "More than Christmas cards."

Definitely hope. Her heart lightened. Fluttered. "I could visit."

"That would be good. When you can get away."

"I could bring pizza."

He met her gaze, his face expressionless. "You heard about that."

She shrugged her bare shoulders. "You warned me how it was. Everybody knows everything on an island."

"And what they don't know—"

"They make up," she finished.

"I sent her away."

She cocked her head. "Before or after the pizza?"

He searched her eyes, and some of the tension left his taut body. "After," he admitted.

"Did she offer you the job again?"

"It doesn't matter. I told her I'm not interested." He caught himself and braced visibly. "Unless you want to talk about it."

She had to bite the inside of her cheek to keep from smiling, overcome with tenderness and affection. He was trying. Despite his own obvious reluctance, he was making an effort to talk for her sake. Which meant she could let it go—for now—for his.

His willingness was everything. Nothing he could say showed his heart more clearly. Except . .

"Jack, are you sure this is what you want?" *That I am what you want?*

"I'm sure. Renee can't offer me anything but the past. My present is here." He cradled her face in his hands. "With you."

Her nose and eyes stung. That was so sweet. More than she had any right to ask for.

And not nearly enough. What kind of future did they have, with him here and her in Chicago?

"Long-distance relationships take work," she warned. "Commitment. Compromise."

"'Compromise is always a good idea. Especially if it gets you what you want.'"

It took her a moment to recognize her words from their very first meeting. "I can't believe you remember that."

His gaze met hers. "I remember every word you ever said to me. Including that you love me."

He robbed her of breath. "I *do* love you. But . . ."

Give me something to hold on to. An excuse to stay. A reason to come back. Tell me you love me.

"You can't give up everything you are, everything you've worked for, to be with me," he finished for her. "I know."

Of course he knew. Or thought he did. Because he hadn't been willing to leave Dare Island. Not for the woman he'd been married to for ten years. Not for the family he'd loved and left.

Certainly not for her.

He liked it here, liked being police chief of a small town in coastal Carolina, serving the people, getting to know them, making a difference in their lives. Part of a population that shifted and renewed itself like the island shifted and was renewed by the tides.

She wasn't sure of her words or her next move. "I'm not leaving *you*."

"I get that. You're moving on with your life."

Without you. The realization ripped her heart.

"No, I meant . . ." *Live in the moment.* Don't take the good times for granted. Because in a blink, in a heartbeat, in the space of a phone call or a man bursting in at the door, everything could change.

My present is here. With you.

She slid her arm over his chest, holding on to as much of him as she could. "I'm still here. Now."

She snuggled close, hitching her leg over his thigh, and kissed the underside of his jaw.

He shivered, his hands flowing over her, her back, her arm, the side of her breast. "You sure you're up for this, sweetheart?"

She bit his shoulder lightly, savoring the hot pressure against her thigh. *Think positive.* "I'm sure you are."

He slanted a smile down at her. "Using sex as a diversionary tactic?"

He really did remember every word.

"Do you have a problem with that?"

"Hell, no," he said and kissed her.

He touched her until she was damp and trembling, until he groaned with need. Because of her head injury, she had to be on top. She crawled over him, shaking, straddling his warm, firm body, claiming him, taking him, making him hers. He let her set the pace, rocking, rocking to the pulse of her body, the rhythm of her heart.

And when she rose over him in the dark, when she arched and he thrust and they both shattered, she owned him.

For the moment.

Nineteen

"Lauren Patterson is having a big book signing in Chicago at the end of the month," Marta said to Jack.

He knew. She'd told him all about it in her last e-mail, which had been full of the kind of newsy details he could have shared with his mother.

Hank lowered the newspaper. "How do you know about some book signing in Chicago?"

Marta raised her brows. "It's on her Facebook page. I'm a fan." She studied Jack over the top of her reading glasses. "I sure would like a signed copy of her book."

Jack kept his face impassive. "You can probably order one from the bookstore."

"Or you could get it for me. If you were going."

He shot her a narrow look, the look that warned drunken boatmen and rowdy Marines that he was nobody to mess with.

But Marta, the mother of four boys, three of them

grown, was made of sterner stuff. She smiled back blandly, waiting for a response.

"At the start of the fishing season?" he said. Dodging.

The summer people were gone. October brought new visitors to the barrier islands. The schools of baitfish, croakers and herring, were already on the move, chased by stripers migrating from the waters north of Chesapeake Bay, followed by flocks of gulls and crowds of serious fishermen. Every weekend between now and January the cheaper motels and rentals would be packed, every beach access crowded with SUVs and pickup trucks.

"I just thought you might. Seeing as you are in the book and all."

"Not by name."

Shortly after her return to Chicago, Lauren had written mentioning that her editor wanted an epilogue, asking permission to include him in her book. She hadn't explained exactly what role he would play, and he didn't ask.

Most of her e-mails were like that, full of facts and details, leaving out the stuff he really wanted to know. *Just the facts, ma'am.*

The longer she was gone, the more he felt her slipping away, being absorbed into her old life—her new life—in Chicago.

Could he fit into that? How could he fit into that?

He'd said yes to the book, of course. What else could he say? She was doing what she should be doing.

But he wanted to be more than an epilogue to her. He wanted to be part of the first chapter of the rest of her life and the happily-ever-after.

"They're talking about it down at the tackle shop," Hank said. "You're quite the hot topic these days."

"I live to serve," Jack said dryly.

"And that's enough for you, is it?"

Jack glared, which didn't faze Hank any more than it had Marta.

"That's why you should go to this signing thingy," Hank said. "Before it's too late."

"I am not discussing this," Jack said tightly.

"Well, you should," Marta said.

"Not with us," Hank put in. "With her. You should listen to me, boy. I know."

"Yeah, because you're all about sharing your feelings," Jack snapped back, goaded.

Hank looked back at him steadily. "No, I'm not. Never was. Never could find the words to say how I feel. Not with my wife. Not with my daughter. Which is how I know that if you keep your mouth shut, you could lose your shot at the best thing that ever happened to you."

THE BOOKSTORE WAS decorated for Halloween, wisps of fake cobweb stretched over the display of books about goblins, ghosts, and witches, a giant crepe paper pumpkin on the wall above the children's section.

But the staff was prepared and the turnout good for Lauren's signing, with lovely stacks of books all over the store and a banner poster with her cover tacked up behind her signing table. The store manager and another bookseller worked the line, verifying purchases and handing out Post-it Notes for the attendees to write their names on. The in-store publicist hovered at Lauren's elbow, keeping her supplied with water and pens.

Lauren took a deep breath and smiled at the next woman in line.

"I just love your book," the woman said.

"Oh, thank you so much"—Lauren glanced at the Post-it Note with the woman's name neatly printed on it—"Amy. I hope you like this one, too."

"Oh, I do. I read it already. I downloaded the e-book at midnight last night. This morning, I guess I should say."

"Me, too," confided her companion.

"Well, I really appreciate that." Lauren hesitated, her pen hovering over the title page. "Should I make this out to you?"

"Yes, please." Amy smiled. "I always buy my favorite authors in print, too."

"Wow. Thank you," Lauren said. *To Amy*, she wrote.

"So, your sexy police chief . . . Does he have a name?" Amy asked.

"Or a brother?" asked her companion.

The woman behind them in line leaned closer. "When are you going to see him again?"

Lauren lifted the pen before she smeared the page. "I'm not sure," she said honestly.

They'd been in touch. Jack called, often at dinnertime, to tell her about his day, stories about Tiger or some routine police call, the progress of the new construction, snippets of island news she could and often did hear from Jane or Meg. She e-mailed: stories about Noah or her mother, her meeting with her advisor, her plans to finish her dissertation after the book launch publicity died down. Except for the fact that she always typed *I love you* above her signature, her e-mails to Jack weren't that different from her communications with Ben.

She swallowed and tightened her grip on the pen. *Live for the moment. Hope for the future*, she wrote in bold, black script.

She wrote that in every book.

Work for the future, she sometimes thought the inscription should be. She was beginning to believe the best shot you had at the life that you wanted was a leap of faith followed by a series of well-thought-out, deliberate steps.

But that philosophy didn't fit neatly on a title page. Or even in an epilogue. Although she'd tried.

Give your readers what they want, darling, her agent, Patricia, advised. *We want to be inspired, not lectured to.*

She smiled. Signed her name.

"Thank you for coming . . ." Another quick glance at a Post-it Note. "Stephanie."

The line moved. She looked up. And . . .

There he was.

Her heart leaped. She dropped her pen.

Jack Rossi, in the flesh, or rather, in a black leather jacket over a button-down shirt and jeans, was hanging back at the end of the line, the way people did sometimes when they wanted an extra word. The stalkers, the weirdos, the aspiring writers.

For a moment she couldn't breathe.

The in-store publicist caught the direction of her gaze and moved closer. "Is everything all right?"

"Yes," she whispered. *Very all right.* More all right than things had been in a really long time.

He was here.

He smiled at her, his dark, hooded eyes, that tiny crook at the corner of his mouth, and everything inside her zinged and pinged and tingled.

"Do you need me to call security?" the publicist persisted.

"No." She cleared her throat. "No, it's okay. I know him."

The women in front of the table heard her and turned. A murmur spread outward. The line shifted back and surged forward, a swell of whispers pushing Jack along like the foam at the crest of a wave.

He stopped in front of her table, his thumbs in the pockets of his jeans. "Hello, Lauren."

"Hello, Jack." Her smile worked its way from deep in her belly to her lips, glowing, spreading. "What are you doing here?"

"I came to buy a book."

"I already sent you a copy."

"I wanted to see you."

Her heart swelled until she thought that it would burst. With pride, with nerves, with happiness.

Jack took a book off the display on the table. Turned it over in his hand to look at her new author photo on the back, the new Lauren with long hair and the tiny gem at the side of her nose.

"How does it end?" he asked.

"You haven't read it yet?"

He shook his head, still looking at her with those dark eyes and that half smile.

Her tongue tied. She had thought—hoped—that the epilogue would speak for her. *I'm working for the future. For our future, Jack.* But the ending wasn't in her hands alone. "It's . . . hopeful."

His eyebrow arched. "Not happy?"

He wasn't trying to torture her, she told herself. He couldn't know that she'd put her heart out there for the world to see. Her hopes, her plans, all in her book.

The book he hadn't read yet.

She smiled wryly. "A wise man once said happiness isn't getting what you want, it's wanting what you've got."

"I've got an alternate ending for you." He put the book down on the table. His fingers brushed her photo, and she felt the caress deep inside. She trembled. He looked from her picture right into her eyes. Seeing her. Loving her. "I put in for a job with the Chicago PD," he said quietly.

She blinked, stunned. "But . . . What?" *Wow.* Not the declaration she was expecting. Not in her plans at all. Everything he'd said about small-town police work crowded into her brain. "You love Dare Island."

He watched her. "I love you more."

Her mouth dropped open. "Jack . . ."

"Hear me out." He reached into his breast pocket and pulled out a small velvet box. A customer gasped. The line crowded closer, cell phones appearing as if they were at a rock concert.

Lauren stood, knocking back her chair, pressing both hands to her heart.

Ignoring the press of people behind him, Jack lowered himself to one knee.

"Oh, my God, it's him," Stephanie said. "From the book. It's Sexy Police Chief!"

Lauren couldn't breathe.

Jack opened the box. Something flashed. A diamond, brightened and blurred by her tears. "Lauren, will you marry me?"

"Yes," she said inaudibly. She said it again, louder. *"Yes!"* She stumbled around the table, joy rising inside her.

Jack stood and pulled her into his arms.

They kissed to the sound of applause.

She burrowed into his chest, hiding her hot face between the lapels of his jacket, breathing in the dear, familiar smell of him. "Did you resign already?" she asked, the words muffled against his shirt.

He kissed the top of her head. "Not yet. I'm waiting for the official offer letter."

"But you're still police chief on Dare Island, right?"

His arms tightened around her. "Why?"

She raised her head, smiling at him through her tears. "Because I just applied for a counselor position at the Dare Island School."

His chest expanded with air. "Moving on? Or running away?"

She answered him with love and perfect confidence. "Looking for a place to call home."

His answering smile started deep in his eyes. "Guess you need to write another epilogue."

"Another book," she said, and stretched on tiptoe to kiss him again.

Turn the page for a preview of
Virginia Kantra's next Dare Island novel

Carolina Dreaming

Coming soon from Berkley Sensation!

GABE SHIFTED HIS seabag on his shoulder, adjusting its weight against the March wind cutting off the ocean. He didn't mind a little wind. Where he'd been, there were no seasons and no privacy, only the stink of metal grease, violence, piss, and Lysol. Like the inside of a ship.

Lying in his rack at night, he used to dream of spring. Spring and women and the sea.

When he got out, winter had still lingered in North Dakota in the dirty piles of snow, in the biting cold. But here, the Carolina sun was warm against his face. The long bridge ahead arched like a gull's wing, skimming between sea and sky.

His heart lifted. It had been eleven years since he first crossed this bridge from the marshy inlet over the flashing waters of the Sound. Behind him, the highway was littered with fast-food chains and beach shops, gas stations and marinas, but this view hadn't changed.

Maybe it was a sign, cause for encouragement.

And maybe he was grasping at straws.

Home is the place where, when you have to go there, they have to take you in.

He'd read that somewhere, Afghanistan or prison. His teachers used to complain he wasn't much of a reader, but that line had stuck with him. Maybe because he'd never had a home. There wasn't anybody who felt they had to take him in, no place he belonged.

Except the Marines, for a while.

He'd screwed that up. He'd screwed up a lot of things.

But there was still a chance that his old buddy Luke would come through with a meal, a bunk, a job. All Gabe needed—all he had any right to hope for—was a chance.

A tall white bird stood motionless in the reeds of a sandbar. The water shimmered to the horizon, reflecting back a wide blue sky painted with clouds.

Gabe breathed deep, smelling salt. *Freedom.*

A pickup rumbled by in a rush of grit and exhaust. He turned his face away, pressing closer to the guardrail. Somehow he'd missed the entrance to the walkway bordering the bridge, so he was stuck trudging the traffic lane with no hope for a lift. He guessed not many happy families headed to the beach in March. Not that happy family groups would be picking up hitchhikers anyway.

Especially not hitchhikers who looked like him.

Sunburn had replaced his cell-block pallor, but he needed a shave and a better wash than he could manage at the sink of some truck stop restroom. He'd zigged and zagged eighteen hundred miles cross-country from the North Dakota State Penitentiary to the North Carolina coast in a jagged, dotted line that left him hungry, footsore, and broke, searching for . . . something.

Whatever the hell it was, he had a better chance of finding it if he had Luke's help. They were the same age, both enlisted fresh out of high school. Even as boots, everybody looked up to Luke. Everybody trusted him. If you were in the shit, Luke would pull you out.

If Gabe couldn't find Luke . . . Well, he'd find something. *Improvise, adapt, overcome*, they said in the Marines.

The bridge crested and rolled smoothly down to the inlet's northern side, a network of sandbars and saltwater channels protected by a man-made wall of rock. Gabe's eye traveled from the beds of rusty pine straw to the municipal sign by the side of the road, its blue-and-gold lettering standing out boldly against the weathered wood. WELCOME TO DARE ISLAND.

A black-and-white patrol vehicle parked in the shade of the pines.

Gabe's stomach tensed. Nothing to do with him, he told himself. He wasn't breaking any laws, wasn't doing anything wrong. But that didn't stop the sick acceleration of his heart.

A car rattled past on its way to somewhere else.

Gabe tramped along the sandy verge, keeping his eyes averted from the patrol vehicle's darkened windshield. He wasn't looking for trouble.

As he drew level with the hood, the door swung open. An officer got out, a rangy, rumpled man in his fifties who looked like every Southern lawman in every chain gang movie ever made, graying hair, mirrored glasses, face grooved like a tractor tire.

Gabe stopped, hand tightening on the strap of his duffel. *Is there a problem, officer?*

But he kept his mouth shut. He already knew the answer. *He* was the problem. He'd heard the words on park benches and in public libraries, on street corners and in cafés. *Move along. Your kind's not welcome here.*

He stood and waited, his heart pounding.

Southern Lawman jerked his chin toward the posted regulations. "No pedestrians on the bridge."

Gabe could have explained that by the time he figured out he'd missed the only ramp for the pedestrian walkway, he'd been a half mile across the bridge. Instead, since he had shit for brains, he said, "You don't look like a crossing guard."

The officer's expression never changed. "You don't look like an idiot. Why don't you save us both some trouble and turn around now?"

"Can't. Sorry," Gabe said with almost genuine regret. He really wasn't looking for trouble. "I'm here to see somebody."

"Is that right." The officer's flat tone made the question into a statement of disbelief.

Gabe nodded, trying to keep his tone easy despite the tension balling his gut. "Luke Fletcher." The officer's face could have been carved from stone. But something in his very stillness prompted Gabe to add, "You know him? His folks used to run an inn around here."

Still did, he hoped. He'd been to their place only once, when Luke had dragged him along after their graduation from boot camp. Gabe had never known a family like the Fletchers. Their easy welcome, their wholehearted acceptance of their son's friend, had sucked him in and left him floundering like a swimmer in unfamiliar waters.

For years after that, Tess Fletcher had sent Gabe care packages, to Iraq, to Afghanistan. The memory of her kindness made his throat constrict.

Over time, they'd lost touch. Just as well. He didn't like to think of Luke's mom sending care packages to prison.

The officer pulled a notebook from his pocket. "Name?"

The knot in Gabe's gut tightened. "You charging me?"

"I'm *asking* you. What's your name?"

"Gabe Murphy."

"Where you from, *Mr.* Murphy?" The slight emphasis was worse than a sneer.

North Dakota State Penitentiary. "All over," Gabe said evenly.

"ID?"

Don't run. Don't lie. Don't make sudden moves. "In my pocket."

The officer nodded, giving him permission to reach for it. H. CLARK read the dull metal name tag below his badge.

Gabe handed over his commercial driver's license. Still valid.

Officer Clark studied it. Studied him. "Be right back," he said, and disappeared into the marked car.

Gabe fixed the bored, I-don't-give-a-shit look on his face that he'd perfected by age ten. His all-purpose expression, equally good for the principal's office and prison.

Through the windshield, he could see the officer tap something into the dashboard and then reach for the radio.

Gabe waited, sweat collecting in the small of his back.

He'd done his time, he had no outstanding warrants, he wasn't in violation of his parole. There was no reason for the cop to detain him.

Unless H. Clark was just looking to fuck with somebody. Which in Gabe's experience, with Gabe's luck, happened all too often.

Returning, the officer handed Gabe his license. No

comment. Gabe relaxed a fraction, tucking the card into his wallet.

"Get in back," Clark said.

Fuck.

As a kid hauled into the principal's office, as a boot dragged in by the MPs, Gabe might have protested. *I didn't do anything.* He knew better now. "Why?"

"You want to see Luke Fletcher. I can take you to him."

Gabe stuck his thumbs into his belt loops, not moving. *Why?* It was for damn sure the cop hadn't offered out of the goodness of his heart.

Clark scowled. "I don't want you bothering the Fletchers. You got business with Luke, you deal with him."

That made sense. Gabe trusted the man's suspicion more than any kindness. Warily, he climbed into the back of the cop car, stowing his seabag on the seat beside him.

When, ten minutes later, the cop pulled to a stop in front of the squat brick police station, Gabe didn't feel betrayed as much as resigned. He never really expected things to go his way.

"I thought you were taking me to see Luke Fletcher."

"Yep."

"He in lockup?" Gabe asked, only half joking.

"Worse than that." Clark met his gaze in the rearview mirror. "He's a cop."

Wait. What?

Luke had always been one of the Good Guys, but they'd raised a lot of hell together over the years. Gabe had trouble picturing his old buddy as a cop.

He slid out of the vehicle, hauled out his duffel. His prison guard look-alike waved him ahead through the station house doors.

And there was Luke, in the flesh, in uniform, and Gabe didn't have to picture anything at all.

"Gabe." Grinning, the tall blond former staff sergeant grabbed Gabe around the neck with one arm. Pounded his back with the other.

Gabe returned his hug. "Luke. You look . . ." *Good*, he decided. The uniform, the life, must suit him. "Very respectable," he said.

"You look like shit," Luke responded frankly. "What brings you to Dare Island?"

Gabe eased back, just a little. "Long story."

"Yeah, I heard some of it," Luke said.

The radio call, Gabe thought. He cleared his throat, aware of Clark and some lady behind a desk, listening in. "When did you leave the Corps?"

Luke's blue eyes narrowed at the change of subject, but he answered readily enough. "Eight months ago. I'm married now. With a little girl."

"Congrats, bro. That's . . ." Fucking weird. Luke, a cop. Luke, a dad. "That's great. I didn't know you had a baby."

"Neither did I."

Gabe frowned. "How old is she?"

"Almost twelve."

"No shit." There had been a high school girlfriend, Gabe remembered. Luke had talked about her some, back in their boot camp days. She'd dumped Luke's ass when he joined up, but obviously things had changed. "So you and . . ." What was her name? Debbie? "Dana got married?"

"Dawn." Luke shook his head. "Long story. I'll fill you in over coffee, and you can tell me what you're doing here."

The middle-aged woman behind the desk—dark hair, dark eyes, bright coral lipstick—swiveled in her chair.

"We have a call. An animal complaint on Shoreline Drive. Sounds like the Crowleys' dog got loose again."

Luke nodded. "I'll take care of it on my way back."

"You going to Jane's?" Clark asked.

"That's the plan," Luke said easily. "I'll tell her you said hi."

"Why? I'll see her myself tonight. But you . . ." His fierce gray gaze speared Gabe. "You stay away from her."

"Maybe I would if I knew who the hell you were talking about."

"Jane," Clark said. "My daughter."

JANE CLARK READ over the builder's proposal for the new enclosed patio at Jane's Sweet Tea House, trying not to think of all the things that could go wrong.

Her savings had carried her through the off-season with just enough left over to pay for this project. But even with the builder's lowball quote, the expansion would take almost every cent she had. What would she do if the walk-in refrigerator went or the fondant sheeter needed repairs or seven-year-old Aidan broke his arm?

She twisted her braid around her finger tightly enough to turn the tip of her finger blue.

You're doing fine. Just try your best, and everything will be all right, she always told Aidan.

Too bad she didn't have a mother to tell her everything would work out. If disaster struck, she simply couldn't go to her father again. Not after all he'd already done for them.

"You don't need to pay until the job's finished," said the builder, Sam Grady, into the silence.

Sam meant to be kind. He could afford to be. The Grady family owned, managed, or developed half the island, including Jane's bakery. But her pride was touched. "Thanks, Sam. But I don't need charity."

"It's not charity. That last storm knocked the hell out of our beachfront properties. I've got more work than I can handle getting everything ready for summer. As long as you don't mind being flexible about the schedule, I can be flexible about payment."

"I can be flexible," she said. *Sort of.* Sam had already given her a break on the project cost. She certainly didn't expect him to pull his crews off more profitable jobs to work on her little patio space. She smiled. "Thank you."

"We'll be out of your hair by Memorial Day." He flashed her the Grady grin, white teeth and charm. "Promise."

Meaning he'd be done with the job before the season started and the tourists came.

Her smile, her whole body, relaxed. "That would be great. Here." She thrust a pink-and-white bakery box at him.

His brows rose in surprise. "What's this?"

"Cupcakes. To say thank you."

"You didn't need to do that."

"I want to." Not because she owed him—which she did—but simply because it made her happy to feed people. "Cappuccino cream for Meg and red velvet for you."

"Can't say no to that. Thanks, Jane."

She followed him to the bakery door, watching as he strolled down the steps and away, hardworking, handsome, successful Sam Grady. A genuinely nice guy, six years ahead of her in school and forever out of reach.

Not her type, she would have said back then, when she was young and stupid and her type meant pretty much any guy her father disapproved of who showed her a little attention.

As Sam reached the end of the walk, a police car pulled

up behind his truck. Sam stopped as the driver's-side door opened and Luke Fletcher got out. The two men greeted each other.

They made quite a picture, Jane admitted, Sam, lean and elegant, with his unruly dark hair and killer smile, Luke, blond and broad-shouldered in his police uniform.

Not that she was looking. Much. Luke was recently married to a lawyer from Beaufort. Jane had designed their wedding cake. Sam was engaged to Luke's sister, Meg. Even if Jane had had time for romance, she didn't poach.

Still, she wasn't immune to a little flutter of female appreciation.

But it was the third man, getting out of the back of the police vehicle, who made her catch her breath.

Travis.

Her heart squeezed and then stopped.

She forced herself to breathe. Not Travis. Her ex wouldn't be out of prison for at least another month.

But the resemblance was strong enough to make her palms grow damp. Long, rangy build, ripped jeans, sun-streaked hair hanging around a stubbled face. Both the hair and his shirt needed washing.

Luke introduced the stranger to Sam. She studied him through the glass door as the three men stood talking, noting subtle differences. The stranger was taller than Travis, or maybe he simply stood straighter. His skin was sunburned, his eyes darker.

But he was definitely the same type. Her type.

Jane shivered deep inside.

Her type left bruises.